Po Man's Child

Po Man's Child
a novel

Marci Blackman

Manic D Press
San Francisco

Thanks to my family, Madigan Shive, Cary Collins, Lila Thirkield, Eileen Myles, Sini Anderson, Michelle Tea, Charlotte Biltekoff, Sara Seinberg, Sarah Brown, Lisa Z., Sunshine Haire, Shelley Doty, Millicent Doty, Jodi Alperstein, Alessandra Ogren, Silas Flipper, Karyn Panitch, Dan Langton, Jewelle Gomez, Keith & Laurie Roueché, Juliette Torrez, and finally my editor and publisher Jennifer Joseph, for their love and support during the creation of this book.

Cover illustration and design by Tracy Cox.

Library of Congress Cataloging-in-Publication Data

Blackman, Marci, 1963-
    Po man's child : a novel / Marci Blackman.

    p. cm.
    ISBN 0-916397-59-9 (alk. paper)
    1. Afro-Americans--Fiction. I. Title. II. Title: Poor man's child
PS3552.L34257 P6 1999
813'.54--ddc21
                            99-6198
                            CIP

For my mother
Harriet Scott Blackman

SUNDAY

Po
1991

Aunt Florida is angry and it's not a good sign. Yesterday the picture of her that adorns my mantle—the one with the cigar in her mouth, and the nickel-sized tar black eyes that glare at you no matter where you stand in the room—tipped over three times. Today all the books on my bookshelf conspired to fall at the exact same moment. And now three mocking liquid shadows dance violently upon my wall even though the candles that cast them burn calm.

"When the Po ladies start turnin their faces down on ya," my mother always warned, "you know they are not happy."

It is four a.m. Mary lies flat on her back, knees bent, hands clasped behind her head, breasts falling off to each side. I'm propped up beside her, leaning on one elbow, my finger circling the labia stencil tattooed across her navel.

"Tell me a story," she whispers in a sultry voice, stopping the motion of my hand with her own.

"Not tonight," I answer, refusing to bite. "Not in the mood."

"Oh," she says coyly, still holding my hand, "but it's not a request." She pinches the skin on the soft side of my forearm, then uses it for leverage as she sits up. It doesn't hurt when she pinches me. It never does in the beginning. We've been through this before. "Tell me the one about your family," she demands.

I let my head fall and rest on her shoulder. "You're not tired of that one yet?" I ask, yawning so she knows that I am. "How many versions have you heard now? Three? Four?"

"So," she answers, still pinching my skin, "tell it to me again." Then letting her mouth slide into the crooked grin reserved for these occasions, junctions in time when she knows she'll have her way, she pinches even harder.

My forearm is starting to burn and it's kind of annoying. I don't want to do this tonight. Something about Aunt Florida's picture lying face down doesn't feel right. "I said I'm not in the mood," I answer again, sternly. "Besides, I'm all out of fresh ideas."

At this last comment, she sits up, tosses her head back and laughs. Her stringy black hair wafts in the breeze stirred up by Aunt Florida. Flanked by the in-your-face arrogance of dancing shadows from the candles, she narrows her pale green eyes and says, "Then try telling the truth this time."

"The what?"

"The truth," she laughs again. "How's that for a fresh idea? Novel concept, isn't it?" The laugh halts abruptly. "When's the last time you told me the truth, Po?"

I sit up on my knees to face her. "Oh, I get it. This is supposed to be some kind of dare."

"No, Po, no dare," she says, coldly. "Just a simple question. Can you remember?"

"You're serious, aren't you?"

She just stares at me.

"You don't think I can do it?" I ask, acting insulted.

Still she says nothing.

"Okay," I smile, responding to the challenge. "The truth? You got it. Starting from where?"

"From the day your parents first met."

On Mary's order, I scoot to the edge of the bed, lay my forearm face up on the nightstand and start talking. "My parents—Gregory Taylor and

Lillian Louise Childs—met and fell in love in 1958. Lillian's last name was Smith then, and at the time she met my father, she had no intention of changing it..."

It's an act, a game we play. Mary picks a spot on my body, any spot; tests how hard she can pinch or bite it, how deep she can cut it, or how long she can burn it. While I recount—without flinching—a story that's never happened.

It must be the fifth or sixth time we've played this game. Mary got the idea from a book one of her fag friends loaned her called *Intellectual S/M*. At first the idea was just intriguing. Kind of like one of those endurance tests the Fitness Council makes you take in junior high school. I was curious to see how long my imagination would hold out. How long I could keep the story going. It wasn't something I expected to like. But being forced to focus so intently on something outside the realm of current pain seems to make the endorphins kick in sooner. Before I know it, for a while anyway, the numbness is nowhere to be found.

This time, whether she calls it that or not, there's a dare involved. She wants the truth, a truth she knows I've never been able to share. And I'm not sure I can now. For as soon as I flinch or falter in the text, the game is over and Mary wins. Otherwise, it continues until Mary believes I've had enough. But I rarely flinch or falter. The real reason Mary stops is because she's had enough. She only tops me because she knows I want her to. She'd much rather have it the other way around. She's never truly understood the numbness that stalks me. Truth is, the levels of pain I endure frighten her. And the thought that I might enjoy the pain is something she doesn't want to think about.

Before the game starts, we agree on a safe word. A word, a non sequitur—usually a color—that I can yell if things get out of hand. Tonight the word is "red," the color of blood, and the spot she has chosen is my arm. It's not coincidence. The small portion of truth I have already revealed is that when I was fifteen going on sixteen, I developed this thing about my arms and cars. A fear that someday someone would forget I was there, halfway in or out, and close one of my arms in the door, roll it up in the window. And though I still can't remember what triggered this fear, the lost moment in time when the bullet ran screeching from the chamber, the overwhelming desire to protect my arms surfaced sometime after the night my parents and I became snow angels.

Everything was spinning. I remember feeling like a flush-faced porcelain doll at holiday time—all hot and bothered and numb—soldered to the plastic floor of one of those miniature snowglobe nativity scenes just after someone has shaken it. Even though I wanted to, I couldn't move. Instead I stood terrified that all the jostling around would cause the bottoms of my feet to rip and tear.

I heard my mother's voice first—wild, out of control. "Goddamn it, Gregory! God-fucking-damn it! I'm not gonna let you do this! I am not going to let you do this!"

But my father was calm. Even in the midst of my mother's rabid cries, his voice soothed, "Lillian. Lil... Lil, baby..."

"What about the kids?" she sobbed, tired and out of breath. "How can you do this to them? How can you do this to me?"

I run from the house, no coat. No one notices the bottoms of my bare feet burned numb in the cold. There in the front yard they're making angels in the snow, my mother on his back, begging.

They are making angels, yelling and screaming and rolling around in the snow. On hot white coals I run from the house, lay my back flat as a board on a flawless patch of snow. Icicle tongues of water drip frigid saliva down the back of my neck, my head crushes its remembrance. Snow white snow. I glue my arms to my ribs, my legs pinch my clit in between, and slowly I breathe. Slowly I begin to move. Ever so slowly I push my legs and my arms out and up until the frozen tips of my fingers touch but do not feel. Then down, arms and legs spread wide; I can touch the sky, I can reach the moon.

"Look! I'm an angel! I'm an angel, Daddy! I can fly."

Ignoring me, my father stands, throws my mother off his back like a fond memory grown indifferent. I remember the hinges on the door of the Falcon squeaking as he pulled it open.

The rules are simple. Once the spot is chosen, it is set; she can never again veer from it. She can, however, add additional means of torture if my tale reeks of bullshit's pungent smell, lacking clarity and attention to detail.

"They were at a party," I go on, still smiling.

"What kind of party?" Mary interrupts, as she walks to the bureau. "Details!" she sings. "Were they with friends or did they go alone? Was it winter and snowing, or did it take place outside, warmed by the hot and muggy stale breath of summer?" She reaches for the cane and cackles loud and hearty, then dramatically raises the thin bamboo stick high in the air before swatting it down on my arm.

"It was a college party," I answer. Matching Mary's playful mood, I pretend to wince from the sting. "A Div party, short for Division. Every year during the six-week winter break between semesters the seniors would throw a big party for themselves. And no, it wasn't snowing. It was cold as a mofo, as my father's friend MacArthur was fond of saying, but not cold enough for snow.

"My mother wasn't supposed to be there. She was a sophomore, just twenty years old. And because it was rumored that other things besides liquor would be on hand, lower-classmen weren't allowed to attend. But my mother's girlfriend, Mavis, insisted on sneaking her in. 'You got to go to the Div party, girl,' Mavis told her. 'Everybody who's anybody makes an appearance at the Div party.' "

While I talk, I watch as Mary rummages in the bureau, the bureau that used to belong to Grandma Margret, my grandmother on my father's side. Before her, it had been Great-grandma Cora's. And before Cora, it had been given to my great-great-grandmother Ida. A gift from Bo Jones, the man who owned half the state. And just to prove the power such wealth afforded, in view of his wife and his children, Mr. Bo took to strolling around town, parading my great-great-grandmother on his arm, daring anyone to say word one about it. Now the bureau had been given to me with instructions to give it to my daughter. If, as with Grandma Margret, I happen to be blessed with only boys, I'm to pass it on to one of my grand-daughters.

The brown leather satchel Mary takes from the top drawer is worn, frayed at the bottom, its drawstrings calling for the comfort of retirement. I speak slowly, make certain my words are measured and audible, focusing all my energy on enunciation. But my eyes never leave her hands, whose fingers—long, white, slender, and sheathed in a pair of rubber latex gloves—are beginning to turn me on.

"My father played vibes and sang in the band," I go on, staring at the gloved hands. "Jazz. The Gregory Childs Quartet. They were the hot new sensation on campus. And after graduating, all but my father—for reasons that will become clear later—would make the pilgrimage to New York to become the pioneers of a new young scene.

"The campus was small, the number of black students on it even smaller. So it wasn't surprising that Lillian and Greg socialized in the same circles even though my father was three years older and a senior. In fact, whether it was passing each other on their way in or out of BSA headquarters or being embroiled in the same five-person debate about a new breed of poets who called themselves Beatniks, Greg and Lillian ran into each other often. But neither ever stopped to take notice until the night my mother's girlfriend snuck her into the Div party.

"At least that's how my father put it. My mother claimed that my father was making passes at her from the beginning, but she didn't trust him. He was shady, she said. And every time she saw him, every time he winked or smiled at her, he was arm in arm with a different girl.

"Shady vibe or no, there was no escaping the attraction, and on the night of the Div party, the night my father made the senior class swoon from his rendition of *This Little Girl o'Mine*, something magical happened. In just a little over a year, while my mother was dropping out of school pregnant with my sister Onya, my father was running around town, handing out cigars, proclaiming that from now on, Gregory Taylor Childs was a certified one-woman man."

From the satchel Mary removes a brand new disposable scalpel, a bottle of iodine, and a package of extra-long cotton swabs, then splays them out across the nightstand. After dipping one of the cotton swabs into the iodine, she begins to paint burnt orange stripes back and forth across the smoothness of my arm.

Taking a deep breath I try to relax but as soon as she unwraps the scalpel from its sterilized disposable package every muscle tightens in anticipation. Its blade is rounded, half-moon shaped. As the white gloves close around its plastic green shaft, it sparkles.

She says she wants the truth this time. But not the whole truth, I'll bet. Only the part that makes a good story. She can't comprehend the real truth. My truth. Even I don't fully understand what's running through my head as I speak. Thoughts like, what does it feel like when the wounds are carved with a dulled and rusted edge? When the hands are not gloved but cold and callused and calculating, caked with the dirt of two solid months in the field? To have them cleaned with salt after? She doesn't want to hear about the curse, about Uncle George. We've been over it before. She can't tag along on this quest I'm on, she says. If she does then she'll be there with me. It's a trip she's just not ready to take. So I go on. On with the story, feeding her the mouthful of truth she's ready to swallow, the morsel with which I'm willing to part.

"They were married at once, in secret. My mother wanted to wait just a little while so she could tell her people in Cleveland: my great-grandma Shirley and my aunt Florida. Grandma Janie, my mother's mother, died in a fire when my mother was a little girl; her father was never in the picture. Shirley and Florida would want her to be married proper, she said. In a church, at least, if she couldn't wear the white dress. But my father insisted, saying that he didn't want to take a chance on his first child being born outside his name. So they said their vows before a justice of the peace and told no one, except my father's younger brother Ray who was needed as a witness, until Onya started showing.

"Although they weren't exactly thrilled about the veil of secrecy (believing that any man who forces his wife to keep her marriage hidden from her family has to be suspect), Aunt Florida and Great-grandma Shirley welcomed my father into the family with open arms. Grandma Margret, on the other hand, was ecstatic. Her prayers had finally been answered. Destiny had smiled on her and she was going to be a grandmother. And though there was some question about which came first (the marriage or the baby), as the day of delivery drew near, she took out her knitting needles and fashioned two pairs of booties—one pink and one blue—for her eldest son's firstborn."

Scalpel in one hand, bracing my arm with the other, Mary's eyes catch mine to see if I'm ready. One word from me and the game stops. Did Uncle George have a safe word? What was running through his head as the whip came down? Stories? Songs of freedom? Anticipation of the end? Did the overseer ever check to see if he was ready? Holding fast to the cadence of my words, I close my eyes.

"The labor was both difficult and long. From the time my mother's water broke, twenty-three hours would pass with all kinds of false starts and interruptions before Onya poked her head from my mother's womb and let out a fierce cry—the first of many protests at having been born at all. But all through the process, between wondering if she had what it took to be a good mother and leveling threats against my father's life, my mother was making plans. Plans to return to school. She would have to wait till the baby was weaned, of course, until Onya was old enough to have a sitter, but as soon as my mother got her strength back, she was going to finish the education she started.

"Unfortunately for Mama, those plans would have to wait. On the day Grandma Margret had looked forward to, the day she was finally allowed to sit unsupervised with her granddaughter, my mother walked into the admissions building to sign up for classes and fainted. Right there in line, after standing there less than half an hour, her mouth went dry, her knees buckled, her body went limp and she fainted. When she came to, one of the admissions ladies was kneeling over her, extending a cup filled with water, asking, 'How long have you been expecting, sweetheart?' Nine months later, my mother gave birth to my brother Bobby."

The first cut sinks deep, creating a hollow that burns. It is long, much longer than anticipated, from the crease in my elbow stopping just short of my wrist. My chest caves and heaves from the pain, like chattel when informed of the existence of free air.

"Where's your blood, baby?" Mary whispers to herself, this time not wanting to interrupt. And though the pearl white dermis is pretty, seemingly innocent lying next to the darker outer layer of brown, Mary is right;

initially there is no blood. Eventually, though, little red dots do matriculate into the hollow's walls, and the latex fingers waste no time spreading the incision wide to release the flow.

All this effort, all this busyness, trying to draw a line, a foothold in the sand, to hold back an enemy I've never been able to see. Aunt Florida called it a curse. The curse of Uncle George. Is it futile, Uncle George? That the conclusion you came to?

Deeper even than the first, the second cut immediately makes the river flow, trickling in forks down the sides of my wrist onto the top of the table.

"Mmmm," Mary sings, green eyes glowing in the first morning light, "there it is." My body starts to tingle. A light swell rises in my head.

But did you get off on it, Uncle George? Did you feel your knees weaken? Your nipples harden? Your body go to shakin? No longer from the beautiful face of pain alone, but from the sheer pleasure of its cheek rubbing against your bones? Did you? Ever? Get off?

"Once again, my mother started making plans. This time, she thought, after Bobby was weaned. This time it would happen. But once again, she was foiled. Just fifteen months after Bobby took his first glimpse of the world, while the nation was still recovering from the death of President Kennedy, my mother discovered another heartbeat thumping away in her womb. A beat that, if allowed to mature, would drum out any remaining hope of returning to school. So she panicked and spoke to my father about the possibility of aborting. Completing her education was her ticket to independence. Without it, she was a cripple who would have to rely on my father for the rest of her life. And what if he died suddenly? Who would take care of her then? But my father was emphatic. Wasn't no way in the world any seed of his was gonna remain unborn.

"Grandma Margret scolded her. Told her she ought to be thankful. And when my mother confided it was too big a burden to bear, that it seemed like she'd been pregnant since the day they were married, Grandma Margret called her an ingrate. 'You lucky the Lord blessed you with children at all,' she said. 'Coulda turned out barren, like Mrs. Felder over in Hamilton. Better learn to look on your burdens as blessins, child. You know it's not everybody the Lord chooses to burden.'"

The third cut is sexy. Water flushes my eyes as the tenuous blade glides without interruption, parting my skin. My head is full. I'm certain it will detach itself and fly away. All my juices—begging to come down—splash violently, ready to boil over.

"Turned out I was a bigger burden than anyone expected." The truth drives on. "After they brought me home from the hospital, the two-bedroom house my parents were renting became cramped. It never was meant to hold more than four, and even that was pushing it. So even though they couldn't afford it, they were forced to find something bigger.

"That's when things started to fall apart. My father wanted to buy. Why should they keep paying all that money to the man, he said, and never have anything to show for it? But they didn't have any money saved, my mother argued. And it would be awhile, at best, before she could look for work. What bank in its right mind would give a loan to a family of five with one measly income and no down payment? Even if it did, the new mortgage would be double the rent they paid now. Rent they barely managed to meet as it was. But again my father insisted. He would give up music if he had to. Get a second job. He refused to argue about it any further. If he had to work three jobs, he said, Gregory Taylor Childs' children were going to grow up on their own land. Six months after I was born, we loaded down a U-Haul with all of our belongings and moved across town into my father's dream house."

I do not see the hunting knife when Mary unsheathes it from its distressed leather casing. Not until it is raised high, poised to rain down, do I catch its gleam refracted in the nervous light of the candles. And not until I see its point spiraling downward do I first consider calling out the safe word. But I'm not quite ready to give in, and as usual, I go on.

"The moment we moved into the house, it seemed my parents started arguing and never stopped. And before long, while my mother stayed home to care for the kids, my father took to gambling and drinking and staying out late. Not only did rumors in town have it that he was no longer a one-woman man, but it was whispered that when he was drunk, Gregory Taylor Childs would fuck anything that moved. Even his brother's wife, that is, if his brother had a wife to be fucked."

The blade stops an inch above my forearm and hovers. I do not move. Slowly it ascends again. This is it. The place in the game I sometimes falter, either by stumbling over the text or by calling out the word. Only it's not a game this time. It's the truth. And as Aunt Florida used to say, the truth has a way of forcing its way out even when you try your damnedest to stop it.

"Eventually, Uncle Ray—my father's brother—did get married, to a white woman named Jessica. And shortly thereafter, as if to fulfill the prophesy of the rumor mill, she and my father started fooling around. The mill couldn't spit out the news fast enough. He's fucking his brother's wife, it said, he's fucking his brother's wife. And the poor brother and his own wife don't even know. What's that they say? The spouse is always the last to know? But Uncle Ray did know. Deep down, my mother did also. They just pretended not to notice."

This time I watch as the jagged blade rises. Again, it comes barreling down, stopping inches from my arm.

"But they couldn't play make-believe forever. And it wasn't long before the truth started to show itself in ways nobody could understand. Out of nowhere, it seemed, Uncle Ray took up trying to kill himself. And my mother just gave up. Like she figured if she couldn't beat the truth, she might as well let it have its way."

The third time, the mesmerizing blade seems to hang, balance awhile at its peak before it starts down. And once in motion it's as though something or someone is trying to resist it. As though if I squinted long enough I could see its tip embedded in the palm of Aunt Florida's blistered, wrinkled, and tired old hand pushing upward to slow its decline.

"Sooner or later, one them was bound to break. Turned out it was Uncle Ray. And when he did, all hell broke loose. When he finally decided to tell my father he knew, he did it with a vengeance. Instead of just trying to take his own life, he tried to take his daughter's as well."

I brace myself for the inevitable. I know the knife is coming down. The truth is on a roll and there's nothing that can stop it. But on the fourth and final turn, instead of raising the knife slowly as she'd done before, Mary unexpectedly stands as though a pair of giant invisible hands has just lifted her to her feet. Then, knife in hand, resting unreliable in her palm, she starts waltzing around the room as if with a partner. But she's not enjoying it. Although her moves appear to be choreographed expertly, with every step she's trying to break free.

"The kidnapping of his daughter was the domino that started the effect. Everything happened so fast, days and events seemed to whiz by in a blur. And by the time they got tired and finished, stood still long enough for us to sort things out, Uncle Ray was in the hospital, nursing a bullet wound to his head, and my parents were bankrupt."

But just as her breasts and the extra skin around her thighs begin to fall into the rhythm of it, just as her hand slips down into that position ready to take over the imaginary partner's lead, her feet throwing in the tricky variances and nuances worthy of the most expert ballroom dancers, almost as abruptly as she started, blade raised high, Mary lunges over to the bed and drives it down...

It wasn't as bad as I thought it would be. That's what I was thinking when I finally heard the phone. I expected it to hurt more, like one of those pains that makes you pray for a quick death. At first, after the blade plunged into my arm, I couldn't think or hear much of anything. Just those words resonating in my head: it wasn't as bad as I thought it would be. The words and a constant ringing. I've since remembered pulling the blade from my arm and getting up from the bed to answer the phone, thinking it had to be stopped. The ringing. It had to be answered.

I remember taking note of the candles as I passed by the mantle. Someone or something had blown them out. Every last one blown right out. Aunt Florida's picture was face down.

I still don't remember how the t-shirt got wrapped around my arm, only that it was still there, sagging and dripping with blood, as we waited in the emergency room. I also don't remember picking up the phone, the actual lifting of the receiver. Just that at some point it was in my hand and the ringing had finally stopped.

"Po, it's Bobby," my brother kept saying on the other end. "Po, it's Bobby," like he didn't think I could hear him or something.

"Oh, hey Bobby, what's up? Uh... listen... it's kind of a bad time, you know? Can I call you back?"

"Po, I'm at the hospital."

"The...? Yeah? What a coincidence. It's kind of a bad time, though..."

"Po!"

"Yeah?"

"I'm at the hospital. Dad had a heart attack. He died on arrival... Po? Did you hear me? I said, Dad had a heart attack. He's dead."

"Yeah, I... Shit! It's just that it's a really bad time right now, Bobby."

"Po!?"

"I heard you, Bobby. But listen, I can't do this right now. I'll call you later, okay? But right now, I gotta go."

Sex and the Speaker
1972

I remember a cry in the middle of the night. It was storming. A branch on the willow my father planted sometime before I became a thought beat Lady Day slow time against the pane on my window. Every so often a light would flash, lighting up the faces on the stuffed animals strewn about my room, the crash of cymbals echoing somewhere off in the distance. I held my breath as I climbed down the ladder from my bed to the floor, for fear of waking Onya who was sleeping in the bunk below. The face on my teddy brightened again, and as I tiptoed to the bedroom door I counted the seconds before the next thundering crash.

The hallway was dark, narrow, and long. The cymbals seemed to have moved closer and the heater hummed low in the closet opposite my door. The smell like burning hair, from that winter's first use, still lingered.

I heard it again. That same cry, faint yet deep and guttural. I looked back to see if Onya had heard it too, but she was still sleeping. When the light flashed again, I started down the hall, running my finger along the wall the way my mother always told me not to. She said it would leave a smudge. I remembered I hadn't washed my hands before I went to bed, and as I inched my way closer to the white door looming at the end of the corridor, I imagined a tiny fingertip-thick black stain meandering down the wall like a wave breaking the length of the hallway. I could already hear my mother's voice the next morning, "Oh no, no, no, no, Po! Get your butt out here, now! Pronto!"

My name is Po. And there's been considerable debate over just exactly how I came by it as a name. My brother Bobby used to joke that it was short for "Po' man's daughter." Leaning sideways against the wall, bow-legged in his pajamas, he'd cross those bony arms over his chest, cock his nappy head back over his shoulders, then laugh loud enough to wake the Lord. "Cause when you was born," Bobby would howl, ears twitching back and forth on the side of his head like an anxious rabbit, "we was so po', Daddy couldn't afford the cab to take Mama to the hospital to get you a proper birth certificate."

"Now that is just not true," my mother would argue, giggling right alongside him. "We named you Po after your great-grandmother, my grand-mother, Shirley Po." And always at the mere mention of Great-grandma Shirley's name, while she was still laughing, a sadness would creep into my mother's voice slow and steady, and her golden brown eyes would glisten longingly like raw honey plucked from a hive before its time. And even though we'd heard it a thousand times before, we'd sit unmoving in our chairs, listening intently until she was through with the oration.

"We may have been poor," she'd begin, shaking her finger back and forth to emphasize certain points, "but not a soul went hungry in Mama Shirley's house. Not a soul. Poor woman would turn over in her grave, bless her heart, if I let you kids think otherwise. From the time I was five years old... not much younger than you are now, Po... when my mother—your Grandma Janie—died in that fire, Mama Shirley raised me up all by herself like I was one of her own. Not a day went by that I missed a meal or didn't have cleaned and ironed clothes on my back. I remember one occasion, when times were especially bad, Mama fed the whole neighbor-hood with nothing but a loaf of bread and a pound of hamburger. Folks were so grateful, you'da thought they were eatin at the Ritz. Children and adults alike would walk by the porch all broken and tired from another day's strain of looking for work (cause, you know, children had to work back then; couldn't afford to just sit around, listening to stories all day), and the smell of that sweet stewed beef would drift through the crack in the kitchen window, down the porch steps and up into their nostrils, callin each one into the house like they were a snake being charmed by a charmer. And no matter how many found their way inside, whether it was one or a hundred, there was always enough for one more. And I'll tell you another thing, when I was sick, not the little colds folks get all panic-stricken about nowadays, but if I had a fever (just as I have always done for each of you), come hell or high water, Mama Shirley found a way to get me to a doctor.

"Po," she finished, "you were named after the finest woman to walk this earth. And I gave birth to you the same way I birthed Onya and Bobby: under her watchful and loving eyes in the maternity ward of Springfield Mercy General. Now don't you let anybody tell you different."

Onya said it was because when they found me alone on the doorstep one cold winter's night, my mother walked around the house for weeks after, shaking her head and crying, "Po chile. Po, po, po chile." And my father, I suspect, even as they lower him into the ground, still claims that the moment they pulled me from the warmth and serenity of my mother's stretched and bleeding womb, I smelled so much like potpourri, they just had to call me Po. But I think it had something to do with my mother's guilt. That she was so torn up over putting her own life before mine, over not wanting to keep me, she couldn't name me anything else.

The next thunder crash seemed to shake the house. As I neared the white door, I heard the cry a third time. But this last one was louder, clearer. I knew it. It was the voice of my mother and she sounded like she was in pain. I turned to go wake Onya, but the long dark hallway talked me out of it. Gently, I pushed open my parents' bedroom door, holding my breath as I entered.

The room was musty and dank, like the smell of boiled sauerkraut. It was so dark, I could barely see my hands as I felt my way inside. I tried to use my ears for eyes, but all I could hear were the whimpering cries of my mother. Finally, when the light flashed again, it lit up the room, and I could see that it was my father who was making her cry.

He had her pinned down naked on the bed. Her arms were spread wide, tied to the top of the headboard with thick pieces of cattle rope. Her knees were forced back over her head and severed pieces of rope hung from her ankles as well.

When my eyes adjusted to the dark, my parents' bodies didn't look like bodies at all. More like porous shadows, with my father's shadow, thick and muscular, moving rhythmic and rapid up and down above my mother's. An outline of a cowboy hat rested on his head, and I remember being confused because we had never owned any cows.

As the sauerkraut smell grew stronger, over and over the shadow of my father slammed itself into my mother's. And with every thrust her cries grew louder until finally her shadow went limp. I thought he'd killed her. I didn't know what to do. Terrified, I ran back to my room as fast as I could and climbed the ladder back up to my bed.

The sauerkraut smell was still stuck in my nose and it reminded me of New Year's Eve. New Year's Eves past as well as present, when Grandma Margret still tries to force feed the stuff to us for good luck.

"What's the matter?" Onya whispered from the bottom bunk.

"Nothing," I whispered back. My heart was racing. I was sure my father had heard me and I was watching the door, waiting for him to burst in.

"What do you mean, nothing? You're lying, Po." I just lay there, silent, watching the door. "If you don't tell me, I'm gonna tell."

"Nothing," I said between clenched teeth. "I just went to the bathroom, alright?"

"Did you wet your bed again? Cause if you did..."

"I didn't wet my bed. I just went to the bathroom." My eyes were still on the door.

"Don't lie to me, Po!"

"I'm not lying."

"Then, if you were in the bathroom, why didn't I hear the toilet flush?"

I just wanted her to shut up. I couldn't get the image of my father pounding away at my mother out of my mind. The hee-hawing of the box spring keeping time with my mother's "Oh, oh, oh." And Onya going on and on about all the things she would tell my parents if I didn't tell her what was up. I pulled the covers over my head and tried to forget I existed. I curled into a ball on the corner of my mattress and waited for the numbness.

It never fails in times like these. That pins and needles feeling after your foot falls asleep that lets you know it's waking up. That it's still alive. It starts slowly at first, in your toes, then spreads like wildfire, through the bones in your feet and ankles, up your calves, around your thighs, into your crotch, your stomach, all the way up to the deep black holes of your eyes, until the black turns to white, emitting thin beams of light as you stare blank into the darkness. But unlike the pins and needles, the numbness is here to stifle the feeling. To bury it. Deep beneath the surface of the skin, down inside the marrow of your bones, allowing you to continue along the path as but another of the living and breathing dead.

"Po, honey, come on," my mother calls from the kitchen. "It's gonna get cold."

It is Sunday morning. Billie is on the stereo singing *Lover, Come Back To Me*, and my father, donned in a brown and yellow dashiki with black and gold beanie, is scatting along beside her, flipping pancakes on the stove. The house reeks of bacon grease mixed with the scent of violets. And the table is set with the usual eight places: one each for Bobby and Onya who are seated and already eating; one for me and my parents; and one each for Hmm Hmm, Debbie, and Try Try, Bobby's three invisible best friends.

When they first appeared, my parents weren't sure how to respond. I was two, Bobby was four, and Onya was six going on sixteen. We were sitting down to breakfast, much as we were now, when out of the blue Bobby asked my mother if she would set three extra places for his friends.

"What friends?" my mother asked, placing a knife and fork next to the plate in front of him.

"Hmm Hmm, Debbie, and Try Try," Bobby answered as he picked up his fork and started drawing imaginary pictures on his plate.

"Hmm Hmm, Debbie, and Try Try?" she repeated, continuing to place the silverware around the table.

"Yes, ma'am," Bobby answered, still drawing.

My mother smiled nervously at my father who was scooping grits and eggs onto Onya's plate. "Well, now, aren't those some unusual names," she said to Bobby. "Do Hmm Hmm and Try Try live in the neighborhood?"

"Debbie and Try Try," Bobby corrected, graduating from drawing to tapping encrypted rhythms on the counter with the butt of his fork.

"What's that, sweetie?"

"Hmm Hmm, Debbie, and Try Try," he said again, banging louder on the counter to emphasize the Debbie.

"Oh. Well, do Hmm Hmm, Debbie, and Try Try live in the neighborhood?" asked my mother as she removed a pitcher of orange juice from the refrigerator and set it in the middle of the table.

"No, ma'am."

"Are they friends of yours from day school?"

"No, ma'am."

"Then where'd you meet em, honey?" she asked, finally.

"Nowhere," answered Bobby, pounding out the syllables of his response. Gently, my father covered Bobby's hand with his own, then plopped two small circles of grits and eggs onto Bobby's plate. As soon as my father was through, Bobby started playing with his food, sounding muted karate cries as he repeatedly stabbed his eggs with his fork.

"Don't play with your food, son," my father said sternly as he set a plate piled high with bacon in the middle of the table next to the orange juice. Nodding his head toward my mother's seat, he suggested she sit down so we could say grace.

But my mother wouldn't let it go. "Nowhere?" she questioned Bobby as she sat down. "You had to meet em somewhere, baby." Carefully, she selected two pieces of bacon from the pile and placed them on her plate.

"No, ma'am," Bobby answered. "I didn't meet em nowhere."

Again my mother glanced nervously at my father. "Anywhere," she corrected Bobby. "You didn't meet them anywhere."

"Anywhere," Bobby repeated, wrinkling up his face.

"Well, if you didn't meet them anywhere, sweetie, how did you all come to know each other?"

"Can we say grace now?" Onya interrupted, rolling her eyes. "I'm hungry."

"You watch your mouth, young lady!" my mother shot at Onya. "We'll eat when I say so and not before. Now Bobby, baby, how did you come to know your friends again?"

"They just with me," Bobby answered, still stabbing his eggs. "Ever since I can remember."

"I said, stop playing with your food, Bobby," my father ordered again.

Bobby set his fork beside his plate and bowed his head.

"Ever since you can remember?" my mother echoed in disbelief.

"Yes, ma'am."

"Well, are you sure they're coming over? It's almost noon, honey. Maybe we should call their parents to make sure they're still coming. Maybe they thought it was next weekend."

"They're sitting right in front of you!" Bobby yelled, annoyed, banging his fist on the table.

Onya started laughing.

"Onya!" my mother scolded. "Eat your breakfast."

"But we haven't said grace yet," Onya said, still laughing.

"I said, eat your breakfast!" my mother ordered. "You too, Po!" She lowered her voice, and said gently, "Now, Bobby honey, do you mean to say your friends have been sitting with us all this time?"

"Yes," Bobby answered, face wrinkling up even further.

"Oh, Lord," she said, looking at my father as though she were pleading for help. "I must be getting old. Now how could I miss you all, when I've been staring right at ya all along? You must be Hmm Hmm," she said, extending her hand to the empty space next to Bobby.

"No," Bobby shouted. "That's Debbie. Hmm Hmm's sitting next to Onya, and Try Try's next to Po."

Onya convulsed with laughter.

My mother threw her a dirty look. "Oh, I'm sorry, baby," she said to Bobby, again glancing at my father. "But I'll tell you what. Instead of dirtying up all those extra dishes, let's you and me pretend to put some food on their plates." She mimed scooping food onto an imaginary plate. "Think they'd like that? See, we can give em some bacon and some pancakes and mmm, mmm, mmm, some-a your Mama's special recipe grits..."

"No!" Bobby yelled, again. "They're not pretend. They're real!"

"Oh, I know they're real to you, baby," my mother soothed. "When I was your age I had a special door in the back of my closet that led to a special room, biggest room you ever saw, filled with all the toys and dolls my mother could never afford to buy me. And do you know what the best thing about that room was? It was so special that only I could see it. No one else could ever find that place."

"They're not make-believe!" Bobby insisted, slamming his four-year-old fist against the table a second time. "They're real!" And when my mother tried to persuade him otherwise, his bony little arm shot out like a giant switchblade across the kitchen table sweeping his entire place setting— silverware, food, and all—to the floor.

"Alright, Bobby," my father jumped in. "That's enough."

But Bobby wouldn't listen. He just kept beating his little fists against the table, shouting, "They're real, they're real!" until my father lifted him onto his shoulder like a potato sack and carried him kicking and screaming from the room. It was well into the afternoon before Bobby finally calmed down. And he only did so because my father extracted a promise from my mother that the next time the family sat down to enjoy a meal, Hmm Hmm, Debbie, and Try Try would enjoy it as well.

The following afternoon, my mother took Bobby to see Dr. Hodges, insisting there was something seriously wrong inside my brother's head. But by the end of the examination, Dr. Hodges disagreed, concluding that Bobby was a well-adjusted and healthy growing boy. Imaginary playmates were a normal stage of development at his age. In fact, they were a sign of intelligence. My parents needn't worry, he said. In time, Hmm Hmm, Debbie, and Try Try would fade away as innocently as they had come to life.

But two years later when Bobby got himself suspended from the first grade for punching a boy in the face because he tried to sit at the desk next to him, then punching him again when he tried to sit at the one in front of him, and a third time when the boy opted for the desk on the other side, my mother returned to Dr. Hodges with Bobby in tow.

"There's nothing wrong with him, Lillian," Dr. Hodges responded. "He's as healthy as any other boy his age with an active imagination and, from what I hear, a pretty good right hook to boot. It was the boy's first day of school, Lillian. A traumatic experience for any six-year-old. Do you remember your first day of school? Trust me," he said, "the imaginary playmates will disappear as soon as he gets over his shock and makes some real ones."

But even after he made real ones, Hmm Hmm, Debbie, and Try Try followed Bobby wherever he went. And though their presence continued to unnerve folks, earning Bobby the nickname of Kooky Spooky, it wasn't long before we all accepted their being around.

At every meal without fail, my mother set places for them at the table. I said hi to them whenever Bobby entered a room I was in. Onya simply pretended that they didn't exist. And my father came to the homespun shamanistic conclusion that Hmm Hmm, Debbie, and Try Try were pieces of my brother's soul. Bobby actually had a jump on the world, he said. At the tender young age of four years old, his only son had mastered something most of us don't get around to until the second or third lifetime: the art of conversing with one's soul.

"Mmmm, mmm, mmm," my mother says as she sits down. "Smell those violets? Mama's here."

My father rhythmically nods his head and smiles, laying a pan-sized flapjack on everybody's plate but mine and Try Try's.

"Dad!" Bobby objects. "You forgot..."

"I know, I know," my father stops him, pouring two small circles of batter into the big iron skillet. "Everything's cool. Just give me one minute." Then lifting the heavy pan with both hands, the veins in his forearms ripple like lighting as he tosses the two cakes in the air.

"Looks like Mama's visiting all the rooms today," my mother continues as the violet smell grows stronger. "Must be something good gonna happen." She smiles and inhales deep. I close my eyes and mimic her, breathing the violets deep into my lungs. If I hadn't been a member of this household the past eight years, witnessing some of its better kept secrets, I'd swear someone was holding a fresh-cut bunch just beneath my nose.

Blue violets were my Great-grandma Shirley's favorite flower. All year round, when she was alive, she'd keep bunches of them in vases in every room of her house. One day about a year after Great-grandma Shirley's death, my mother woke up claiming someone had scattered violets all over the living room floor, swearing that as she lived and breathed, Mama Shirley had finally come home. It was the first time in a year my mother had gone a whole day without crying. The first time in twelve months she didn't awake complaining of a pit in the bottom of her stomach. "Mama's home," she kept whispering to herself. "Mama Shirley has come back home."

According to my father, when Aunt Florida called to bear the bad news, my mother was pregnant with my brother Bobby, and her doctor, fearing the emotional strain might cause her to lose the child, forbid her to attend the funeral.

"She never got over that one," my father told us. "Never forgave herself for not going anyway."

Still my father wasn't all that convinced about the Day of the Violets, as Uncle Ray came to christen it. He rose early that day, had been raking leaves in the yard. And by the time he got back inside, a mysterious whistling wind had already swept through the house, blowing the last of the violets through the open sliding glass door onto the edges of the patio.

But Uncle Ray, who after a night's worth of drinking had just stumbled through the front door looking for a place to crash, put his hand palm down on the Bible to prove he'd witnessed the entire scene. "I saw em, Greg," Uncle Ray slurred to my father. "I'm tellin you, man, I saw em. Barely got the door closed behind me when all of a sudden them violets just up and started dancin. Two-steppin. Swishin around in circles. Gatherin up momentum till they turned into this big ol fat lady wearin one a them straw bonnets. Price tag hangin down and everythang. I couldn't believe my eyes, man, but I knew it was Mama. Had to be. Who else you know be wearin them sorry-lookin ol hats come rain or shine?

"Then when Lillian come round the corner from the hall into the living room, all feeble and broken like someone had sucked the last of the life out of her...Aw, man! Mama just wrapped her arms around her like she was a big ol wool blanket. And never let go till that wind came, callin her home. Saw it with my own eyes, man. These two, right here. Swear."

Whatever Uncle Ray saw, the day of the violets gave my mother an opportunity she'd missed by not attending the funeral. A chance to say good-bye. And even though it was a little disconcerting to walk into a room full of flowers that weren't there, a certain comfort rested over our house when the violets came calling. My mother may have been the only one who truly believed it, but their presence allowed us to hope something good was never too far behind.

I can see my mother now, the image of her, that Sunday morning at the kitchen table. It bleeds through these pale green walls as clear as the gray of the sky seeps through the bars on my window. She's dressed in a white linen suit jacket with matching skirt, sky blue silk camisole beneath, and blue leather pumps. Her hair's combed back and tied in a bun. Gold hoops dangle from her ears. Autumn Red lipstick graces her lips. As she tucks a napkin into the front of my shirt and my father adds a small pancake to the two pieces of bacon on my plate, try as I might, I just can't reconcile the image of my parents that stormy winter night—and so many nights since—with the one before me now.

"Intercourse," Onya had called it when I finally told her. "Mom and Dad were having sex-u-al intercourse."

I wish I could say it all made sense after that; that learning sex was something in which my parents and other grown-up people commonly engaged eased my mind about what I'd seen. But I hadn't told Onya about the ropes. I hadn't told her about the nasty names my father sometimes called my mother. Or about the strange sensation I felt watching them, how I ran my finger along that wall so many nights in anticipation. And how I crouched down hidden in the corner, just inside the door and watched. Watched as my mother rode my father like an unbroken horse. Licked my lips with envy as he neighed and whinnied and pawed the ground. And that the reason I was late for Sunday brunch every weekend was because I'd only gone to sleep a few hours before. Lain awake all night replaying a singular piece of footage over and over and over.

"You okay, babycakes?" my mother asks, kissing the top of my forehead. She feels my neck with the back of her hand, then brushes my ponytail off to the side. Starts rubbing my shoulders. My father clears my plate, picked-over pancakes still on it.

"Sure wish you'd eat more," my mother adds, worried.

"Oh, she's alright, Lillian," interrupts my father. "Aren't ya, Po?" As he speaks he pauses in measured beats, bopping his head up and down to the music. "Ate the bacon, didn't she? Protein. Building blocks for the muscles. Why she's so lean." He's wiping down the table. As usual, Hmm Hmm, Debbie, and Try Try haven't touched their food. My father wraps it up in cellophane and stores it in the refrigerator. "She'll be alright," he mumbles to himself. "Be alright."

Pressing the fullness of her lips against my forehead one last time, my mother twirls me around in my chair. "Go on now, sweetie," she whispers. "Get your clothes on. We don't wanna be late."

I can hear my parents' voices, low and grumbling, as I traipse through the foyer on the way to my room.

"I wish you wouldn't constantly usurp my authority, Gregory," my mother complains.

"What are you getting at now, Lil?" His tone has changed. The laid-back-everything's-cool-jazz-man has blown the scene. This is the voice he uses under cover of darkness. The one of disdain. The one that so thoroughly despises its co-interlocutor, tolerating it just long enough to teach it a valuable lesson. I've heard that voice before, recognize it from my excursions down the hall.

"Every time I tell the kids to do or not to do something," my mother argues, "you override me. Every time I show some concern about their well-being, you dismiss it like it was a piece of candy. And it's not just the kids either, Gregory, it's at parties, in the store, you name it. I'm sick of this shit," she ends. "It's tiring."

"Lillian," my father starts, "I really think you're overreacting..." But his words are lost in the echo of her heels against the tile of the kitchen and family room floors. And once again, as I rest my hand on the knob of my bedroom door, I feel the numbness burning through my ankles as his big tenor voice falls in step behind Billie.

The room is empty. Bobby and Onya already have their coats on and are out on the patio playing Jacqueline Jacqueline. I close the door and lock it behind me, then run across the floor to my bed. By the time I lift the mattress and reach for the knife, the numbness is already past my knees. I have to hurry. I hide under the covers, and press the tip of the blade down into my thigh. Not deep, just enough to break the skin. And the fact that I wince when it does tells me there's still time. Time to stop it before I'm deadened completely. Slowly, I carve three thin lines, scratches really, along the inside of each thigh. It's dark under the covers, so I can't see the blood. But I know it's there, little dots that coagulate almost before they surface. When my mother knocks on my door to see if I'm ready, I feel my legs reawaken as the numbness begins to dissipate.

"Po," she says as she tries the door. "Time to go, honey."

"Coming," I answer, scrambling to hide the knife back under the mattress.

"Why is this door locked?" she yells, jiggling the handle. "Po, you alright? What's going on?"

"Nothing," I answer, catching my breath as I open the door.

"Look at you, you're still in your pajamas. What's the matter, honey, don't you feel well?"

"I'm okay," I mumble, wondering if three cuts will be enough this time.

"You sure?" she asks, feeling my forehead. "You look a little pale."

"I'm sure."

"Well, you don't feel warm or anything. So I guess you must be. Now stop procrastinating and get that dress on. We don't want to miss the Minister's speech."

We were on our way to hear the Speaker. Preacher Man, Uncle Ray called him. Saver of souls. Leader of the lost. Light o'the blind. It was Commencement Day. And Uncle Ray's girlfriend, Jessica, was graduating from the college. The Speaker was scheduled to deliver the address.

When we arrived, the whole town was there milling about, smoking cigarettes, greeting folks they hadn't seen in a while. Up on stage, a group of five Motown hopefuls jumped up and down, stomping out their version of *Tears of A Clown*. I clung tight to my mother's leg, following her every turn.

"Lillian!" a voice yelled over the crowd. It was Jessica, standing atop one of the risers near the stage. She waved to us and held up a finger, signaling for us to wait, then floated through the crowd as if she were walking on air.

Again she sang my mother's name. "Lillian!" Her cheeks had been kissed by the new spring sun and her blonde hair sparkled, blowing slightly askew in the wind. She and my mother embraced, holding each other long and tight.

"Gregory," Jessica said to my father, accepting his peck on the cheek. "It's been a long time."

"Yes. Yes, it has, Jessica," he said, beholding her as he stepped away. "And, by the way, may I say you look positively radiant?"

"You may, you may," she said smiling, then extended her arms wide and twirled around like Mary Poppins, showing off her graduation gown. "So tell me, Gregory," she said when she was finished. "Where do you think that no good brother of yours has run off to now?"

While my parents and Jessica talked about life after graduation, and what she thought she might do, I decided to go find Onya and Bobby. But they'd long since run off and all I could see when I pulled away from my mother was a sea of swaying eyes attached to blurred faces, staring at us like we were mannequins on display. Even after I turned back around, I could still feel them, their eyes, penetrating and accusatory, uttering all the words their mouths dared not. Words that, remaining hidden protected by the shadows, would grow and fester until a more perfect and certain time. I could feel the scratches turning to scabs on my thighs as I listened.

What's she doing with that nigg...?

Just look at her, blushing and giggling like a schoolgirl.

But what does she see in their kind anyway?

Oh, I just couldn't imagine.

Well, whatever it is, it ain't nothing she can't come by in her own backyard.

Strong words. Hate words. Words that divide.

Damn, man. Another brother gone down.

What's up with that shit?

Who she think she is anyhow?

Like she ain't got enough to choose from without comin over here.

Well, fuck him, then. We ain't good enough for him, fuck him. Ain't no thing.

Damn, man.

"So did Ray tell you the news?" I heard Jessica saying as I drifted back, clinging to my mother ever tighter.

"No, what news?" my mother asked, stroking my head.

"Yeah, baby. What news?" Ray echoed, throwing his arm around Jessica as he strolled up.

"Oh, come on, Ray. You mean you haven't told them?"

"Told em what?" Ray asked, throwing his hands in the air, feigning ignorance.

"Ray!" Jessica shrieked.

"What news?" my mother demanded, impatient.

My father just stood there, half-grinning.

Jessica returned the smile. "We've decided to get married," she announced.

Uncle Ray looked at my father and grimaced, shrugging his shoulders as if to say he couldn't help it.

"Married?" gasped my mother.

Jessica's smile spread all the way across her face. "Isn't it wonderful, Lillian?"

My father's eyes hadn't left Ray's; the corners of the sardonic smile hadn't moved.

"Wonderful?" my mother questioned, squishing my face in her ribs. "Oh, Jessica, are you sure? You don't think it's a little too soon?"

Uncle Ray just kept shrugging his shoulders.

"Well," Jessica started as the President called for the audience to take their seats and for the graduates to assume their positions on the risers. "We've talked about it. Now that we're both finished with school, if not now, when? Besides," she added, just before running off, "I'm pregnant."

As Onya and Bobby ran giggling back to our seats, the Speaker started in on how we were approaching a new time, a new era in which brothers and sisters of all races would hold their heads high in solidarity. That Dr. King's and Brother Malcolm's efforts had not been for naught, they were only the beginning.

"And what they don't know," he enlightened, "what they don't want you to know, is that both Brother Martin and Brother Malcolm were on the same stage together at Selma. Yes. That's right. Together. At Selma."

The Speaker's legs seemed to move all on their own, gliding effortlessly back and forth across the stage, with the Speaker's voice, lyrical and dissident, stressing the second to last syllable of every other word.

"They said *Mal*colm wouldn't *speak* at *Sel*ma. Said he would not *go* to *Sel*ma. But there he was. Yes, there *he* was. *On* stage. With *Mar*tin. At *Sel*ma. Think about why, as you prepare to say good-bye to this... esteemed university. Think about why they did not want you to see *Mal*colm and *Mar*tin to*geth*er in solidarity. Think about what would happen if we all. *Right* here. *Right* now. Shouted. Up to Je*ho*vah. I am, *Some*body! I said, I am, *Some*body! Come on now, let Him hear you. I am *Some*body!"

Within seconds everyone in attendance had risen to their feet, letting the words lift each countenance, rush of emotion, every voice.

"*I am*," we all shouted up to the heavens, "*Somebody!*"

I am Somebody!

Shit
1977

From the moment we walked through the door, it smelled like the devil himself had taken a shit.

"Oh my Lord!" my mother cried, craning her neck to the side as she opened the door.

"Whew! Hold your breath, Po!" warned my father. Holding his nose, he straddled the threshold as if he were stepping over a three-day-old body.

I begged not to go inside, but my mother insisted. "Bobby!?" she yelled, dragging me behind her.

"Bobby!?" echoed my father, with a little more disdain. They marched through the house like soldiers, checking every room, opening and closing every door to every cupboard and closet. I pulled up the rear. Again they yelled my brother's name, but there was no answer. Bobby and my parents no longer knew each other.

"It ain't nothin," Bobby said the day I asked him. "Seem like one night we all went to bed friends, woke up the next morning strangers."

My parents were tired. Of each other, of us. The heaviness in their shoulders confessed it. Even when they were standing upright, shoulders high and proud, their spirits stooped.

They were planning to send him away, and Bobby knew it. It's the reason he let himself stop. Said if he was forced into going someplace, he was sure enough "gonna stop" before he got there. And stop he did. Stopped doing his homework, stopped going to school, stopped playing music, going to sleep, getting dressed. Just stopped. Lifted that waterpipe up to his mouth, and stopped.

He'd been in his room the whole time, alone in the dark, watching reruns of *The Untouchables*.

My mother banged on the door. "Bobby?!" she said as she went in. "Why's it so dark in here? Didn't you hear me calling you?"

"Uh-uh," he answered, standing and lighting a cigarette. "What's up?"

"What's up?" Her eyes took in the room. "You don't smell that?"

"I smell it," Bobby replied, shrugging his shoulders. "Why I closed my door."

"Closed your door? It didn't dawn on you to go see what it was making the whole house smell like Hades?"

"Don't know nothin bout no Hades. Smelled like shit, so I closed my door."

"Uh-huh..." my mother said, staring at him hard and cold. "Why's it so dark in here then? What's going on?"

"Ain't nothin goin on. Watchin t.v..... that's all."

"Watchin t.v.?" She eyed him close. His hands fidgeted in the pockets of his pajamas like they were searching for loose change. The cigarette burned slow, dangled from the corner of his mouth. His eyes, brown and hollow, looked down at the floor. "Then what's that burning over there?"

"Incense."

"Incense?"

"Yeah, what else would it be?"

"Well, now, I don't know, why don't you tell me?"

"Lil!" My father's voice trembled as it called to us from the bathroom.

"Understand," my mother cautioned, pointing her finger at Bobby as she turned to go. "We're not through here. You got that? This conversation is not over. And you better do something about that cigarette!" she added on the way out. "The day you begin to pay your way in this world will be the day you are old enough to smoke in my house. Come on, Po."

After Onya went off to school, it was rare that my parents left Bobby at home alone. Not because he needed a sitter, at fifteen years old Bobby could care for himself; it was the house they were worried about. Ever since the morning everybody woke up strangers, they believed if the house came crumbling down on top of Bobby, he'd still be hunched over in that chair, beneath all the rubble, cradling and sucking on that pipe, taking no notice of the draft that now chilled his bones.

But this night was special, an occasion. One of my father's old jazz buddies—the cat who for reasons unknown never faced his audience—was playing a sold-out show in the city and could only give us three comps; otherwise, whether he wanted to or not, Bobby most certainly would have gone with us. As it was, for the hour and a half we gazed dreamily upon the player's back, amened and hollered as something in the music pouring out of that concealed and muted horn reached in and massaged our souls, Bobby was left alone to make his own music, whichever way he deemed fit. And my parents never quite let themselves relax about it.

While the rest of us gave each other permission to be lifted up and carted away on that something's back, believing all would be okay as long as the music continued on, my father's foot tapped a little bit too long behind the beat, my mother repeatedly checked her watch, shifting awkwardly in her chair, and both of them sucked down way too much of the devil's brew for its effects to ease their minds.

My father was still in the hall when we got there, about two steps back in front of the door, his face washed with shame and resentment. Shame at having been there at all to see it, resentment at having to live from that day forward with the knowledge of it.

"Well, what is it?" my mother urged, as we ran toward him.

But he just stood there, staring, the hallway never seeming longer. And all the while we were running, legs tripping and stumbling to get to the spot in which he stood frozen, his face was tearing itself up trying to turn us back. *You don't want to see this*, it said. *You don't want to know.*

"Sweet, sweet Jesus!" my mother mouthed silently, covering her mouth with the back of her hand.

It started on the doorjamb—a single pleading handprint on one side, a cupful carelessly splashed on the other—running all the way back the length of the vanity, past the side by side set of sinks, the toilet, ending in the bathtub. Shit. Splattered on every available surface: white patterned walls, blue tiled floor, polished brass faucets, double full-length mirror. As though someone had taken the entire bucket of an outhouse, braced themselves against the sides of the doorjamb and heaved, emptying the pail of all its contents, leaving no spot untouched. And there lying smack dab in the middle, despondent and naked, was my Uncle Ray flopping around like a fish, shit still oozing from his asshole.

"Quick, Gregory," my mother motioned hurriedly to my father. "Bring me a bucket and some towels."

Perhaps my father was too busy trying to steady his hand when she spoke, or was hard at work trying to woo the night's liquor tab back into his stomach when my mother sought his help. For he did not, could not, or would not hear. Instead, holding the one hand with the other, he stepped gingerly into the living room and over to the piano. Beanie cap pulled down over his eyes, he played straight through till dawn one minor chord after the other, while my brother slept and my mother and I cleaned, until he was sure all feeling had gone from his seen-too-much body.

Watching him go, my mother breathed, took off her coat and kneeled beside Uncle Ray. With her bare hands, Billie's *Strange Fruit* banging out on the keys in the background, tears flowing as she went, she began to clean the shit from my father's brother's face. "Po," she said, quietly. "Go get a bucket of water and some towels."

Ray and Jessica had had another fight, and Bobby couldn't remember anything after he let Uncle Ray in. Just that when he told him we were in the city, Uncle Ray wanted to wait. Bobby returned to his room.

But judging by the trail of empty pill bottles strewn along the hallway from my parents' bathroom to ours, Uncle Ray had been through my mother's medicine cabinet, swallowed every pill that remained of every prescription for Valium, Librium, and Percodan my mother had ever been given, marking the second of what would be five suicide attempts in a span of seven years. Each, except for one, more serious than the last, and all unsuccessful.

We started to look on him as some kind of larger than life superhero, becoming a crowd of spectators, waiting for his next feat.

"It's like he can't die," I said in awe the last time Bobby let me hang out in his room. "No matter what he does to himself, he just can't die."

"Yeah, well, guess some people just ain't meant to die," Bobby answered. His voice rang low and quiet, like he was speaking from experience. Then all of a sudden it perked up, and he laughed so hard his shoulders shook as he whispered, "Hey, maybe he could be the fifth member of the Fantastic Four. Can't-Die-Man: you can hang me, gas me, shoot me, and shit on me, but I still won't die."

When she heard it, my mother told Bobby he was sick, that he needed help. But secretly, when she was alone on the nights when the house was quiet, she laughed along with him. We all did.

The first time Uncle Ray tried to kill himself, Jessica drove her '65 Beetle nonstop from the city clear through to our driveway, into the backyard, and onto the patio. It was Sunday afternoon and cold, overcast. The weatherman had said first snow. Onya was at cheerleading practice, Bobby and I were watching television, my father was alone at the store, my mother was on the sofa with a book, listening to Ella.

Cradling Lisa Marie in her arms, Jessica emerged from the car wearing a bright yellow halter top, a mini-skirt, and big thick dark sunglasses that failed in their attempt to hide what had become a bulging black eye. Her step was heavy, tired. An overnight bag hung from her shoulder.

"Something wrong with the driveway?" my mother asked, ignoring the black eye. She lifted Lisa Marie out of her mother's arms. The shiner was impressive. Varying shades of blues and blacks and purples. It wrapped all the way around the bridge of her nose, past the bottom crease of her eye socket.

"Oh, you know," Jessica responded, letting the bag slide to the floor before collapsing onto the sofa. "It's Sunday. Never know who might come to visit the Childs family on a Sunday. Wanted to make sure I left plenty of room for parking. Got a cigarette?"

My mother laughed and tossed a pack of Salems onto the table. "Little cold for that top, isn't it?"

Jessica didn't answer, just rifled through the overnight bag until she found a lighter, then lit her cigarette.

"You sure have got your mama's eyes," my mother cooed to Lisa Marie, who only two weeks before had made it through her second birthday. "Ice cold blue, sittin up in your daddy's brown round face. So how soon can we expect him?" she finally asked.

Jessica inhaled deep and exhaled long. Her eyes scanned the room, searching.

"Greg's at the store," my mother answered, responding to the question that hadn't been asked. "Alone."

"I don't know," said Jessica, shaking her head. "I took Lisa Marie and barricaded the door. He tried, but he couldn't get in. Soon as I heard the front door close and the car pull away, I didn't wait around to find out. Could be at Margret's, could've just gone to Stop-&-Go to refill his bottle. I don't know.

"He said it was over, you know. After the birthday party, he said it was going to stop. We talked. He was bouncing Lisa Marie on his knee. Funny thing is," she laughed (though it sounded more like a hiccup), "I believed him."

"I'll go call Greg," my mother said, handing over Lisa Marie. "And see if I can't find us something for that eye."

She returned from the kitchen with an ice pack, two empty wine glasses and a bottle of Cabernet Franc. As instructed, Bobby and I went through the house locking all the doors and windows, pulling the curtains tight. The front door was to be opened for only two people: Onya, who any moment now was due back from cheerleading practice, and my father, should he have a change in attitude and close the store early. But under no circumstances, she made it clear, was Ray Childs to step foot in this house.

"Just once," Onya complained when she got home, "I wish I could live in a normal house with a normal family. Rachel and Katelin's families eat dinner every night at six o'clock sharp."

"Then don't you mean a white house?" Bobby responded, sharply. He was sitting in the corner playing an imaginary game with Hmm Hmm,

Debbie, and Try Try. I could feel the hate in his voice. So could Onya.

"No," she shot back, revealing the hurt in hers. "I mean a normal house that doesn't have twelve-and-a-half-year-old boys running around in their pajamas talking to imaginary people or fathers who come home drunk in the middle of the night saying they just won your best friend's family store in a poker game and the friend once she finds out won't speak to you anymore. Not to mention the spirits haunting this place, parading around knocking things over like they own it, or uncles who beat and stalk their wives, forcing you to lock yourself up in your own home like you were some kind of prisoner."

"That's enough, Onya," my mother ordered, stubbing out her cigarette while lighting another.

"Now, see, that's exactly what I mean," Onya went on, ignoring her. "Rachel's family discusses things when someone has a problem, and Katelin's family has once-a-week family meetings…"

"I said, that's enough, Onya. You are not Rachel, and you are not Katelin, and we are neither of their families. If your history classes haven't taught you that, honey, I'm sorry. You'll just have to settle for 'that's the way it is' until they do. Now if you are uncomfortable sitting in this room with this family, I suggest you go to your own."

Onya turned to go.

"Wait," my mother stopped her. "Bobby, apologize to your sister."

"Apologize!" he squealed, looking up from his game. "Why? Cause she wants to be white?"

"I said, a-pol-o-gize."

Onya waited impatiently, shifting her weight from one foot to the other, the water building up behind her eyes threatening to run and take Onya with it. Bobby said nothing.

"Bobby!" my mother nudged.

Still he said nothing. Just whispered something to Hmm Hmm, Debbie, and Try Try, rose to his feet and shuffled off to his room. Onya ran to the one we shared, slamming the door behind her.

"Now all we need is Ray," my mother looked at Jessica and sighed. "All we need is Ray."

But Uncle Ray didn't come. Not that night, nor the next, nor the one after. My father came through the door around eight-thirty, arms overflowing with McDonald's bags. But Uncle Ray was a no-show. In fact, for the next three days, house shut up tight as a fortress, children forbidden to go anywhere but to school and back, we heard not so much as a peep from Uncle Ray until the night of the third day, when just like Lazarus he rose. Just two-and-a-half weeks after his baby girl's second birthday, Grandma Margret called from the hospital to report that Uncle Ray had hung himself from a drainpipe in her basement.

The doctors didn't know how, but Uncle Ray survived. There was no brain damage that wasn't already there before the hanging and his voice would have a new gravelly quality due to near asphyxiation. But their true bewilderment lay in the space between the base of his head and the tip of his spine—his neck was perfectly intact. And as far as they could tell, it had to be something in the way he tied the noose. There was no other explanation. If asphyxiation and lack of oxygen didn't get him, the broken neck should have.

For three days, little curious men in white coats, headlamps beaming from the center of their foreheads, stethoscopes hanging from their necks, poked and prodded and thumped, asking question after question after question until everyone was about to drop dead from sheer exhaustion. In the end, after all the releases had been signed, it was agreed —Uncle Ray was to live immortal in the annals of medical science.

But in my father's eyes, he had fallen. Outside the hospital, after he slapped Ray on the shoulder and said, "Hey, glad you made it, man," after he held Grandma Margret in his arms, whispering, "I know, I know," while she cried thanking her maker, my father confided to my mother that he didn't care what catastrophic event happened, what desperation had suddenly befallen him, sure as she was standing there, rest assured he would never ever attempt to take his own life. Any man who did, in his opinion, was no longer a man. Our lives, he insisted, had been fought for, delivered to us on palls and backs of blood, we were not worthy to take it upon ourselves to end them in despair. Especially over the fidelity of some damn white woman.

When my mother talked about fear, that maybe his disgust was mired in the knowledge that Ray was his brother, and that white woman or no, he wondered if it couldn't happen to him as well, my father said no. When she spoke about being human, argued that none of us, no matter how certain, knew for sure how we'd react in a given situation until we came face-to-face with it, again my father said no. And when she whispered that maybe Ray's song was sung a little too close to home, that just maybe, at one time or another, he'd shared some of those same thoughts of suicide himself, my father looked at my mother and said, "Woman, now I know you're crazy!"

And so it happened on the night his feet lagged a little too long behind the beat, while my mother and I cleaned and my brother slept, face awash in shame, my father turned his back on his brother to play away his feeling.

"Lillian?" Uncle Ray mumbled, after my mother had washed all the shit from his body, except his privates, which she was about to do next.

"Yes, Ray," she answered, running the worn cloth through the crack in his cheeks, over his scrotum, and last, his penis.

"I fucked up."

"No, you didn't, baby."

"Yeah, I did. Fucked up big time this time."

"No, baby. Not big time. Wouldn't be here if it was big time. You just got a little messed up is all, like we all do, all the time. But you're all cleaned up now," she said, dropping the soiled rag back in the bucket. "You're all cleaned up now. Help me get him to his feet, Po."

With one arm draped around my mother, the other sprawled around me, minor chords pounding away in the background, the three of us dragged, crawled, and everything but walked down the hall to my parents' room and over to the bed. After covering Uncle Ray with a blanket, we sat down to catch our breath.

"You alright?" my mother asked, laying her hand on my shoulder.

"Yeah," I lied. "You?"

"Oh yes, baby," she smiled, hugging me tighter in that moment than I will ever remember. "I'm alright. I'm alright."

Normal People
1991

"Self-inflicted," Bobby read from my chart. He stood at the foot of my bed in the standard uniform of the Ministers (a trim black suit loose in the shoulders, cropped at the ankles), reeking of the Armani aftershave that had become his trademark. He held the clipboard an arm's length away as though it were a contaminated newspaper clipping he was reading aloud to the flock, demonstrating yet another example of the painted demon's uncanny ability to trap and ensnare one of its sistahs.

"Deeply incised wounds of the forearms and antecubital fossae," he continued. "Accompanied by several hesitation cuts, apparently self-inflicted. Patient is a twenty-seven-year-old African-American female who has requested admittance under 72-hour watch for further observation and rest... Well, girl," he grinned slyly, hanging the clipboard back on the bedpost. "The sickness got you good this time, didn't it?"

I didn't answer.

To exorcise the sickness, also known as the white man's disease, was the reason Bobby believed Allah had sent him to me. And other than reading my chart, his reference marked the first words spoken by either of us in the fifteen minutes he'd been in the room.

"It was over that white girl, wasn't it?"

Still, I didn't respond. Just sat on my bed, staring at him, trying to figure out how he got here so fast. How he'd found out.

"Po," he said, rotating his neck and throwing his shoulders back, trying to shake off his disgust. "Don't you know that girl ain't nothin but Lucifer in disguise?"

"If she's such a devil, why are you so nice to her all the time?"

"Come again?" he asked, raising his eyebrows.

"Every time you see her, you're always going out of your way to make conversation."

He adjusted the clip on his tie and smiled, then strolled over to the white plastic visitors' chairs on the other side of the room and sat down. (Each room had two. Aside from the bed, they were the only places to sit.) "Let the devil think he's got you fooled, Po," he said finally, pausing to cross his legs. "He relaxes, becomes weak and vulnerable." He clasped his hands loosely around each other, then slowly let them rest on his crossed thigh. "But Ol Scratch got another thing comin, lil sis," he went on. "It's me who's foolin him."

His confidence made me smile. "You foolin the devil, Bobby?" I asked.

"Killin him with kindness, Po, killin him with kindness."

"Yeah, well, maybe that's what I'm doing, too."

"What, foolin the devil?" he laughed.

"Sure, why not?" I shrugged.

"Aw, girl. Sleepin with him is more like it."

"You think your way's all that better? I thought you were supposed to be one of Allah's foot soldiers."

"To the grave, girl," he chanted, lazily placing his right fist over his heart. "To the grave."

"Then don't you think the devil's fully aware of who's fighting on the other side? How you gonna fool somebody, Bobby, if he already knows who you are? Better be careful, bro. Underestimating your enemy's liable to make you as vulnerable as he is."

"Ah, but see now, that's where you wrong, lil sis. Ol Scratch is greedy. Overconfident. Got his hands embedded in a thousand pots all at the same time. Probably even thinks he can sink those clawed hooves into my bones.

But I'll tell you what, he don't even know the direction I'm comin from. And if he gets lucky enough and figures it out, Allah's got a million more comin right behind me."

I never realized how much Bobby reminded me of my father. The trim cut of the suit. The bobbing up and down of his head as he spoke. The sardonic smile that never left his lips. And mixed up somewhere in all the madness spewing from his mouth, the tenor of his voice charmed and soothed, making even the air feel light.

"So what you gonna do, Po? Just sit up here and...," he glanced over at the clipboard, "... rest?"

"Looks like the plan for now," I said blankly.

"The plan, huh? What about the job?"

"What about it?" I shrugged again.

"What about it? You think that ol white man at the typehouse just gonna let you take a few days off, then return to work like nothin ever happened?"

The floor nurse poked her head in to tell Bobby he only had five more minutes.

"Gotta make a move sometime, sis," he finished, collecting his coat and starting for the door. "Can't just sit in here gatherin moss forever."

His righteousness started to grate on me. "Time running out on me, Bobby?" I asked.

"Time's runnin out on ol Scratch, girl. But Allah's got all the time in eternity and the patience to wait it out. He'll get you back home. Bet on it." For the first time, as he rested his hand on the door, he stared into the webbing on the bandage, almost as though he were looking through it deep into the wounds. "Saw Ray the other day," he said. His eyes didn't move.

"Yeah? He recognize you?"

"Naw, girl. You know he all tore up on that poison."

"Yeah, sometimes I wish I could forget." I paused and lowered my voice. "Do me a favor, Bobby."

"What's that?" he asked, looking up.

"Keep all this between me and you?"

"Little late for that, ain't it?" he said, laughing awkwardly. "Lot more folks than me and you up in this place."

"You know what I mean. Don't tell Grandma Margret."

"Why not? Fraid she'll find out just how sick you really are?"

"No, I just think she's got enough to worry about right now. Don't you?"

"Yeah, guess you right, Po. How bout that? For once we actually agreein on somethin."

I sighed and looked at the floor. "Was a time when we agreed on a lot of things, Bobby."

His eyes studied the bandage. "Will be again, Po," he said at last. "By the grace of the good Lord, Allah, there will be again. Alright then," he added, shaking his head as he opened the door. "Check you in a few, girl. Oh," he stopped, turning back. "Funeral's Thursday. Think you be done restin up by then?"

"Hard to say, Bobby. Thursday's a long way off, you know."

"Yeah, guess it is, girl," he answered, fingering his hat. "Guess it is, at that."

When the door closed behind him, the musk of the Armani loitering in his wake, I thought about Bobby running around in his pajamas, playing with Hmm Hmm, Debbie, and Try Try, and wondered if Allah had fought for their souls as much as Bobby believed He was fighting for mine.

The first time I cut myself I was seven years old. It was back in 1971, about a month after Aunt Florida, on what had come to be her last visit, suddenly took ill and died in the hospital. Truth be told, it wasn't so sudden. Seems Aunt Florida had been in the fourth stage of uterine cancer and, according to the emergency room doctor, she'd known about it for some time. My mother refused to believe him saying that if Aunt Florida truly had been sick in that way she would have told someone. And even if she hadn't, my mother added, one of us would have sensed it. "Grief is more likely," she argued. "Florida Po, bless her heart, died of plain and simple down-home grief."

Aunt Florida was really my great-aunt, Grandma Janie's sister, the youngest of Great-grandma Shirley's two children. Because she always made a point of talking to me like I was grown, she was my favorite of all the relatives. The grief my mother was so certain had killed her was the off-spring of standing idly by, helpless, as she watched her longtime companion, a woman named Gooch Johnson, waste slowly away from liver disease.

Unlike Grandma Janie, Aunt Florida never married. And to hear her tell it, she never intended to. She was perfectly happy, she said, sorting mail at the post office down on 23rd Street and helping Great-grandma Shirley look after my mother. But despite her intentions, even though the law never recognized it, married was exactly what she'd become.

"I was just fine with things the way they was," she'd always remind us. I remember sitting next to her on the sofa, watching the smoke make rings in the air as she puffed on her cigar.

"What'd I need with another body to care for?" she'd continue be-tween puffs. "Let alone another miserable life to cry over. Watchin the clock when they a few minutes late from work. Wonderin if they got jumped or not on the way home. Still don't know what the Lord was thinkin," she said, patting my head as she exhaled. "The way I saw it, and still do, I guess, I had all I could handle worryin bout your mother and Mama."

The Lord, it seemed, disagreed. And just a few days after Aunt Florida's thirty-fourth birthday, after letting her get settled in the comfortable cush-ion of being alone, He decided it was time to give her some more. Just minutes after her co-workers surprised her with birthday cake and candles, the 23rd Street post office supervisor ushered Aunt Florida into his office and closed the door behind her. She was being promoted, he told her. He was taking her out of the sorting pool and putting her behind the counter. Aunt Florida was to be the Postmaster General's new liaison to his 23rd Street regulars.

Aunt Florida didn't like it. Didn't like it at all. At best it was a bad sign. "You have to remember," she said, "this was 1955. Whoever heard of a Negro sellin postage to white folk in 1955?" But along with the promo-tion came a significant increase in pay. And bad sign or no, in addition to taking care of my mother and Mama, sellin postage to white folk was ex-actly what Aunt Florida did, until Gooch Johnson swaggered through the double glass doors of the lobby to get a look at the colored woman working her own window at the post office.

"I remember that day like I remember the day you was born," she told me. "There I was, carefully counting out Mrs. Oldenberg's change. You know in those days, a colored person couldn't afford to make no mistakes. But if you was gonna try your luck and mess up anyway, Mrs. Oldenberg was not the one to try it on. So there I was tryin my damnedest not to mess up, when in through the door walked the most beautiful black face I'd ever seen. And proud too. Dark, shiny, and proud, with black shiny eyes to match. I had to count Mrs. Oldenberg's change three times before I got it right.

"Every head in the post office turned to behold that face, like they was suddenly lookin on royalty. And right in the midst of all their starin, ol Gooch took her place in line like she'd been doin it all her life, darin any of em to say word one about it. 'Heard they gave one of us our own window down here,' she whispered in this deep throaty voice when she reached my window. 'Decided I had to come check it out for myself.' And that was all she said. Not one word more. Just stared at me awhile to see what I was about, then slid ten cents across the counter to purchase a single stamp before walking out those doors just as proud as when she had walked in."

Gooch, it turned out, worked in a nearby factory and had learned of Aunt Florida's mixed fortune when she overheard the foreman discussing the matter with one of the men. From then on, everyday at half past noon she appeared at Aunt Florida's window to purchase a single stamp. To most ears, never more than formalities passed between them.

"Afternoon, Miz Po."

"Afternoon, Miz Johnson."

But it wasn't long before they became sweet on each other and decided to share their lives. Immediately, the rumors and insults flew, from folks outright threatening to kill them to the ladies of the neighborhood standing on their stoops and raising their eyebrows whenever the pair passed by. But Aunt Florida and Gooch paid them no mind. And for thirteen years, they bore the other's burdens as they would their own until Nixon won election in 1968 and Gooch finally lost her battle to liver disease.

Three years later, Aunt Florida called my mother and told her she was coming for a long overdue visit.

In the weeks after Aunt Florida's death, the air around the house hung low and heavy. Every room was flush with the essence of violets. Not the fresh-cut scent we'd all grown used to, but the stale wet soup of sad and weeping ones. Even Great-grandma Shirley, it seemed, believed Aunt Florida passed before her time.

"Mama's crying again," my mother would whisper every time a breeze would stir the soup simmering beneath her nose. Then all of a sudden she'd close her eyes and tilt her head to the side as though she were listening to it speak. The soup. As though in its brewing, it was preparing her for something.

I used to watch her and wonder what she heard, and why, no matter how I tried to mimic her, I couldn't hear it as well. It all felt so silly and foolish, standing there in the middle of the hall or the living room, arms overflowing with one load or another, heads tilted to one side, waiting for secret words of wisdom that never came. And yet, in spite of all my doubt, a small part of me always held my breath, hoping that the good times the violets foretold were real, wishing they would hurry up and get here.

We tried to function as normal as could be expected. My mother rose early to fix breakfast before Onya, Bobby, and I trudged off to school. My father skimmed over the newspaper before he went off to work each morning. Billie sang the blues from sunup to sundown, but all our movements were clouded in distraction. Especially my mother's. Every time she set out to complete some chore around the house, whether it was running the vacuum or gathering up dirty clothes for washing, in mid-chore she'd forget what she was doing and move on to something else. Before long, we never thought twice if we found a carton of milk where the vacuum cleaner should have been, or stumbled upon a bag of dirty laundry sitting on the curb in place of the garbage can. We'd just pick up whatever the out-of-place item was and put it back where it belonged. Once my father even found his can of shaving cream frozen solid inside the freezer. So it was easy, when the time came, to remove one of my mother's paring knives from the kitchen drawer and hide it under my mattress without her noticing.

I got the idea from a story Aunt Florida used to tell, called the Curse of Uncle George. Uncle George was a slave. "A crazy one, too," Aunt Florida would say, with a penchant for running away and getting caught. But that wasn't what made him crazy. "Shoot," she'd add. "If there's a soul in captivity who hasn't been whipped for runnin at least once, I'd like to meet him." What made folks look at Uncle George sideways, she said, was that every time he ran and got caught, the lashing he gave himself was worse than any the overseer could have imagined.

All told, he ran five times through entanglements of birches, poplars, and chokecherries, looking for something called freedom. And each time, after the overseer brought him back and made an example of him, Uncle George found some way to mutilate himself even further. Whether it was ramming his head against the trunk of a tree until it burst open or chopping off his middle and index fingers with a pick ax, he always managed to outdo the overseer. After the third time, when Uncle George swallowed an entire can of lye that ate up most of his insides, the overseer stopped trying. And the next time Uncle George ran, since he was obviously doing a better job of it, the overseer decided to save himself some energy and let the nigger punish himself.

Uncle George didn't disappoint. As soon as he was turned loose after being dragged back on the end of a rope for the fourth time in a row, while the rest of the plantation shook their heads in disbelief, he took hold of one of the overseer's branding irons and burned his master's initials into every reachable spot on his body.

"It was like he was chastisin himself for gettin caught," Aunt Florida said. "Either that, or somewhere along the way, he stopped runnin for freedom and started runnin open-armed toward death. You know, figurin the two were one and the same. Either way, he was still a fool. Everybody know death got its own timetable. And only a fool would try to change it."

The fifth time he ran was his last. The overseer was nearly doubled over in hysterics when he brought him back, like he couldn't wait to see what new castigation Uncle George had in store for himself. He wouldn't wait long. As soon as he cut him loose, before he could gather his wits to stop him, Uncle George reached for the overseer's rifle, stuck the barrel inside his mouth and blew his head off. Rushing death or not, if being free was truly the same as dying, Uncle George had finally found freedom.

"Now you know," Aunt Florida would end to scare us. "Damn curse has been with us ever since. So watch yourselves," she'd warn. "Ain't none of us safe." And anytime Onya, Bobby, or I would get out of line, or a certain relative would get up the gumption to lose his mind, Aunt Florida would blame The Curse.

"Now what'd I tell you all bout actin like Uncle George," she'd yell before sending us to our room. "You know what it is," she'd whisper to my mother under her breath, when we got news of the latest cousin to crack. "It's that ol Uncle George thing showin its ugly butt again."

Aunt Florida died before I could to tell her about the numbness. The lack of feeling that had begun to consume me day and night. Maybe Uncle George was consumed by it too, I wanted to tell her. Maybe the overseer's whip made him feel again, and his own further retribution was an attempt to keep that feeling alive. Maybe he wasn't rushing death at all. In time, I decided Aunt Florida was wrong. It was a curse alright, a man-made one even, but Uncle George wasn't the maker. He just passed it on. At one time or another, it made visits to us all, and now it had found its way to me.

So it wasn't from idle curiosity that I turned to the knife. Nor was it, as Bobby and the ward counselor believed, an attempt to escape from a hostile world of worrisome and unwanted demons. The act of drawing my own blood with one of my mother's paring knives was born out of the desire to feel. To prove to myself that I could.

After Bobby left, the floor nurse told me I was wanted in the counselor's office.

"Hi, Po," she said when I entered. "My name is Cheryl Foster. I'll be your counselor during your stay with us." With her hand, she motioned to a chair across from her desk and told me to have a seat.

Cheryl was a pale and skinny white woman whose young face and eagerness to see me get well told me she was fresh out of graduate school. The reason she sent for me, she said, was to learn about the events leading up to my arrival on the ward. The knowledge, she confided, would help her determine the best course of treatment. She also needed to determine, she added while flipping through the manila folder that contained my file, if I still posed a threat to myself.

"So," she smiled, resting her hands on the folder, "wanna tell me what happened?"

"Not really." I crossed my legs and leaned back in the chair the way Bobby had done back in my room.

"Says in your file that you tried to slit your wrist. Is that true?"

"Not exactly."

"Not exactly," she repeated, nodding her head up and down as though she had anticipated my response. The smile was still frozen on her face. "Wanna tell me what that means?"

I tried hard to keep from rolling my eyes. I knew when I checked myself in here that I'd have to go through this. That I'd have to play along with the charade of being suicidal. A part of me just wanted to tell this woman the truth. To shock her. I didn't try to kill myself, I wanted to yell, I was in a heavy scene with my lesbian lover and we got a little carried away, okay! But I can't tell you that. I can't tell you that people carve each other up in my world. Shit all over each other and whip one another until we have trees on our backs just for pleasure. Because it's beyond the realm of comprehension in your world, so you and yours have made it illegal. And if I tell you that, you could send me to jail. Even though you've been trained to understand my need to end it all, to take a razorblade to my wrist in a final effort to escape the mounting pressure, you will never relate to my need to keep the numbness at bay. Because understanding that will force you to admit that you're just as dead inside as I am.

"Means I wasn't trying to slit my wrist," I answered, finally.

"Okay. So you weren't trying to slit your wrist, but you did give yourself a pretty serious laceration along your lower forearm," she said, glancing at the bandage. "Did you mean to do that?"

I didn't answer.

She clasped her hands firmly together, leaned over the desk, and looked deeply into my eyes to convey the seriousness of her words. "I'm not here judge you, Po," she said. "I'm here to help you. But I can't do that if you don't talk to me."

Still, I didn't answer.

"Do you want my help?"

"Not really."

"Okay," she said, sitting back in her chair. "Then why did you check yourself in here?"

"You got the file."

"Yes, I do," she answered, opening the folder. "It says here that you requested admittance for further observation and rest. Is that right?"

"The 'rest' part is. 'Observation' is the doctor's word."

"Okay, so you don't need observation. Let's talk about what you need to rest from?" She was smiling again.

I scooted to the edge of my chair and decided to be nice. "Life," I said, returning her smile. "Doesn't everybody now and then?"

"Well, I suppose so. But I'm not sure everybody finds it necessary to take a knife to their wrist to get it."

"That was an accident."

"What was?" She knew she had touched a nerve.

I looked down at the bandage.

"Okay," she went on, reading from the file. "But there were also hesitation cuts, smaller ones that weren't as serious. Were those accidents as well?"

"No."

"So you cut yourself on purpose. Have you done this before?"

I decided to play along. "Sure."

"Often?"

"Sometimes."

"And why do you feel the need to cut yourself?" She was taking notes as she spoke.

"Why not?"

"Surely, you must have a reason."

"Yeah? What do you think it is?"

"I don't know," pausing to look up. "That's why we're here, remember? Are you depressed?"

"No."

"Are you trying to cut out some part of you that you don't like?"

I laughed out loud, I couldn't help it. This fresh-faced woman was trying her textbook best. "No," I said.

"Why do you laugh?"

"It's funny."

"What's funny?"

"You thinking you know so much about me. You don't know anything."

"You're right, I don't. So why don't you tell me something?"

I wondered if this woman had ever listened to Billie. If there was ever a time when she was unable to face the music without singing the blues. I was debating whether or not to tell her the story of Uncle George when the floor nurse entered the office and whispered something in her ear.

"Do you know someone named Mary, Po?" she asked when the nurse left.

"Why?"

"She's in the lobby. It seems she's pretty anxious to see you. Was she there when the accident happened?"

I just stared at her. I was finished talking. As my mother would've said, this conversation was over. The counselor read my look correctly.

"Okay, Po. I guess that's enough for now." Cheryl Foster jotted a few more notes, closed the folder, and slid it in her desk drawer. "We'll pick up where we left off tomorrow morning in group. Maybe it will be easier for you to talk among people with similar experiences."

I walked back to my room, anticipating what Mary would say first. I wondered how long she would wait before demanding to see me. On a whim, I started to skip down the hall, making believe I was a washed-up Golden Age starlet who'd been locked away in an asylum for the last thirty years, feigning excitement over the notion of two callers in one day. Who could it be this time? I wondered aloud to the blank internal stares of the medicated patients lined up along the wall. A fan? My long lost niece or nephew? Perhaps it was death, complete with top hat and tails, coming to take me for one last ride in his carriage.

I wasn't that far off. When Mary entered my room, she looked like death was all around her. Her face was pale and gaunt, and her eyes were cold.

"A rest?!" she yelled when she closed the door. Immediately she began squeezing her hands over and over, as if she were wringing a stubborn drop of water from a rag before placing it on the line. And though the tears chose to wait until later, the pacing commenced as soon as she saw the bandage. Back-and-forth and back-and-forth she started to walk, from the thick metal door as it latched behind her to one putrid-green wall after the other, stealing hurried glances at the bandage each time she reversed direction.

"I'm tired, Mary," I tried to explain. Even the session with Cheryl required more effort than my body was willing to offer.

Her eyes, pale and green like the walls, squinted and fixed on me as though they failed to recognize the wiry tan legs swinging from the bolted-down bed in front of her as those of the woman she'd been fucking the past two years.

"Sitting there freezing in that emergency room," I tried again, focusing on the section of floor outside the path of the pacing. "In that concrete-walled room with no windows, remembering and not remembering, timing the spaces between each splash of blood, as it spread in diaspora across the sea of linoleum, all those people sobbing and coughing and moaning, I just suddenly felt so tired. You know? Like my legs, arms, and feet all looked back and turned to stone, relieving themselves of their burden to move, my neck and shoulders yelling, 'Get ready, hands, it's fallin. This head is comin down. We done bore this weight too long.'"

"Listen, baby," she said, stepping up the rhythm of the pacing. "It's not that I can't appreciate your being tired. I know you're tired. You deserve to be tired, exhausted. But, honey, normal people take vacations when they need a rest. They take long relaxing walks along the river and go fishing, escape to isolated cabins in the woods. Do you understand what I'm trying to say, Po? Go visit an old friend for awhile. Shit! Check yourself into one of those fancy-ass health spas or terrycloth retreats where they provide for your every need and teach you how to macramé. Shut yourself up in your goddamn room and unplug your fuckin phone, but baby please realize you don't belong here."

"What's the difference?" I asked.

"What?" She stopped pacing for instant and then started up again.

"What's the difference, really, between one of those chi-chi health spas and here? I mean there really isn't one, when you think about it."

"Po, people do not choose to check themselves into mental institutions just because they need a rest."

"No? Well, maybe they should." I couldn't tell her that it really wasn't much of a choice. That after they stitched up the wound and started grilling me with questions, my head felt like it was about to fall off. That I tried to leave, but my arms and legs played tricks on me and refused to move. How I sat there, trying to lift my feet off the floor, knowing that soon I'd have to answer. Then it hit me. Rest. I needed to rest and figure things out. Right here, right now. Just for a few days until things started to come around.

And the longer I thought about it, the more it made sense. I could finally stop giving myself that headache, worrying about how I was going to get out of there. Physically. Pillars of stone posing for my feet and legs. How was I ever going to make it from the cot to the door, for instance? From the door to the exit? The exit to the house? All the way back to my room to pick up those books that had fallen? If I stayed, I wouldn't have to think about that anymore. I wouldn't have to think about anything. Not the shadows, not Aunt Florida, not the phone, not a thing.

"But why?" she asked, tears starting to fall. Her hands were red and welted from the wringing. The unwavering clomp of her work boots against the linoleum was making me dizzy. "Why didn't you tell me what was going on? I thought we were in this together, baby. You could've at least sent word. Did you even think about what I was going through out there, waiting for you to come out, wondering what you'd told them? If they'd called the cops? Whether or not they were going to treat you?

"Then you didn't come out, and no one else did to talk to me either. And that bitch in reception: 'You're not a family member, miss. We can only give out information to family members.' Well, they can just go fuck their family members for all I care! I was going crazy." She was reaching a hysterical pitch.

"Keep your voice down," I hissed.

"If you had only told me. I mean, all I could think was to call Bobby."

Mmmmmmmm. "So you called Bobby."

"If you had just told me something, baby. Anything, you know? Like what was going through your head at the time. Maybe together we could've worked something out."

"Damn, I should've known."

"Don't you see, Po, I had no choice. They wouldn't let me see you. I was involved in this too, remember? What film do you think was running through my head? How do you think I felt, watching the blood hit the floor?"

My head was spinning. "What'd you tell him?"

"Who?"

"Bobby! What'd you tell him?!"

"What do you mean what'd I tell him?"

"Just what I said. How'd you get him to let you come back here? What did you tell him?"

At last the pacing stopped. Backing up against the cold metal door, she slid down its frame into a half-sitting, half-squatting position, cupping her head in the now welted and wrung-out hands. Then slowly, almost against her will, she said it. "I told him you tried to commit suicide," she whispered. "I didn't know what else to say. I didn't know what he would do. What he would think. I just wanted... I needed to see you. Talk to you. Find out..." She was looking for absolution, comfort, assurance that we were still okay.

"It was an accident," I said, finally. "It's okay. The phone rang and fucked everything up. Next time we'll unplug it."

But there wouldn't be a next time, and no, it wasn't okay. Not the accident itself, or even that other road we could have traveled, the one that passed through the town of knowledge called she would have done it willfully. It was the foul taste of the groveling that sickened me. The revealing of yet another weak spot in a once thought sturdy countenance. Until this morning, just like her masters before her, Mary could have whipped me silly if she'd wanted to, then cut off my feet to keep me from running away. As long as she didn't freak out or grovel later, everything would have been fine. As long as she'd meant it. And if she hadn't, as long as she made me believe every ounce of her being had, we could have gone on. But from the moment she slumped down sobbing against a cold metal door, cupping her head in a pair of welted and wrung-out hands seeking absolution, our journey was over. Never again would she be able to give me what I needed. No, it would never be okay. And we both knew it.

MONDAY

Debbie's Dead
1976

We each fought the curse in different ways. Like Uncle George, Uncle Ray thought he could beat it by putting an end to his body. I tried to cut it out. Onya attempted to drink it away. And Bobby decided to get rid of it by killing off the pieces of his soul.

The first to go was Debbie. And though we never discovered how or when he did it really, as the killing of souls must always be, we all supposed it was violent.

It was the summer of '76. The country was beaming with confidence and hope, instilled by a little-known peanut farmer who had won the Democratic nomination for President. There was no threat of rain, but the air was thick, hot, and wet.

The surplus of moisture was caused by an accident over at the laboratory. A chemical spill that clouded the environment with so many hazardous materials, the mayor was forced to shut down the town. In addition, he advised all those who didn't have emergency business to please remain inside. So even though it was late Monday morning, because everybody was home, it felt like Sunday.

Despite the stifling heat, everyone was busy. Onya was preparing for cheerleading camp. Between trips to the sink for water, she was knocking over vases and lampshades, turning cartwheels across the living room floor.

But it was her first summer as counselor, she complained, when my mother told her to stop. If she wanted to be invited back, she needed to make an impression.

"Then make it in your room," my mother ordered. "It's too hot for you to be jumping around like that anyway. And unless they're giving out ribbons for how much of my good crystal you can destroy, I see no cause for you to go on breaking up my house."

Billie was busy singing about being down so long that down no longer worried her. And my parents were busy huddled around the card table with Ray, Sumner, and MacArthur, dabbing sweat, discussing which might be the better way to handle the Klan.

"Well, I say we meet em down at the county line with a bunch of semi-automatics," Ray said in his gravelly voice, banging his fist on the table for emphasis. "Scatter those honky-tonk asses all over the woods."

"Semi-automatics!" Sumner countered. "Fool, you been watchin too much television. Can't you just see us now? You, me, Mac, Greg, and that little ol white wife a-yours, standin out on somebody's county line with some semi-automatic weapons we done got from Lord knows where, tryin to turn back a hundred-some-odd souls in white sheets with that many more guns than we got. Just where we s'posed to get all these from in the first place? You been runnin with Stokely and Geronimo behind our backs? Made some connections we don't know about? And even if we did manage to catch up to em in number, who you think the police gonna arrest first? Damn, Ray, if I didn't know you better, I'd ask Greg what you been smokin."

"Ey man," Ray shot back, leaping up from his chair. "First off, you leave my wife outta this. Second, motherfucker, I don't like your tone. And third, you know goddamn well every black sonofabitch up in this town got his hands on some kinda piece."

"Oh, no!" my mother broke in. "Wait! Wait! Wait! Wait! Wait! Have you lost your mind? Have you forgotten? My children live in this house!"

Ray and Sumner glared at each other across the table.

"Now, you want to go and disrespect each other with that foul language," she continued. "Fine. Just do it someplace else."

"Lillian's right, brothahs," MacArthur chimed in, running his tongue along a pair of snuff-stained lips. "We all family here." He rubbed the top of his head like a crystal ball as if it would show him the future, then placed his hand on his chest and bowed toward my father. "No disrespect, Greg, Lillian," he offered sheepishly.

"Yeah, man," Uncle Ray added, sitting back down. "I was outta my head for a second. This fool," pointing at Sumner, "got me all caught up."

My father glanced at my mother, then back at Ray. "Don't worry about it, man," he said, smiling.

"Me too, Greg," Sumner threw in, half-hearted. "But we still ain't figured out what we gonna do about the Klan. Brothah Truly says we ain't got much time, man. Says they marched through Hamilton Saturday last and burnt up two churches. Left a note, too. Painted in big red block letters on the sidewalk. 'Tell all them educated niggas,' it said, 'we comin their way next.'"

Sumner, Truly, and MacArthur, along with my father and Uncle Ray, were all members of the Black Student Alliance—the BSA. Without the aid of the BSA, Uncle Ray would have never been admitted to the college. Not because he wasn't smart enough or didn't have the grades; to hear my mother tell it, he held the highest GPA in his graduating class. The Alliance, my father told us, was founded to put pressure on the Board of Admissions, so that bright black hopefuls like my Uncle Ray wouldn't have to jump through the same hoops my father and my mother had to get an education. But like most upstart causes with good intentions (fanatic or otherwise), once the BSA started to wield a handful of power, simply keeping an eye on the secret doings of the Board of Admissions was akin to tossing the remains of a bone to a ravenous pack of dogs. It just didn't satisfy. In time, the maneuverings of the Board took a distant back seat to knowing the whereabouts and activities of the KKK, the FBI, Nixon, and ultimately each other.

In addition to having its hand deep in the pocket of every fistfight, riot, and race war this side of the Ohio, along with keeping detailed dossiers on each of its members, the Alliance had a special file (locked neatly

away in a safe somewhere) on every prominent, or even potentially prominent, member of the community.

"Hell," Uncle Ray once joked, "they got a sheet so long on that Preacher
Man of yours, they not only can tell you the color of his shit, but the odor
of it, how often he takes it, and the value, or lack thereof, in its nutritional
breakdown."

The BSA was now the Black Student Alliance in name only, leaving
the Board of Admissions free to discriminate at will, our bright black hopefuls
left alone to fend for themselves.

"Your point is well-taken, Sum," my father responded to Sumner. "But
it'll have to wait. Even the Klan won't strike on a day like today. And right
now, brothahs, the nourishment of my family seeks my attention. You're
welcome to join us," he added, then excused himself to search for a box of
grits.

As my father started to fix brunch, and Billie moved on from stating
her right to sing the blues to begging sympathy from the weeping branches
of a willow, my mother made sure all the condiments were in order: butter
on the toast, juice and water in the pitchers, sugar in the sugar bowl. Sumner
and MacArthur grumbled something about losing time as they shuffled
from the card table to the kitchen counter. And everyone, it seemed, either
harmonized in silence or wept along in solace to the blues of the Lady.

For once I wasn't the last to sit down. And when my mother finally
got around to telling Onya to stop all that nonsense and wash up for breakfast,
after stopping to pour another glass of water, she actually listened. No one
noticed that Bobby was missing until my father—for the second Sunday in
a row—skipped over Hmm Hmm's plate and Bobby failed to complain.

"Where is Bobby?" my mother asked, startled.

"Bobby!" my father yelled to the back of the house. "Better get while
the gettin's good!"

He rounded the corner still and calm, bony yellow hands hanging limp
at his sides, eyes beady and tight, the circumference of the pupils appearing
to have shrunk a full size overnight. My mother thought it was the illness.

"What's the matter, honey?" she asked, moving toward him. "Don't
feel good this morning?"

Bobby didn't answer, just stood behind his chair, frail arms dangling, staring at the three extra places lining the table.

"Bobby, sweetie?" my mother tried again, this time feeling his forehead. "You okay?"

"What's the problem, little man?" MacArthur drawled, yellow teeth smacking stained lips. "White man got you down?"

"Probably just the weather," my father answered, filling his plate with bacon, eggs, and grits. "Nothing a little food won't cure. Come on, Lillian," he soothed, "he'll be alright; let's eat."

Bobby's sickly appearance was nothing new. It had been with us for some time. Six months ago, his skin started to turn progressively yellow, his eyes a continuum of pale and hollow. The doctor said he had hepatitis. But on the Monday morning that felt like Sunday, my mother was right—his pallor had changed. Though it wasn't from illness, at least not the one my mother was thinking of. It was because he had made a decision, a settlement, and followed through. Bathed his entire body in the murky chalk-like waters of the well of resolve. And though it would be awhile before I fully understood, on the morning we all proselytized with Billie on the salacious pleasures of being down, Bobby had begun his battle with the curse.

Onya knew before the rest of us. Whether she'd inherited Aunt Florida's powers of sight and divined it, or had simply witnessed something my parents and I had not, no one knew.

Everyone stopped eating. The clang of silverware dropping against my mother's good china resonated as all attention riveted on Bobby. Even Billie decided to give the blues a much needed rest.

His hands moved first, slowly, as though his mind-strings were pulling them, willing them to rise, the infirm and bony fingers wrapping around Debbie's plate like a noose around a neck, carpal veins bubbling as their grip tightened.

At once, the maternal shadow of concern darkened my mother's brow, lifting her from her chair, while my father's hand reached slow and steady across the table to still her, then eased her back down.

Bobby's feet moved next, pivoting and stepping as though some outside force were guiding them, plate and hands barely clearing the table as he turned. Each step was deliberate, called, marking a path through an emotionless abyss, leading him first to the stove where, veins still bubbling, the skeleton-like fingers scooped Debbie's uneaten grits back into the pot kept warm for second helpings. Then over to the sink where three times in succession he rinsed, washed, then rinsed again, until like his father he was sure all germs were gone from the plate that belonged to the piece of his soul that offended. Aside from the progressive jaundice and the ever-diminishing size of his pupils, the hollow expression on his face never changed.

"Debbie's dead," Onya revealed matter-of-factly after the third washing. My mother told her to hush, then rose from the table to wrap her arms around Bobby's broken shoulders. Neither of them spoke. Onya guzzled another glass of water. Sumner and MacArthur, each mumbling something about things getting "just a little bit too freaky up in here," suddenly remembered they had to be someplace. And Uncle Ray excused himself, deciding now would be a good time to make that trip to the bathroom. My father just sat there, motionless, watching.

"Debbie's dead," Onya stated again. "It happened last night."

"Onya!" my father tried to stop her. But his voice was barely above a whisper and lacked its usual command.

"It happened in bed," she went on. "But she didn't die in her sleep."

"Onya!" my father repeated. And though this time his voice rang strong and forceful, it did so too late. The riddle had become her song.

"Debbie's dead," she sang in the all-knowing tone of a sixteen-and-a-half-year-old. "It happened last night/it happened in bed/but she didn't die in her sleep."

Ignoring Onya's song, my mother whispered to Bobby that he had cleaned enough. She knew all about cleaning, she said. It was time to let it go. When he turned around, he looked directly at my father. His pupils had disappeared. Only the whites, and the red lines winding their way through them, remained. My father looked away. My mother took Bobby by the hand and led him past me in an eerie procession accompanied by the funereal twang of Onya's death knell. The whites and red lines stared straight ahead. On impulse, I reached out my hand to touch him, then drew it back immediately. It may have been the hottest day of the year, but Bobby's skin was ice cold.

"So what happened?" I asked Onya after breakfast.

She was packing her bag for cheerleading camp and ignored my question. "Do you think I should take the red sweater or the white one?"

I plopped down on our new double bed, the one that came with the bedroom set Onya had begged for when she turned sixteen.

"Dad!" she had argued. "It's my sweet sixteen. Do you know I'm the only one in my class who still sleeps in a bunk bed? I can't even invite my friends home for sleepovers, it's so embarrassing. If I can't have my own room, the least you can do is let me have a real bed." So now, instead of sleeping on top of each other in two different beds, Onya and I slept side by side in one.

"White or red?" she repeated.

"Isn't it a little too hot for a sweater?" I asked, draping a wet rag over my face.

"They're my letter sweaters," she barked at me. "I have to take at least one. White or red?"

"Red... So tell me what happened!" I demanded.

"What are you talking about?" she asked innocently, sipping a tall glass of water. She removed two pairs of pleated white shorts from the dresser drawer and put them in her suitcase.

"With Bobby. How did you know?"

"Po, he cleared Debbie's plate from the table. Wasn't it obvious? If you ask me, he should have killed all three of them. It's not right, fourteen-year-old boys playing with imaginary dolls. You should hear the way my friends talk. Why do Mom and Dad put up with it?"

"Yeah, but you knew before. Besides, they're not dolls."

"Oh God! Don't tell me you actually believe they're real? Take it from me, Po, that brother of yours is a real freak."

"He's your brother, too," I shot back. "And I didn't say I thought they were real. I just said they weren't dolls."

"Yeah, well, whatever they are, it's not right. And Mom and Dad should do something about it. Anyway, I saw." She paused and looked up. "Black eyeliner or brown?"

"You saw him do it?" I asked, astonished.

"No, stupid! I didn't see him do it. How am I gonna see somebody kill something that isn't real? Black or brown?"

"Then what did you see?" I insisted.

Onya ignored me. "Black or brown?"

"I don't know, both."

"Oh, loads of help you are. Here, the least you can do is help me sit on this." Her suitcase was completely overstuffed. "I saw why he did it."

"What do you mean?" I asked, sitting on top of the bag while Onya zipped.

"Just what I said," she grunted. "I mean, I saw."

She was parched, she remembered. In the early hours of the morning that Bobby decided to kill off a piece of his soul, the curse forced Onya to bolt from a sound sleep and grope for a glass of water. But the only water to be had was in the kitchen. And as she reached for her robe at the foot of the bed, she thought she heard voices. Hushed, anxious, and whispering ones, that drifted through the crack under our bedroom door on the back of a draft blown in from the foyer. Voices that fell mute as soon as she rubbed the sleep from her eyes.

Gasping for breath as she slipped on the robe, she listened again for the voices but the thirst distracted her. No matter how hard she strained her ears, all she could hear was the rushing sound of water. Ice-cold water to quench an unquenchable thirst.

She never heard the creak in Bobby's door as she fled to the kitchen, never heard the patter of his shriveled-up yellow feet as they ran into the foyer, then disappeared through the open front door. Fact is, at one o'clock in the morning, as her own feet, dark brown and smooth, carried her across the colored brick tiles of the foyer, Onya was so overwhelmed by thirst, she never even noticed the front door was open.

If she had noticed, she might have been tempted to follow. Might have bounced down the stairs in time to see Bobby crouch inside the shadow of the giant oak tree that darkened the sidewalk. Had time to get suspicious, prepare herself for what she was about to see. But she didn't notice. And as it was, when Onya threw her dehydrated body over the edge of the sink, anticipating the sensation of the life-saving fluid sliding down her throat as she placed a glass filled with ice under the tap of the moonlit faucet, the scene playing out in front of her on the other side of the kitchen window took her so by surprise that all she could do was drink more water.

When she raised the glass to her mouth, her eyes glanced through the window just in time to see the distorted images of my father and Jessica, arms and lips locked tight in a passionate, heated embrace.

"My mouth was so dry," she remembered. "Like I couldn't get enough water." Her voice grew flat, trance-like. She thumbed through the pages of the handbook titled *Things Every Cheerleading Counselor Should Know* without ever looking at them. "Have you ever had that?" she asked. "That feeling of knowing that no matter how much you drink you will never be able to get enough water? That's how I felt when I saw them, like I couldn't get enough water. So I just kept on drinking, watching and drinking. Glass after glass after glass, but still it wasn't enough. It was the weirdest thing, Po. My mouth was so dry, I just couldn't get enough."

Because they were drenched in moonlight and Onya was shrouded in darkness, Jessica and my father never saw her, nor did they see Bobby. But Onya did, crouched low and hidden in the shadows. And when she finally convinced her eyes to pull away, stop the gluttony long enough to take in some of the other early morning sights like the shadows cast from the forty-odd oaks and willows my father planted before we were born, she saw Bobby's emaciated yellow hue rise to its feet and glide slowly into the house.

My father and Jessica kissed one last time before Jessica ran up the street to her car and my father bounded up the stairs behind Bobby.

Onya remained hunched over the sink until sunrise, thinking about shadows. Shadows as shade. Shadows as the colorless, scantily clad reflections of ourselves. Shadows as protective coverings, like wings, shielding us from observation. The shaded, darker portions of the photograph, representing the duller, less illuminated fragments of the whole. She never did get enough water, and it would be a long, long time before she ever would.

As it turned out, my father was right. Even the Klan wouldn't strike on a day like today. They came instead under the cover of darkness, while our bellies hung full from a Monday supper of pan-fried chicken, mashed potatoes and gravy.

Uncle Ray was helping my mother dry the dishes when MacArthur and Sumner's shouts threatened to bring the house down, their fists and shoes pounding and kicking against the front door like an explosion. My father was playing the piano. Onya and I were reading in our room. And Bobby was sleeping.

"Greg! Lillian! Open up the door! Open the door, man! They here, they here! Open up the door, man, they here!"

"What on earth is going on!?" my mother shouted as she ran from the kitchen.

The double wooden doors to our closet started shaking. "Come on," Onya yelled, grabbing her glass of water as she ran. "Let's go!"

My father had already opened the door when we got there. My mother and Uncle Ray stood, anxious, behind him. Bobby was still in his room.

"Y'all look like you done seen a ghost," Uncle Ray laughed as Sumner and MacArthur tripped inside, eyes popping out of their sockets.

"Damn right, man," Sumner responded out of breath. "Bout a hundred of em, wearin white sheets."

"They carryin torches, Greg," MacArthur added, shaking. "They carryin torches."

My father locked the door behind them, then ushered everyone into the living room.

"Shit, man!" Sumner went on, pacing back and forth in front of the piano. "I told you we wasn't ready. I told you! Now we outta time. We got to do somethin, Greg!"

"Damn!" MacArthur shouted, quickstepping opposite Sumner. "And I just know one of em was that racist cop, Dewey. Be a fool not to recognize them slick black shoes."

"Alright, alright!" my mother ordered. "Now everybody just calm down."

"Ain't no time to be calm, Lillian!" Sumner countered, sweat pouring from his temples. "We got to act and we got to act now!"

"I said, calm down!" my mother repeated, looking at my father. "We won't accomplish anything if we lose our heads."

"Lillian's right, Sum," my father cautioned as he moved toward him. But Sumner kept pacing, yelling and screaming "Punk ass" this and "Fuckin cowards" that as he went. My father stepped in his path to stop him, putting his hands on Sumner's shoulders.

"Get your hands off me, Greg," Sumner growled. His hair was wild and his eyes were scared. "This is about business."

"Now... Now, hear me, man," my father grunted, using all his weight to hold Sumner still. "Listen to me, Sum, listen to me. Lil's right. We've got to act with clear heads."

"But we got to do somethin, Greg," Sumner seethed, starting himself to tremble and shake. "We got to do somethin."

"We will, man," my father assured him, pulling Sumner to his chest and holding him. "We will. I promise. But first, we've got to catch up to our heads."

Rumor on the street had it the Klan had already set fire to the Baptist church over on Hyde and was now on its way to torch BSA headquarters, which was the reason Sumner and MacArthur had hightailed it over to our place. Reluctantly, it was agreed: we were outnumbered and caught off guard. We needed to regroup, my father said. Retaliate. Find out who they are, then take them by surprise. But for now, we had to set up our defense.

While my father started loading and handing out pistols, my mother, Onya, and I started securing the house: locking the windows, closing the curtains, fixing long metal rods behind the sliding glass doors. MacArthur and Sumner took up positions at the kitchen and planter windows. And as my mother went to rouse Bobby from his illness-induced sleep, Uncle Ray headed for the front door.

"Where you goin, man?" Sumner yelled from the planter.

"I gotta go find Jessica," Ray answered as he opened the door.

"Man, forget her," Sumner responded. "Ain't nothin gonna happen to her."

"Ray," my father stopped him, holding a shotgun loose at his side. They were standing close, too close, breathing the other's breath, mouths saying one thing, eyes another.

"She's doing research at the college, Greg."

"Think, Ray. They're going after the BSA, they're not about to burn one of their own. But if you get caught in the street, man..."

"She's my wife, Greg. I got to." He vanished through the front door, just as my mother was leading Bobby into the foyer.

"Was that Ray?" she asked.

"Jessica's at the college," my father answered indifferently.

"And you didn't stop him?" she asked, astounded.

My father shrugged his shoulders as if to say it wasn't his affair.

"We tried, Lillian," Sumner chimed in from the planter. "But he wouldn't listen. You know his stupid ass ain't got no sense."

"He'll be alright, Lil," my father said to her. "He'll be alright." But my mother just shook her head in disgust.

MacArthur and Sumner settled back into their lookouts, as Onya, Bobby, and I nestled around my mother on the sofa. While my father paced back and forth with his shotgun, Bobby put his head in my mother's lap and began to cry. Slow soundless tears at first, building to loud, wracking, violent sobs. Nobody spoke or tried to soothe him. And though outside it was as quiet as it must have been when Onya stood hunched over the kitchen sink battling her thirst, at one time or another in the days that followed, we all swore we could hear the hoots and hollers of the Klan as we kept watch.

Beloved
1991

"I'm going home tomorrow," Lilah told the group. But even though the staff had arranged the morning's breakfast chairs to form the 'circle of intimacy' (an environment that would prep the group for sharing), we could barely hear her over the hacking of Sylvia, the phlegm ghost.

Come Tuesday, Sylvia will have been on the ward three months, the exact amount of time her doctor gave her to set things right with her maker, if she still insisted (as had been the case for the last thirty years) on sleeping with the cancer stick. "Alright!" she finally hacked at him, catching the green and yellow spittle in the heirloom handkerchief her mother had given her. She'd do it. But not before she smoked one final cigarette. Savored, one last time, the bittersweet pleasure of her Daddy's Georgia homegrown. Then, she promised, she would quit the stick for good. And though the reasons she chose to close the book on her life in this place would be forever lost on the rest of us, she spent every page of its final chapter in a constant frenzy trying to keep that promise.

Pity for poor Sylvia, it was never to be. Not because the quitting of a thing so long accustomed proved too difficult a task. Had she been able to make it that far, quitting might have seemed relatively easy. It was the smoking part Sylvia had lost the hang of, the ability to relish even the memory of her Daddy's Georgia homegrown. For in all the time she graced the ward with her presence, roaming and rattling the halls like an ethereal Nebuchadnezzar, the eternal coughing spell never ceased long enough for her to finish a single cigarette. At any hour, day or night, old Sylvia could be seen clamoring down the hall, bald head gleaming in the florescent lights, green examination gown split down the middle of her ghostly white back, dragging the linoleum floor behind her, holding a burning cigarette high above her head as though some sentient being had revealed that the cigarette's position there would prevent her from coughing.

For three solid months she haunted the ward, hacking up phlegm, blood, food, and everything else time managed to stick in her craw. In the odd moments the spell caught a case of the leniencies, voting to give Sylvia a break. By the time she managed to swing the arm down and hurry the cigarette to her lips, the cigarette's fire had already burned its way to the filter, forcing her to stop, search for and light another, leaving just enough time for the arm to shoot back up in the air before the coughing began again.

Today Sylvia must have sensed the end, for she executed the ritual with more than her usual aplomb. The arm stood up a little straighter. The wrist, with index and middle fingers crooked to support the burning cigarette, hung at a precise ninety degree angle. And the hacking simply outdid itself. So much so that Lilah had to repeat her announcement.

"I said, I'm going home Tuesday!" the skinny middle-aged black woman yelled. Her eyes were wide and dark like her skin, and were careful not to stay fixed too long in any one direction. Even as she spoke, they darted around the room like they were making sure she wasn't being followed. I'd seen them before, those eyes, in Bobby and Uncle Ray when they were sick and in need of a fix. But this woman wasn't sprung, at least not on smack. Hers was an addiction to the predictability of surroundings, the holding pattern that life brings.

In concert, we all scooted to the edges of our chairs and strained our necks to hear.

"How do you feel about that?" Cheryl the counselor yelled back.

Like last time, Lilah was scared. Wasn't sure if she was ready to go back to the outside, though she did look forward to seeing her girls. She'd been on and off the ward a total of three times, but at Lilah's insistence, the girls had never visited. They were too young, she reasoned the first time, unable to understand. The second time, she and her husband agreed it would be better if they spent a few months in Sandusky, keeping time with their grandmother. And in the seven months she'd survived this last go around, now that they were old enough, Lilah just couldn't convince herself it was right for them to see her here. "This ain't no place for children," she argued, sucking on her bottom lip between words. "Ain't no place for nobody."

Though there was that one morning, three months ago. Perhaps Lilah had allowed herself to forget. Completely erase from memory the morning the sun slid its fingers through the bars on her window to paint shadows on the wall. The day she traded in the ward-issue no-slip slippers for an actual pair of shoes. Wrestled down the fear just long enough to walk the entire length of the linoleum, ignorant of the commotion surrounding the arrival of the phlegm ghost, to hand the desk nurse two dimes and ask to use the phone.

She woke that morning feeling different. Not strong, bounding with some new combination of hope and courage. Just different. Altered enough to call her husband and tell him it was time. "Bring em on," she said. "I wanna see my girls."

But as the days counted down, the ward all abuzz with doubt as the celebrated event drew near, once again Lilah's body became gripped with fear. The same fear that had driven her back to the outstretched arms of the smiling nurses three times running, just days after she'd been released. And at the ill-fated hour, when her husband sat stiff-backed in one of the ward's donated visiting lounge chairs, their two girls sitting obediently on either side, hair crimped and bowed above the brown skin glistening in their Sunday best, Lilah remained frozen behind a locked bathroom door, crouched low and trembling beneath the stainless steel sink, screaming, "I can't, I can't!" at the orderlies trying to coax her out.

She was afraid of the legacy, she said. The one written in the blood of survival awaiting her on the outside; represented in every disillusioned face that pushed its way screaming through the double glass doors on the main floor.

From the time she was a little girl, Lilah had been pulled aside and hiked up on the knee of one aunt or another whose job it was to recount the history. Stories of strength and resistance. The women in her family had always been strong, they told her. From the unnamed and undocumented, credited with poisoning their masters, to the Mary's and Kate's burned at the stake for setting fire sometimes to entire plantations, on down to those who taught themselves and their children to read and write the language of their enemy guided by nothing but the light of the moon. Even though they perished, she was told, their refusal to succumb under so devilish a fire bore strength and determination in her four and five times great-aunts and grandmothers to do the same. Lilah was no exception. In time it would be her turn to impart the legacy to her own children.

Each account began with the recitation of the gene. The S-trait. We are a race of survivors, they implored. The evidence was scrawled permanently on our backs in the shape of a sickle cell. A cell that enabled us to last for weeks on end, packed up in each others' excrement like sardines for the eating, denied the privilege of food and water. You would not be here, they told Lilah, if your people hadn't fought back and, yes, survived.

But the legacy carried too much weight for Lilah's diminutive shoulders to bear. Too much pressure. How was she to recite the great gift of the legacy when all her girls wanted to know was why the security guard followed them down the aisles of the supermarket? How could she call on its power every time there was a paperclip or pen shortage at the office, and she was the first one questioned? And what good did learning about a stupid sickle cell do her youngest the first time she ran home from school crying, having gleaned the significance of the color of her skin? Even the greatest tale of bravery, she reasoned, could only suit her daughters in the armor to endure. Never would it prevent a single arrow from being slung, nor shred the banner of significance flying from its shaft.

So while her husband sat stiff-backed, her daughters sitting obediently beside him, crimped and bowed in their Sunday best, Lilah cradled the elbow of a silver-plated drainpipe, riddled with fear.

"Doesn't look like today's going to happen," the smiling desk nurse apologized to Lilah's husband. "Maybe next time."

But this time Lilah hoped things would be different. Prayed she'd at least be able to make it longer than the standing three days. The new apartment would help. It would give her a fresh start. The old house was too big to keep clean anyhow.

Admittedly, she was nervous. Didn't know if her marrow was strong enough. On Cheryl's lead, the group cajoled and coddled, reminding her of the tremendous progress she'd made. She would be fine, Cheryl assured. Just like the last two times, we all had the utmost confidence in her. Lilah simply needed to have it in herself. If, for some reason, she again found it difficult, impossible to cope, she needn't worry; we would all still be here, glazed over in smile, welcoming her back with open arms.

We heard the laboring footsteps of the floor nurse long before she interrupted the circle and busied ourselves with chatter, pretending not to listen as she whispered something about a visitor in Cheryl's ear. I watched as the worry lines around Lilah's mouth began to relax a little, becoming aware that for the first time in the twenty-nine hours since I was admitted, the ward was almost quiet. Even the beleaguered hacking of the phlegm ghost had faded to recent memory.

After the nurse had gone, Cheryl assured Lilah one last time, then adjourned the meeting, exclaiming, "My, my, time does fly, doesn't it?" As I got up from my chair, she informed me that Mary was waiting in the visitor's lounge.

The desk nurse was keeping a close watch on us through the little glass window that opened into the visitor's area. We'd been in the lounge just ten minutes and already we'd had another argument. Mary was convinced that the reason I freaked out and checked myself in here was because she had failed to take care of me.

"I wasn't the one who freaked out," I whispered, trying to keep the desk nurse from hearing our conversation. "And even if you hadn't, it wouldn't make any difference."

"Oh, so what are you saying?" she whispered back, rolling her eyes. "That after spending a day in this zoo, you've miraculously come to your senses?"

"I'm saying that we just don't understand each other, Mary. My father just died, and you haven't said word one about it."

"Yeah, well, I didn't know you two were all that close," she muttered defensively.

"He's still my father," I insisted.

"Po, you haven't said two words to the man in two years, and ten years before that."

"So it's not supposed to affect me?"

Mary shook her head back an forth, like she always does when she's frustrated with me. "Look, I'm sorry," she said. "I didn't know."

"That's just it, Mary. You never know. You're always trying to do or say what you think I want. You never just act on your own."

"Well, excuse me for trying to be sensitive to your needs." She opened her purse and started rummaging through it. "Gum?" she asked as she un-wrapped a piece and stuck it in her mouth.

"No, thanks," I answered, glancing up at the desk nurse. She was still watching us, with a suspicious look on her face. "Look," I said to Mary, eyeing the nurse. "Maybe this isn't a good idea. Maybe you should go back home. We can talk about things when I get out."

"Oh, right, and leave you all alone in this place, so you'll have another fuck-up to add to your list." She didn't get it. "Tell me, Po, where does this one rank? Below the fucking tree, or above it?"

A chokecherry tree. That's what I told Mary I wanted her to put on my back. Over the years, the numbness had gotten worse. Guess I figured since I couldn't feel anything as it was, there might as well be a reason.

We were twisted among the sheets of the wrought iron bed she'd found on the sidewalk in front of her studio. It was our first real argument, occur-ring just minutes after the first time we combined S/M play with sex.

After fisting and making me come for the third time in a row, scream-ing and nearly falling to the floor, Mary pulled me back on the bed to recover, then planted subtle kisses on my nose and forehead.

"You know," she whispered, producing three heavy duty extension cords from under the bed. "Funny things happen to electrical cords in the middle of the night."

Laughing at her own joke, she used one of the cords to tie my wrists to the headboard and with the others knotted each of my feet to the sides of the bedframe. "That too tight?" she asked, slipping a leather hood over my head and fastening the straps. I said no and closed my eyes.

Mary is a trust fund baby. The kind that feels guilt and embarrassment every time one of her working-class lovers discovers she has a six-digit bank account.

"It's no big deal," she was quick to explain when I asked. "My parents died in a car accident when I was five and left me some money. Too bad I can't use it to buy them back." She was raised by her grandparents, the ones on her father's side. Until she turned eighteen, they were in charge of the money. Their plan was to teach her to appreciate the values in life, send her to the finest schools. A Catholic boarding school until the age of fourteen, then on to Mother Theresa's Prep Academy for Girls. In their minds, there was no question Mary would go on to Harvard or Yale to study medicine, law, or some other reputable secure profession that would prevent her from squandering the money. Then, after graduation, she would settle down with some nice fine upstanding young man—a fellow student, perhaps—from a good line, and start a family.

Good Catholic girl that she was, Mary followed her grandparents' rules until her eighteenth birthday when the money officially became hers, then informed them that there had been a change in the program. Her plans for herself were different, she said; she was moving out to experience life on her own. She would finish prep school, but she was not going to college.

As expected, her grandparents fought it; tried to prove legally that Mary couldn't be trusted with so much money. She was too young, they argued; already she'd demonstrated an inability to make sound decisions. Their son had worked hard for that money, too hard to let a girl barely of age piss it all away. But their meticulous planning and the efficacy with which they carried out its design backfired; the judge ruled to the contrary. There was nothing in Mary's make-up or history suggesting such a thing would happen. In fact, he asserted, her grandparents should be proud of the way Mary turned out. She was an excellent student and she knew the value of hard work. Her record and reputation at both the boarding school and Mother Theresa's stood unblemished. She had to face life's little pitfalls at some point in time. Since the original documents were all in order, there was no reason that time shouldn't be now. Mary waited until after the court's decision to tell her grandparents she was gay.

From the beginning, sex between us bordered on the perverse. Although Mary was wrestling with her own demons about God and bondage when she first took my order that day in the cafe, we were two months into the relationship before we talked openly and called it what it was. We'd wake in the mornings, bruised and confused from the dark places we'd traveled the night before. Then upon rising, over cigarettes and coffee, we'd talk about our individual plans for the day, not about what happened.

At first, Mary wanted to submit to me. Turn the tables, she said, fulfill my wishes, serve my needs. But my needs demanded that she be dominant. I wasn't in this for retribution; I got involved with Mary for one reason only: like Uncle George, I believed I needed her to help me feel.

She didn't know if she could do that, she answered. In relationships past, she had always topped, but with me, it was different. She didn't know why, she said, letting her hair fall in her face as she folded into a ball at my kitchen table. It just was.

Mary never said why she was attracted to me. To be honest, I didn't really care, but I imagine it had something to do with her Catholic upbringing. "You know those Catholics," MacArthur used to say, "always takin in some lost soul, tryin to assuage that guilt."

After fastening the hood, Mary began to weave a knife around my breasts. Figure eights, in and out and in and out, coming to rest, pressing hard against my nipples. I would find out later that she drew blood. She called me names: bitch, whore, slut, worthless. But never nigger. Never the one I wanted. She reminded me that at any moment, if she felt like it, she could slit my throat, then balanced the knife on my pubic hair and told me she knew I wanted it, wanted the knife inside.

I lay still and silent.

"You want this?" she asked, pressing the blade against my labia. "You want my knife inside you, gutter bitch!?"

"Yes," I whispered, muffled through the hood.

"What was that?" she commanded, pressing harder. "I can't hear you, bitch."

"Yes," I said louder. "Yes, I want your knife."

But she refused to give it to me. Instead, she told me that I'd been bad. That I had mumbled. And that now I was about to find out what happens to sluts who mumble and don't behave.

She loosened my wrists and untied my feet. Then flipped me onto my stomach and reknotted my hands. She left my feet free. The cord was too tight, cutting off my circulation. I slid my wrists back and forth to loosen it, but it didn't help.

"Aw, did I tie it too tight?" Mary asked, laughing. "Am I hurting the little whore's little wrists?"

I shook my head no; the mockery in her voice told me that if I answered yes, she would tie them tighter.

"I didn't think so. Now get up on your knees!" she ordered.

As I crawled to my knees, she started to flog me. Soft and fast initially, then hard, slow, and rhythmic. At first I thought she had doubled-up one of the extension cords, but soon realized (when she shoved its handle deep inside me) that it was a whip. A cat-o'-nine-tails, I would discover in the morning, with metal beads tied to the ends.

In the beginning, I felt nothing. But as the whip slowed down, each lash began to feel as though it were ripping up my skin. And by the end, when the measured strokes of rawhide began to soothe, I got off on them. Wanted them. Needed them. I wondered if this was how it was with Uncle George. If, when the overseer had tired, when there were no more bare patches of skin to rip open, if Uncle George had begged him not to stop, as I was begging Mary now.

But she did stop. Something about the urgency inside my begging must have scared her, she said later. Abruptly, she put the whip down and untied my wrists. Carefully turned me over, then removed the hood. Gently, she pressed her lips against my eyelids, brushed her cheek softly against my nose, ran her tongue slowly across my lips.

"I'm sorry," she whispered over and over. "I'm sorry."

When I opened my eyes, her face glistened with sweat. She was massaging the blood back into my swollen hands. "Are you okay?" she asked.

I nodded and smiled.

"Let me take a look at your back."

She helped me sit up, then traced the fresh welts with the tips of her fingers. "Mmm, nice," she hummed. "Those'll stick around a few days." Wrapping her arms around my shoulders, she kissed the back of my neck and held me. Slowly, we started to rock. Neither of us spoke, just rocked, slow and steady.

I hadn't expected to like it. Truth is, I hadn't expected much of anything past beating back the numbness, though even that was short-lived. Already, as Mary began to drift off to sleep, the numbness started to crawl up my legs again. Lying on my back in the darkness, I could feel my body twitch as it cried out for more.

"I want a tree," I whispered, staring up at the ceiling.

"What, baby?" she answered, nuzzling her nose into the nape of my neck.

"A tree. A chokecherry, like Sethe's."

"Like who?" she asked, groggily.

"Like Sethe's in *Beloved*, that book by Toni Morrison." I turned on my side to face her. "Remember?" I started to explain. "Sethe was pregnant with Denver. She and Halle decided to escape from Sweet Home on the underground railroad. But the night before they were about to run, School Teacher took Sethe from her quarters, strapped her against the whipping post, then opened up her back with cowhide. Lashed her so long and hard the welts fused together to form a chokecherry tree: trunk, branches, leaves and all. Killed all the nerve endings in her back. That's why she was so strong, you know, that's why she survived. The branches on the tree lightened the weight of the burdens forever trying to keep her down.

"I want you to put a tree on my back," I said again. "I'll be Sethe, and you can be School Teacher."

"You mean role play?" she asked, confused.

"Sort of, only I want you to use a claw whip, a real one. No safe words, stopping only when the nerve endings are gone, dead."

"Po," she yawned, "that's sick." She was starting to wake up.

"Is it?" I asked, somewhat amused that she was finally starting to understand.

She sat up in bed and rubbed her eyes. "Think about what you're saying."

"I have," I answered, sitting up across from her. She was shivering. I pulled the blanket up around her neck to cover her.

"This is crazy!" she said, doing that frustrated head-shake thing. "A claw whip?" she repeated. "It'll kill you!"

"Maybe, maybe not," I answered. "Didn't kill them. Didn't kill Sethe."

"Po, this is stupid!" She was getting angry. "If this is supposed to be some kind of twisted joke," she said, "it's not funny."

"I'm not joking," I answered. "Why are you getting so mad?"

"Why am I getting so...? Jesus, Po!" she pleaded, grabbing my hands and pulling them into her chest. "Sethe was a character in a book, baby! A disturbing book at that. And what's up with this *them* you keep talking about?"

"Sethe was based on reality." I was starting to get annoyed. "And you know damn well who *they* are."

"Yeah, well," she whispered. "I think you're going a little too far on this one." She threw off the blanket and climbed out of bed; started pacing around the room. "This is ridiculous," she laughed nervously. "I don't even know why we're discussing it." She stopped pacing and looked at me. "I'm not School Teacher," she said quietly. "I can't go there with you."

"Fine," I said, ending the discussion. "I'll get somebody else. But remember," I added, pulling the blanket over my head and lying back down. "You're a hell of a lot closer to School Teacher than you think."

"Fuck you, Po!" she screamed. "Just fuck you! Now I'm some kind of evil overseer? I never do anything you don't want me to."

"Yeah?" I answered. "Well, now I want you to do this." I stuck my head out from under the blanket and stared at her. It was some time before she answered.

"I can't," she murmured. "I won't." Then slammed her fist against the wall and stormed out of the room.

I woke in the morning wrapped in the sheets alone without any pain in my wrists or back. It was raining. The city clock chimed eleven times. I rubbed the sleep from my eyes and got up to find Mary. She had fallen asleep in the bathroom, curled up like an infant in one end of the footed tub. There was no water. An ashtray filled with cigarette butts sat on the ledge of the tub beside her. Her neck and shoulders were squished in the corner. Drops of rain echoed down the drainpipe that ran past the window. I made coffee and brought some to her.

"Hey," I whispered, shaking her gently before handing her the mug. "Stay like that much longer and it'll be permanent."

"God, you sound like my grandmother," she answered, clearing her throat.

"Wanna talk?" I squeezed into the tub beside her.

"How's your back?" she asked.

"Sore," I lied.

"I'm supposed be taking care of you, remember?" She took a sip of her coffee.

"Yeah, well, I slept in a warm bed last night."

"Po," she said, getting serious. "You know I can't do what you're asking, at least not now."

"I know," I answered.

"And I know you think this thing you're fighting isn't about me. But it is, you know? If we go there, I'll be there with you. Then I really will be School Teacher." She started to cry. "I'm just not ready for that."

I set down my coffee and put my arms around her, held her. I've since forgotten the number of times the clock tolled that day, but we stayed like that until well into dark, adhered together, lodged in the bathtub, wrapped inside the blanket of the drainpipe's music, thinking but saying nothing.

There was no more mention of the chokecherry tree after that. We both knew we were short on time. With each new sunset, every second of our lovemaking took on a new urgency. And with the sole exception of the accident, after every scene Mary took care of me as she was trying to take care of me now.

We were still in the visitor's lounge. Mary had become distracted by Agnes the slasher, who was visiting with her parents at the table across the room. In a cruel reminder of her emotional instability, which she blamed entirely on her parents, Agnes had greeted them in short sleeves, and both Mary and her parents glanced nervously about the room, trying hard not to notice the railroad tracks creeping up her arms. Battle markers, Agnes called them, for all the times she had failed.

Agnes was the first face I saw (leaning over my bed, examining my nose ring), when I woke from the five-hour sleep I fell into after checking in. And it was Agnes who first briefed me on the various maladies afflicting the patients on the ward.

"Cool septum ring," she said, as I opened my eyes. "So you're the other slasher. Sorry," she added quickly, registering my confusion. "I looked at your chart. Is that alright?"

I rubbed the sleep from my eyes without answering.

"Hi," she said, extending her hand. "I'm Agnes, Agnes Tate. But everyone around here calls me 'the slasher'. Except the nurses, of course. At least not in front of me. I'd have their jobs if they called me that in front of me. Oh, I know," she said, holding up her hand as if I'd interrupted, "they have a field day when I'm not around, when they're in their tiny little nurses' quarters, smokin cigarettes and eatin cakes and chocolates. That's why they're all so fat, you know. Sittin around gossipin about all us crazies, eatin cakes and chocolates between rounds. It's true," she added, nodding her head up and down. "Just look at their asses. But it's cool, as long as they don't do it in front of me. Hey, you got a cigarette?"

I motioned toward my jacket, which was draped across one of the plastic chairs.

"Rule number one," she said, as I handed her the pack. "Smoke only in the smoking lounge, never in your room. Ain't that the shit?" She pulled some matches from her pocket and lit her cigarette. "The smoking lounge?" she asked as she exhaled. "Like we're all guests at the Hyatt or something." She skipped over to the bathroom, threw the burnt match in the toilet, then skipped back. "But I do it anyway," she said, smirking. "What are they gonna do, take away my cigarettes? Yeah, they tried that once, but they won't try it again." She pointed to one of her scars. "That's where this came from. Pocketed one of them plastic picnic knives they give you at meal time and sharpened the fuck out of it. They tried it with Sylvia, too, ya know. You met the phlegm ghost yet?"

I shook my head no.

"Boy, was that ever a fuck-up. They had to take up a collection and buy her a whole new case before that one was over with. But they don't really care, ya know? About the rules and shit. It's all just frosting to cover their fat asses with the insurance companies. You don't mind me being in your room, do ya?" she asked, as though she suddenly realized it might be a problem. "I mean if you do, it's cool. It's just that I saw you when you checked in and, except for that big bandage you got wrapped around your arm, you looked kinda normal. A helluva lot more normal than anyone else around here." She backed away from the bed and started poking around the extra sheets and blankets in the closet.

"I don't mind," I answered, looking around the room for the hidden camera. "Think I could have one of those cigarettes?"

"Oh yeah," she said, embarrassed, handing back the pack. "Sorry about that. Ya know I had a shaved head once." She waved her hand at my head. "But my parents made me grow it back; said I looked like a skinhead. Actually, you know, you coulda done a lot worse than wakin up to me. Coulda been one of those lame-ass doctors who's only interested in recordin your progress for the article he's writin for some medical journal. Or maybe that gag-and-barf chick, checked herself in here a month ago for shock treatments to make herself stop. You believe that shit," she yelled, laughing. "Volunteering to have someone hook electrodes up to your brain?" She pointed to her head and made little circles in the air with her finger. "Loco. Know what I mean?"

I nodded.

She sat down on my bed and started to get comfortable. "Yep, Po," she said, like we were old friends. "If you were expectin to get any kind of privacy around here, you come to the wrong place. See that door?" pointing to the door. "No lock. Nunna the doors got locks." She looked at the floor and thought for a second. "Except for the ones in lockdown. But those are all on the outside. You sure do sleep a lot, Po," Agnes said, getting up to snoop around the room some more. "They don't got ya on meds, do they?"

Again, I shook my head no.

"Good. Whatever you do, don't ever let em get you started on meds. So how'd you get a name like Po, anyway?"

"It's kind of a long story," I managed to spit out.

"Don't wanna talk about it, huh? That's cool. I should probably be goin now, anyway. Let ya get acclimated and all. Course, you're just a 72-hour girl; you won't be here long. But if you need anything in the meantime, I'm in the next room. Thanks for the cigarette. I'll return the favor tomorrow when my parents come; they're bringing me a whole carton. Remember," she said, as she opened the door, "name's Agnes, Agnes Tate."

"I brought you a change of clothes," Mary said finally. We were both looking over at Agnes. Her parents had forgotten her cigarettes. Her face was bright red and her voice grew deeper and louder.

"And I called the type house," Mary went on, distracted.

"Oh, yeah?" I said. Agnes was getting louder and louder. "What'd you tell em, that I tried to off myself and ended up in the nut house?"

"No," Mary said, irritated. "I told them you were in an accident."

"I don't care what those fuckin doctors say!" Agnes yelled at her parents. "I want my cigarettes."

"Everything okay in here?" the desk nurse asked through the little glass window.

"Everything's fine," Agnes's mother answered. "Isn't it, Agnes?" Agnes just sat there glaring, gritting her teeth. She shoved her hands between her legs to keep them still.

Trying to stay focused, Mary picked up where she left off. "They said as long as you bring in a doctor's note, everything'll be fine."

"Oh, great!" I responded, looking down at my wrist. "Why don't I just show em my little crazy person's band? What do you think they're gonna say when they realize the doctor's note is from a shrink?"

"Should have thought of that before you checked yourself in here," she quipped.

I didn't respond.

"Look, I'm only trying to help, okay?" she blurted.

"Thanks."

"Well, for what it's worth," Mary went on, "they also said to tell you to have a speedy recovery."

"As in, don't miss too much work or they'll fire me?" I asked dubiously.

"As in, maybe they give a shit, Po."

"Oh, right. And that's why they threaten to can anyone who complains about working twelve-hour shifts with no overtime."

"Hey, at least you have a job," she scolded.

"Yeah, easy for you to say," I snapped back. Mary just sat there, stunned, eyes glaring at me. Bastard, they screamed. It was a reflex; I didn't mean to say it. The words just slipped out. "Sorry," I whispered, but I knew it was too late. The damage had been done.

Agnes was out of control. Her face was rigid with anger and she was stalking the lounge. "Fuck you and your fuckin paid-off doctors," she was screaming.

"Everything still alright, Mrs. Tate?" the desk nurse asked again.

"Yes, Nurse Ratched!" Agnes yelled, whirling and lunging for the window. "Everything's fuckin fantastic! Peachy!" she screamed, banging her arm against the pane. The orderlies were in the room in seconds, placing Agnes in a chokehold while a nurse administered medication.

"Come on now, Agnes," one of them said. "Don't fight it, darlin. We'll have you feelin better in no time."

"You two, out of here!" the second one barked at Mary and me. "Now!"

"Have a nice life, Po!" Agnes screamed, kicking to break free. "You'll be gone by the time I get back. Agnes Tate!" she yelled. "Remember, Agnes Tate." And then she was gone, vacant, as though the life that was just sucked out of her had never really been there at all.

"There we go, Agnes, there we go," the first orderly soothed. "We're all better now. We'll handle it from here," he told the nurse, who ushered Agnes's visibly shaken parents from the room.

Mary and I watched from outside the glass.

"I should go, too," Mary said, dazed.

"Yeah, probably best," I agreed, pretty exhausted myself. "Thanks for the clothes."

"Hey, what are girlfriends for? So, I'll see you tomorrow?"

"Sure."

"Should I bring anything?"

"Maybe some cigarettes," I answered, then watched the orderlies drag Agnes through the swinging double doors at the end of the hall, as Mary hugged and kissed me good-bye.

We Don't Need No Music
1979

"It'll be small," my father promised. An intimate little gathering. Just family and a few friends. We didn't want Jobe, Jr. to get wind of it, he said; it was still a sore spot.

Then Truly called two days prior to ask if he could bring his lady and two of her girlfriends. MacArthur dropped by the store to say he was bringing his "pardner." Uncle Ray said Jessica's parents were in town. And Grandma Margret was so proud and excited, she invited the Bid Whist girls and told them to bring their cards. Then Truly's lady's two girlfriends turned into five, all of whom had boyfriends. MacArthur's pardner turned out to be two army buddies on leave, who invited their platoon. Jessica's parents, who were in town for a convention, wanted their newfound friends, Bob and Irma, to meet their daughter. And there was not one of Grandma Margret's Bid Whist girls that didn't have her own son or daughter who didn't bring their family as well. Sumner was still in the county lock-up awaiting sentencing so we didn't have to worry about him.

Before we knew it, my father was making trips back and forth to the store for spirits, my mother was turning out deviled eggs and potato salad faster than anyone thought possible, and what began as a small intimate little gathering of friends and family grew into a real live bonafide celebration.

The sun was high and the house full. The chemical spill from nearly three years ago had finally left the atmosphere. Onya had come home from school. Stevie was on the stereo singing about superstitious writings on the wall. MacArthur and his army buddies pushed all the furniture out of the way so folks could have room to get down. And except for Bob and Irma (who were cowering off to the side, drinking without speaking to anyone), at one time or another, everyone got around to talking about Sumner.

"Boy shoulda had more sense," one of the Bid Whist girls' sons said.

"You know he's always been a hothead," someone else added.

"Time bomb is more like it," MacArthur threw in, sucking on the end of a cigar. "Just a-tick, tick, tick, tick, tickin away."

"Now, you all have to remember something," interrupted my father, as he refilled their glasses with champagne. "Sum was upset. And he had reason to be. After all, we did promise to retaliate."

"Yeah," MacArthur conceded, exhaling a cloud of smoke from his cigar. "But how you s'pose to retaliate with just one person, Greg?" he demanded through the cloud.

"As I remember it, Mac," my father said, raising his eyebrows and tilting his head to the side (implying that Sumner's predicament was MacArthur's fault), "it was you who filled his head with all that talk about Dewey and his shoes. Sumner just couldn't let it go."

"That was three years ago, Greg," Mac responded, defensively. "And it still ain't no cause to go off half-cocked, beatin up on some police officer—an off-duty police officer at that—with a baseball bat. A soldier's got to have more sense than that, Greg. You know it as well as I do."

"Maybe so," my father agreed reluctantly. "Maybe so."

"Still woulda liked ta seen the look on ol Dewey's face, though," MacArthur added, crouching down behind an imaginary wall and laughing. "When my boy Sum jumped out from behind the barbershop, all wide-eyed and crazy, swinging that bat."

"Must have been something," my father mused with him. "Must have been something at that."

Bobby situated himself in an out-of-the-way corner and watched it all dressed in his pajamas, wearing a strange smile on his face that didn't have anything to do with the festivities.

It was the five-year anniversary of the store, almost three years to the day since the Klan marched through town setting fire to the Baptist church and BSA headquarters.

"Are you aware of what they say, Greg?" Jessica's father posed to mine, offering a toast.

"What's that, James?" My father asked, raising his glass.

"The first five years of a small business is said to be the toughest."

"Well then, Mr. MacIntyre," my father said, smiling, patting him on the back. "I guess we're over the hump."

By nightfall, it seemed the whole town (with the sole exception of Jobe Jr.) was dancing, drinking and playing cards in our living room. Heads full of alcohol, stomachs flush with my mother's potato salad, my parents' little gathering of friends and family carried on well past three in the morning. And even then, nobody so much as hinted at leaving, not even the Bid Whist girls, who were having more fun than they'd had in years, challenging the younger folks to rise and fly. Bobby disappeared into his room sometime before the sun went down. And as the cries and laughter threatened to raze the foundation, Onya and I lay awake, staring at the ceiling, wondering if it would ever come to an end.

My father won the store in a card game. Poker. Pulled a natural four-of-a-kind to Jobe Smith, Jr.'s inside straight. It was four o'clock in the morning before he finally made it home, bursting and stumbling through the door like a drunken tornado. Onya and I thought he was a burglar.

As he staggered into our room, donned in his lucky pinstripe poker shirt, dragging Bobby behind him, my mother ran screaming down the hall.

"What is going on in here?!" she yelled, trailing my father into our room.

"Up and at em!" my father slurred, flipping the switch to our bedroom light, so that it flashed off and on. "Uppy, uppy!" he laughed. "Come on, Po, Onya! Uppy, uppy!"

"What time is it?" Onya asked, rubbing her eyes.

"Celebration time, my dear," he sang. "It is time to celebrate."

"Gregory Taylor Childs!" my mother yelled, as she sailed into the room. "You've been drinking."

"Right you are, Lillian," my father answered, turning around to face her. "Right you are, indeed." He dropped to his knees like he was proposing. "Babydoll," he said, "welcome to the rest of your life." Five plastic wine glasses and a bottle of cheap champagne trembled uncertain in his arms. "Compliments of Mr. Jobe Smith, Jr., himself."

"What on earth are you talking about, Gregory?" my mother asked as he started to pour.

"Lillian," he said, belching and raising his glass. "You are now looking at the proud new owner of the Party Shack."

"Oh, shit!" my mother answered, rolling her eyes. "Now I've heard everything."

"But the Smiths own the Party Shack," Onya said, confused. "That's Caroline's store."

My mother moved to take my father's arm. "Alright, Gregory," she said, holding back her anger. "Come on, you've had a little too much to drink. Let's turn out this light and let the kids go back to bed. Onya, Po, go on back to sleep. Bobby, go back to your room, sweetie."

"No, Lil!" my father yelled, spilling champagne on the floor as he jerked his arm away. "Don't treat me like one of the children. We own the Party Shack!"

"Gregory, this is ridiculous!" she yelled, reaching for his arm again. "Just come to bed and let the kids go back to sleep. If you still insist we own the Shack in the morning, we'll talk about it then."

"No, Lil!" he insisted, stepping back out of her reach. "I'm serious. Where do you think I've been all night?"

"Evidently," my mother answered, "getting a little too cozy with a bottle." She collected Bobby in her arms and turned to leave. "Look, you can stay up and continue this charade if you want to," she said, walking toward the door. "But the kids and I are going back to bed."

"No, Lillian!" he yelled again, swallowing what was left in his glass, then throwing it to the floor. "Listen to me!"

My mother halted abruptly in the doorway. She was still holding Bobby's hand when she pivoted to face my father.

He took a deep breath before continuing. "I was out at Truly's, playing cards," he confessed. "I know, I know," holding up his hand to register her disapproval. "But it was my lucky night, Lil. You should've been there. Mac was there, so were Sumner and Ray. I'm telling you, baby, it was beautiful. Won every hand but one. Poor ol Jobe didn't know what hit him. Sure was determined, though, I'll give him that much. Couldn't let me leave, he said, till he'd recouped some of his losses. Said Edna would kill him if she found out how much money he'd dropped. So I said, 'Alright, I'll give you one last chance. One hand of five card, winner gets up and walks... with whatever he's got.'

"Ol Jobe ordered Sumner to deal, and that's when Miss Lady Luck reached through from the other side and patted my shoulder. Would you believe it, Lil? Sum dealt me a natural four, straight off the bat. One three after another. Last card was a nine."

My mother was quiet. She just stood there, unmoving, hand on her hip, taking it all in. Bobby and I leaned back on Onya's bunk and rubbed our eyes. Onya just sat there with an anxious and troubled shadow creeping over her face.

My father went on to say that since the rules of the house required jacks or better to open, it was his bet. Face straight as a board, he pushed his entire night's winnings to the middle of the table. "But ol Jobe was short, see?" he told us, his usually deep voice getting higher and higher as it filled with excitement. "And he was dry," he went on. "Didn't have a single bill left in his pocket."

Panic-stricken, Jobe ripped out a check from his checkbook and signed it, leaving the amount blank.

"Check's no good here," my father said quietly as he relived the moment.

"What?!" cried Jobe, certain he had misheard.

"I said, your check's no good here," my father repeated sternly.

Jobe slammed his fist on the table and started screaming. Squealing that my father knew he was good for it. But soon the painful realization set in. My father had no intention of changing his mind, and Jobe turned his appeals to Truly.

"House rules, Jobe," Truly said, shrugging his shoulders. "Nothin I can do."

"But he done took all my cash, Tru," Jobe pleaded. "What I'm s'posed to do?"

"Guess that's it, then," my father cut in and started scooping up the cash to leave.

As my father spoke, his eyes glazed over and faded as though he were no longer here talking to us in our bedroom, but instead was back in the game. Huddled around the rickety table in Truly's dank back room, living again the night Lady Luck used her double-edged nails to cut through the fabric and pat his shoulder.

"Aw, hell no!" Jobe yelled, standing and pointing at my father as he started to leave. "You can't just walk outta here with my money like that!"

"What you gonna do, man?" my father answered, giving Jobe one last chance to come up with the bet. "How you gonna call?"

Little beads of sweat appeared on my father's forehead as he recounted the tale. Jobe just stood there, he said, legs shaking and trembling with fear, glaring at him from across the table. In desperation he dropped to his knees and pleaded with Uncle Ray, Sumner, and MacArthur to help him out.

"Sorry, Jobe, man," they answered in unison. "We tapped."

As my father's voice reached an octave higher, the little beads of sweat turned into goblets that dripped down the sides of his face. His eyes remained glazed and distant. "And that's when he blurted it out," my father laughed, doubling over and holding his stomach. "Down there on his knees, like he was begging for mercy. He said, 'I'll put up the Shack.'"

"You gonna what?!" Sumner yelled in disbelief. Each in his turn, the others tried to talk him out of it. Sumner going on to advise him against being a fool. Truly reminding him of the lateness of the hour and that he'd had too much to drink. Uncle Ray offered to drive him home, even though Jobe's house was eight miles in the opposite direction from which Uncle Ray was traveling. And MacArthur just sat there, perched high up on a stool like a king on his throne, smiling at the shenanigans of a fool.

Still ol Jobe would have none of it. "I ain't goin nowhere!" he yelled. "I'm callin with the store."

He refused to leave until my father revealed his hand. He had paid to see it, he said. Then swore on his grandfather's grave that if my father didn't do so, he would spread word throughout the county that Gregory Taylor Childs was a liar, a swindler, and a cheat.

As the goblets of sweat started down his neck, my father's new high voice became at once quiet and animated. His eyes were still distant. "I put down the nine first," he squeaked. "Reversing the way Sum had dealt them to me. "Then one by one I lay down each of the threes."

"Aw, shit!" Sumner whispered to no one in particular. "Jobe, man, you a bigger fool than I thought."

Jobe's face was stricken like he had just received news of a loved one's death.

"What you got, Jobe?" Uncle Ray asked.

But Jobe didn't answer. Just sat at that rickety old table, clutching and staring at his cards. It was Truly who finally pried them loose. Tried to match those cards every which way possible, my father said. But in the end, everyone agreed: the best Jobe could do was a straight.

"You bet your store on a motherfuckin straight!" Sumner yelled.

Uncle Ray told Sumner to shut up, then whispered to Jobe that it was time to go home. But as he pulled back Jobe's chair to lead him from the table, my father stood up and blocked their path.

"Don't mean to break up your little party, gentlemen," my father said, smiling like the Reaper. "But there's still a matter of payment."

"Tomorrow, Greg," Uncle Ray answered, as they stepped around him. "It can wait till tomorrow."

"Fraid not, Ray," my father countered, grabbing Uncle Ray's arm. "Tomorrow's a new day, my brothah. Memories tend to fade in the dawn of a new day."

"What you want him to do then?" Ray asked, jerking his arm away in disgust. "Give you the keys so you can sleep in there tonight? The man just lost his life, Greg. It's late, go on home to your family and deal with the particulars tomorrow."

The sweat that began as little beads on his brow now poured down my father's chest in streams. Dark wet stains spread across the armpits of his pinstripe lucky poker shirt. What he wanted, he calmly told my Uncle, was the pink slip.

"The pink slip?" Uncle Ray repeated, tearing up his face. "Look at him, Greg."

Jobe was standing facing the door, staring blankly at his empty outstretched hands as though they were still holding the losing cards.

"Does the man look to you like he can even find a pink slip right now?" Uncle Ray asked my father. "Let alone sign one over?"

At last, MacArthur, who had said nothing during the entire hand, jumped down from his throne and cleared his throat to speak. My father had a point, he informed Uncle Ray. "Man shows his hand, he deserves to be paid."

Finally, after the ensuing argument in which already heated tempers flared even hotter, my father and Uncle Ray reached an agreement. They would write up an IOU, a promissory note that Jobe and my father could sign. Truly, Ray, MacArthur, and Sumner would ratify it as witnesses.

For the first time since he knelt down on his knees, the lucky poker shirt saturated with sweat, my father focused his eyes and looked at my mother. Slowly, he reached into his pocket, produced a wrinkled piece of paper and handed it to her. Clearing his throat before he spoke, he whispered, "We own the Shack, Lil. The Party Shack now belongs to the Childs."

Oddly enough, my mother didn't seem to care, just folded up the promissory note and handed it back to him. "So it does," she said, looking down at the floor. Her voice was filled with sadness. "So it does."

"What's the matter?" my father asked, confused. "This is good news! Now all those things we dreamed about doing for the kids, we can do. What's the matter with you? This is a good thing!"

"Been a long night," my mother sighed, looking down at Bobby who'd lost the battle to the sandman around the time Jobe said he wasn't going anywhere. "Now that it's over," she said wearily. "I think we should all try to get some sleep."

"But what about Caroline?" Onya asked, as my mother woke Bobby to take him to his room. "What's going to happen to Caroline?"

"Caroline'll be fine, baby," she said, turning off the light. "Go to sleep. We'll talk more about it tomorrow."

My father watched her as she turned to leave. "Lil," he whispered, when she passed back by our room. "Lil?"

But there was no answer. And when we finally heard the door close to my parents' room, my father fumbled in the dark for his wine glass, picked up the champagne, then stumbled into the living room.

"You think it's true?" I whispered to Onya, as Billie's *I Don't Want To Cry Anymore* started up on the piano.

"I don't know," she said, quiet and muffled from the bunk below. "I don't know."

It was true. The appearance of Uncle Ray and MacArthur at our front door the following afternoon confirmed it. Sumner and Truly sent word that their names on the promissory note would suffice in their absence, but it happened just as my father had told it. We were now the proud new owners of the Party Shack. But my mother wasn't the least bit proud.

"Look at it this way, Lillian," MacArthur jawed. "Now, you ain't never again got to work for the man, long as you live. Ain't got to take no more dictation and Greg can just throw that dirty lab coat right on in the garbage."

We were all seated around the coffeetable in the living room. My mother and MacArthur lounged in the two armchairs. Onya, Bobby, and I sprawled across various spots on the floor. My father sat on the sofa with Uncle Ray. Both held ice packs to the sides of their heads.

"I suppose that remains to be seen now, doesn't it?" my mother said to MacArthur. "You ever own a business, Mac?" she asked while lighting a cigarette. "What makes you think working for ourselves will be any easier than working for the man? What if we can't make it work?"

"Lillian," Mac answered in all seriousness. "Anything beats workin for the man. Besides," he added quickly, winking at my father, "with you and Greg runnin things, I know it'll work out. I got what you might call faith."

"I guess I just don't see what's so wrong with the way things are," my mother responded, speaking more to my father than to MacArthur.

"Damn, Greg," MacArthur said, shaking his head. "Your woman always this hardheaded when her ship comes in?"

My father shrugged his shoulders and pointed to his watch.

"Maybe I just don't like the wind it rode to get here," my mother answered, annoyed.

"Well," Mac conceded, bowing his head. "S'pose I ain't got much of an answer for that one, Lil. Cept at least I know better than to stick my head back there by the horse's tonsils, if you know what I mean? Speakin of which," he added, turning to my father, "I see you gettin all anxious over there, Greg, but you know I'm just tryin to bring Lillian around."

"Do that on your own time," my father ordered, standing up to leave. "Let's go."

"Alright, alright," MacArthur answered, throwing his hands high in the air as though he'd just been stopped by the cops. "Ain't got to tell me twice. Don't ever let it be said MacArthur Fields stood in the way of no man tryin to collect his money. Nice conversin with ya, Lil."

"I'll phone," my father said over his shoulder as he grabbed his keys and started for the door.

"We'll be here," my mother retorted as she lit another cigarette.

"Grab a jacket, Greg," MacArthur said on his way out. "Might be August, but it's cold as a mofo out here."

Nobody seemed to care about who Jobe would work for now, how he would feed his family. Except for Onya, who followed my mother around the house asking, "What about Caroline? What's going to happen to Caroline?" The store had been in Jobe's family since before he was born, before he knew enough of the Bible to know why the older kids teased him about his name.

"What kind of a name is Jobe, anyhow?" one would chide.

"Jobe, Junior, at that," another would add.

"Your great-granddaddy named Jobe, too?"

"Slave master give him that name?"

" 'I believe I shall call you Jobe,' slave master say. Jobe Smith." Then the laughing and rolling around in the grass would begin before Jobe had a chance to respond.

My father called from the store to say things didn't go so well over at Jobe's. He got his pink slip, alright. But Edna, it seemed, got a little crazy and threatened him with a shotgun. Told him as he approached the steps that if he came any closer she was going to blow his head off. MacArthur was the one who talked her out of it, reminding Edna that she didn't know thing one about firearms. Before she knew it, he told her, she was liable to shoot Jobe's, Caroline's, or her own head off. It took a little while, but Edna finally gave in, dropping herself and the gun in a pile on the floor. She was still lying there, weeping on the throw rug, when my father emerged from the back room, with Uncle Ray and MacArthur, cradling a manila folder.

At Uncle Ray's urging, my father promised to do right by Jobe. Told him that he would do whatever he could to help him save face in the eyes of the community. As far as the town was concerned, he said (as well as Grandma Margret), the two of them had entered into a legitimate business arrangement. A friendly takeover, so to speak, in which my father assumed ownership of the Shack in exchange for helping Jobe raise his head above an irreversible stream of debt.

No one ever asked how my father happened upon the means to affect this generous bailout, nor how it came to pass that on an unusually cold afternoon in August Edna Smith threatened to blow his head off with a shotgun she didn't know how to use. Everyone just went about business as usual, changing only their "How ya doin, Jobe?" to "How ya doin, Greg?" when they dropped by the Shack to pick up their weekend six-pack of Strohs.

In addition, my father told Jobe he was welcome to stay on awhile until he found something more permanent. As it turned out, the time came when he was of little use to anyone because he could no longer pull his head out of the bottle.

Whether my mother liked it or not, the Party Shack was ours now, and as my father told Onya after he staggered drunk into our room, it was time to celebrate.

The five-year anniversary party was raging, with no signs of letting up. "This is ridiculous!" Onya screamed as the constant thump thump thump of music started shaking the bed. "I need my beauty sleep."

"We could turn all the clocks forward," I offered, sitting up in bed.

"Won't work," she disagreed. "They're too drunk to notice."

"Then we should just tell them," I moaned. "Tell them that we're trying to sleep."

"No. It might work for a minute but as soon as our backs are turned, they'll forget all about us. Let's take the music."

"What?" I asked, confused.

"The records," she answered, laughing. "That'll show em. We can sneak around through the patio and take all the records. They're mine anyway, damn it! They'll have to leave if they don't have any music."

At first Onya's plan worked brilliantly. We crawled through the patio door on our knees. Onya eased the volume down to make the song that was playing appear to be over. I grabbed the records, and waited for her outside. We sprinted back to our room, giggling and out of breath, then collapsed onto the bed to wait for the discovery. Except for the talking and the frequent bursts of laughter, the house was quiet.

Jessica was the first to notice. "Hey," she slurred. "What happened to the music?"

"Put on another record, woman!" Uncle Ray yelled from across the room.

"I can't," she laughed. "They're gone."

"What you mean, gone?" somebody hollered.

"Just what I said. Somebody stole them. Even the plug is gone," she shrieked. "We can't even play the radio."

That's when the cackles started, falling in step one after the other. Until the house became an early morning drunken chorus of laughter.

"I think someone's trying to tell us something," my mother cried between bursts of laughter.

"Three someones," my father added.

"No matter," MacArthur drawled as he started to clap his hands to an imaginary rhythm. "We don't need no music."

"That's right," my father echoed. "Keep that beat, Mac," he said, joining him. "We don't need no music," he sang over the rhythm. "We don't need no music." Clap, clap. "We don't need no music. Come on. We don't need no music. Hey! We don't no..."

We barely had time to bury our heads beneath our pillows before everyone, including Bob and Irma, had joined in behind him. "We don't need no music." Clap, clap. "We don't need no music."

For one solid hour, they belted out inebriated four-part harmonies, while my father threw in verses from *Bye, Bye, Blackbird* between choruses. *Bye, Bye, Blackbird* sung with every type of phrasing you could imagine. Then, after all but killing the poor little bird, he ran through every verse of Billie's *Travelin' Light*, Sarah's *Black Coffee*, and Nina's *Mississippi Goddamn* before he was done. And when the last person stumbled drunkenly through the front door, bumping into walls and tables on their way out, the house stank so much of morning breath and spilled vodka, Onya and I might never have fallen asleep had our bodies not been so riddled with exhaustion. But exhausted we were. And after laughing and shaking our heads at the absurdity of it all, we were just starting to doze off when the hush of my parents' voices tiptoed past our room.

"Better sleep fast," my father whispered. "Got a hell of a mess to clean up before the store opens."

"Don't remind me," my mother sighed. "Seems like the only two people who didn't show were Jobe and Mama."

"Sure was something," my father laughed, as they opened their door.

"Sure was," my mother answered. "But seriously," she said, "what do you think happened to Mama? I expected the house to be filled up with violets tonight."

"Oh, you know," my father laughed. "She's probably up there gettin busy with one of the saints."

"Gregory Childs," my mother scolded, laughing. "You are wrong, wrong, wrong. Must be mad at us for something though." She added, "You know Mama never misses an opportunity to party."

"Well, whatever it is," my father yawned before closing their door. "I'm sure she'll let us know. You can bet your life, she will let us know soon enough."

Soon Enough
1979

Our rest was short-lived. Not one hour after the house recovered from shaking long enough to settle into sleep, in the middle of dreams none of us would remember, at four-thirty in the morning breaking the silence of the night like a plane exploding and lighting up the sky, the phone rang. And after letting it ring a total of ten times unanswered, the caller had to hang up and dial again before my father would wrest himself from his sleep to see who it was. Even Bobby woke up for this one.

If only it had been a wrong number or an intoxicated partygoer calling in a panic to say that she'd forgotten her purse or he'd misplaced his wallet, we might have gone back to sleep. If it had just been one crisis, as opposed to three, each on the heels of the other, we might have been rescued. But there were three, and from them the family never recovered.

The caller on the phone was Jessica. She was the first.

"He's got Lisa Marie!" she screamed through the receiver. "That fucking asshole took my baby!"

"Jessica... Jessica," my father tried to calm her. "Calm down... Jessica... calm... calm down. Okay... okay, tell me what happened."

We were all perched on my parents' bed and could hear Jessica's voice through the receiver as though she were transmitting through a two-way radio.

"What happened?" my mother urged.

"Ray's got Lisa Marie," my father answered, cupping his hand over the mouthpiece.

"What do you mean, he's got her?" she asked.

"I don't know!" my father snapped, waving his hand at her to be quiet. "That's what I'm trying to find out!"

As had become commonplace, Uncle Ray and Jessica had another fight on their way home from the party. She must have had more to drink than she realized, Jessica told my father. Let things slip that shouldn't have. She cried and screamed hysterically. My father sat down on the edge of the bed, listening patiently, while the rest of us whispered and huddled around behind him. Although we were only able to decipher coded bits and pieces, to Onya, Bobby and I, two things were sure: Uncle Ray had found out about my father and Jessica, and in retaliation, he had kidnapped Lisa Marie.

"He knows!" Jessica yelled through the phone. "No, I will not calm down! That bastard took my child! He's knows, Greg. Goddamn it! He knows!"

"It's going to be alright, Jess," my father comforted, scooting as far down the side of the bed as he could without falling off. "It'll be alright! Where has he taken her?... Okay, now listen... Jess, listen to me!" he ordered. "Call... call the police; I'll be right there."

"Knows what?" my mother asked as he hung up the phone.

"Ray kidnapped Lisa Marie," he answered, slipping on his pants. "Jessica says he has a gun."

"I'll get my coat," said my mother.

"No," my father stopped her, pulling on his. "I'd better handle it."

"What do you mean, you'd better handle it?" she grilled, grabbing her overcoat. "You must be out of your mind if you think you're going without me. And you didn't answer my question. Just what is it that Ray's supposed to know?"

"One of us has to stay with the children, Lil." Unlike my mother's, his voice was rational and calm. We all followed as he started down the hall.

"Onya is more than capable of looking after Po and Bobby," she argued, hot on his heels. "What does Ray know, Greg?"

"Now's not the time, Lil," he said, opening the door. "I'm leaving. If you're coming, come on." My mother told Onya she would call with an update, then snatched up her purse and ran through the door behind him.

The update came more than two hours later, when my mother phoned from the hospital to say that Uncle Ray had attempted another suicide. Upon returning home from the party, after paying and saying goodnight to the babysitter, Uncle Ray ended the argument by punching Jessica in the stomach, then woke Lisa Marie and drove her to Grandma Margret's. Once there, he shoved Grandma Margret aside and barricaded himself and the girl in my grandmother's guest room. After several failed efforts—on the part of the police, my mother, and Grandma Margret—to talk him down, with the five-year-old still in his arms, Uncle Ray placed the barrel of a loaded .38 against the roof of his mouth and squeezed the trigger. When the paramedics wheeled him through the hospital doors, intravenous needles sticking out of both arms, no one, with the possible exception of Uncle Ray, believed he would make it. Along with the police, Jessica, and Grandma Margret, my mother said that she and my father were holding vigil in the emergency room, awaiting the news.

What the update didn't tell us, what we were forced to sew together from the worn-out tatters of conversation we overheard in the weeks to come (much of which we already knew), was that by the time my parents arrived at Grandma Margret's, the police had already cordoned off the area. That even after my father produced two government documents, identifying him as Uncle Ray's brother, they refused to let them through. And that it was Jessica, not my grandmother, who was escorted to the other side of the yellow tape to prove his identity.

"Greg, Lillian," she gasped, visibly relieved as they led her over. "Thank God, you're here!"

"You know this man?" one of the officers asked, shining a flashlight in my father's face to help Jessica see.

"Of course I know him," she snapped. "He's my husband's brother! Oh God, Lillian," she cried to my mother, trying to embrace her from across the tape. "He's got my baby. He's lost it. Talk to him, Lil, he'll listen to you."

My mother just stood there, one hand holding onto her purse, the other lodged in the bottom of her overcoat pocket.

"What are you doing?" Jessica yelled at the officers as she backed away. "Don't just stand there, let them through!"

"So what did Ray find out?" my mother asked while they rushed toward Grandma Margret who stood with the negotiator behind the lead police car.

Jessica was silent.

"I told you, not now, Lil," my father answered.

"No matter," my mother sighed, "I'm sure Ray will tell us soon enough. Margret?" she called to my grandmother when they approached.

My grandmother turned to embrace her, then held on tight. Too tight, it was remembered, refusing to let go. "Heaven help us, Lil," she cried into my mother's shoulder. "My baby's got himself all tangled up this time."

My father stood off to the side and watched while Jessica talked with the negotiator. Every time they tried to talk him into handing Lisa Marie over to my grandmother, Grandma Margret told her, Uncle Ray would hold the .38 to the child's head and laugh hysterically.

"Think I don't know what you're up to, white man?!" he'd yell in that gravelly voice from the upstairs window. "Think I don't know that soon as my mama walks out with my little girl, you gonna give her to that white bitch? I'll see my little girl dead fore I see that happen."

"Fuck you! You bastard!" Jessica would scream back. "Give me back my baby!" and the negotiations would stall. When the SWAT commander radioed that his team was in position, my mother asked the negotiator if she could try.

"Ray," she shouted through the megaphone. "Ray, it's Lillian."

"Forget it, Lil," Uncle Ray laughed, screaming from the window. "Ain't gonna work this time, baby. I'm too far gone."

"No, you're not, Ray," she answered. "Not yet. And I know in my heart of hearts, you don't want to see anything happen to that child. Ray," she reasoned, "whatever's happened, no matter how bad, it doesn't have a thing to do with Lisa Marie. She's your baby, Ray, your flesh and blood. Let me come up and get her. I promise I'll keep her right by my side until we can sort things out. Please, Ray," she begged, "give this up before somebody gets hurt."

"Ain't gonna happen, Lil," he yelled, brandishing the gun. "I hate to disappoint ya, sweetheart, but it ain't gonna happen this time. Now where's Greg?" He squinted into the police lights and their shadows. "Lemme talk to that highly respected brother of mine."

As my mother handed the megaphone to my father, the SWAT commander informed the negotiator that one of his men could get a clear shot at Uncle Ray without hitting the child. The negotiator told him to wait.

"Where you at, Greg?" Uncle Ray hollered again. The nickel plating on the gun sparkled in the floodlights of the police cars.

"I'm right here, Ray," my father shouted from behind the lead police car.

"Where?" Uncle Ray asked, craning his neck to see. "I can't see you, man," he yelled, alarmed. "Step on outta the shadows where I can see you."

As my father started to move, the negotiator blocked his path. "It's alright," my father said. "I'm his brother. It's alright." Then stepping out from behind the police car, he stood under the streetlight where Uncle Ray could see him.

There was relief in his voice when Uncle Ray announced, "There you are, businessman. I just wanted to see if you were laughin. How come you ain't laughin?" he asked, then waited as though he truly expected a response. When none came, he yelled, "Look at ya, standin there lookin all concerned and shit. You might be able to hide it from them," he brandished the gun some more, "but you can't hide it from me; I can see right through your ass. Deep inside, you just bustin a gut. Cause it's funny, ain't it? Po Ray. Po, po pitiful Ray. Stupid sonofabitch just doesn't get it, does he?"

"I'm not laughing, Ray," my father yelled through the megaphone.

"Well, I got news for you, bro," Ray went on, ignoring him. "You don't get it either. Don't none of us get it. Was it good for ya, Greg? Was my wife good to ya?" This time he didn't wait for a response. "I hope so, man. Go ahead and laugh. Laugh, respected businessman. But you know what? We all po man, Greg. You just another pawn in the system like the rest of us."

My mother clutched her purse and stared at my father. Jessica hid her face, sobbing uncontrollably.

"A po black fool, just like me. Cause while the two a you were lyin up in bed laughin at ol po Ray, that white bitch was laughin at you. But that's alright. It's alright, man," Uncle Ray's stream of words abrubtly halted, and he suddenly placed the barrel of the gun against Lisa Marie's temple. "Me and my po little girl just decided we ain't gonna play this game no more."

Before the SWAT team commander could give the order to shoot, my mother screaming, "Ray, no," in the background, he withdrew the gun from Lisa Marie's head, shoved it in his mouth and pulled the trigger. As the gun, Lisa Marie, and Uncle Ray fell tumbling to the floor, the commander and the SWAT team leapt the stairs to the house, with my mother and Jessica screaming in tow behind them.

"Get the ambulance," somebody yelled.

Grandma Margret tried to follow, but my father grabbed her and reeled her into his chest. As the ambulance pulled to a stop on her front lawn, its siren muted, the flashing lights dressing everyone in red, my grandmother beat her fists against my father's chest until she began to weep. Even muffled, her moans blanketed the air like the cries of a wounded animal, ensnared and scared in the hunter's trap.

In the weeks that followed, the tatters of worn-out conversation focused on Lisa Marie. She never even cried, it was remembered. Even as the three of them were falling, the girl, the gun, and Uncle Ray plummeting to the floor, she never made a sound. And when my mother and Jessica finally made their way up to the guest room, parting a sea of blue uniforms to get to her, the child lay stretched across the floor, still and silent, watching the blood drain from Uncle Ray's head, the way she used to marvel at her George of the Jungle mobile, when it turned in circles above her crib.

The third crisis occurred while my parents were still at the hospital. Uncle Ray was still hanging on. In his rush to pull the trigger, the doctors said, the barrel must have slipped. Instead of blowing apart his brain, which would have killed him instantly, the bullet made a clean exit behind his ear. Considering the nature of the trauma and the inordinate amount of blood loss, the cerebral damage was minimal. The next twenty-four hours, they warned, were the most critical.

As soon as my parents arrived at the hospital, they made arrangements with Truly and his lady, Aisha, to open the store. And just three hours after my mother called Onya to say that she and my father were going to remain at Uncle Ray's side until he was out of danger, we received another call, a distress signal from Aisha.

There had been an accident, she told Onya. Truly was making a delivery out on Route 68 to a customer who had phoned in an order for a party she was throwing. Immediately, Aisha said, they had trouble filling the order. Not only did the customer call back three times to change it, but the store was so busy, by the time Truly finally got on his way, the delivery was an hour late.

It was well into the dinner hour on a Monday night when he left so, lucky for Truly, there was very little traffic. As he sped along the deserted two-lane highway, the car bounced into then out of an unusually deep pothole, causing all four tires to leave the road. And as the car became airborne, the box of wine sitting on the seat next to him tipped over on its side; one of the bottles fell to the floor. Since he was already late (and because the bottle seemed so easily within reach), instead of pulling off to the side of the road to pick it up, Truly figured he could save time if he retrieved it while driving. But just as his fingers were primed to wrap around the bottle's neck, the car hit another pothole and the bottle rolled out of reach. Checking first to make sure the highway was still deserted, he pulled his eyes from the road to locate it, then picked up the bottle and put it back in the box. The whole maneuver took only two seconds but when Truly returned his eyes to the road, he discovered that he had drifted into the oncoming lane of traffic, heading full-speed toward the only other car on the road. Before he had time to turn the steering wheel, force the brake to the floor in a futile effort to stop, he was caught up in the wreckage of a head-on collision of which he had been the cause.

My father had to be notified at once, Aisha told Onya. Truly, she said, for the most part was doing alright. He was taken by ambulance to Springfield Mercy General. Aside from a crushed and nearly severed right foot that would cause him to walk with a limp the rest of his life, he suffered only minor scrapes and bruises. It was the other car Aisha was worried about. The driver was okay, but somehow, the passenger—the driver's wife—got twisted up around her spine and there appeared to be nerve damage. It was too soon to tell, she said, but the attending physician had already called in a specialist to determine if the paralysis was permanent.

After hearing her name paged over the hospital's intercom, my mother met the news of Truly's accident with silence.

"I suppose we should've seen it coming," she whispered finally, then went on to say since nothing could be done from the hospital, they would have to deal with it when they got home. "Call Aisha at the store," she told Onya. "Get the name and phone number of Truly's doctor. Tell her I said to call Truly's family and let them know what happened, then close up the store and go on home. Your father will check in with them both later."

At least there was some good news, she sighed into the receiver. Looked like Uncle Ray was going to pull through. It had only been a few hours, but his heart was beating stronger and his condition was stabilizing. After instructing Onya to put a box of fish sticks in the oven for dinner, my mother told her she would call when she knew more.

"Been a long day," she murmured quietly before hanging up the phone. "Guess soon enough came sooner than expected."

TUESDAY

A New Era
1991

Bobby had a surprise that couldn't wait. At ten o'clock in the morning he phoned the desk nurse, demanding that she pull me out of group and put me on the phone. Impossible, she told him. Hospital policy. Pulling me out of group would severely hinder my healing process. But after a testy argument in which Bobby swore by the hand of Allah that he would descend upon the hospital with all his soldiers bringing the wrath of his maker with them, the desk nurse threw up her hands and complied. Everything was set, he gloated, when I picked up the receiver. He would arrive within the hour. It was simply too big to wait for visiting hours. No, he would not tell me over the phone. He just wanted to prepare me, he said. Make sure I would be around.

"And just where is it I'm supposed to go?" I asked him.

"Well now, that's just it, ain't it, Po? Just when somebody thinks they know where you is, you up and go someplace else."

"Yeah, well, given the circumstances, Bobby, even for me that would be a bit hard right now."

"That's what I'm sayin, lil sis. Ain't no tellin with you." In any case, he added, he'd be down in an hour.

I was lying on my bed, reliving the day Truly had his accident, when

Lilah knocked on the door to tell me about the Speaker. Three hours had passed and there was still no sign of Bobby.

"Am I interrupting?" she asked, sticking her head in and smiling.

"No," I answered, sitting up, "I'm just killing time, waiting for my brother." I motioned for her to come in. "He called this morning to say he was bringing me something special. But ain't that just like family? Call you up, tell you to stay put cause they're comin right over, then never show. Guess it must not be too special, right? Missed you in group this morning. Everything okay?"

"Oh, yeah," said Lilah, as she sat down in one of the plastic visitors' chairs. "I was just in with my doctor, gettin my outpatient stuff straightened out."

"Shit, that's right! Today's the big day, isn't it?" I snapped out of my stupor. "You excited?"

"Sort of," she answered, face grimacing a little. "It hasn't really sunk in yet. Little too nervous, I guess."

"Yeah, I know what you mean." I got up from the bed and offered her a cigarette.

"Thanks," she said as I held out the lighter.

"So how long before your husband comes to break you outta this joint?" I asked, pulling up the other plastic chair and sitting across from her.

"I thought it was gonna be this mornin," Lilah answered, looking for someplace to ash her cigarette. I got up and retrieved the styrofoam cup I kept next to bed, setting it on the floor between us. "But the head nurse stopped me on my way to breakfast and asked if I wouldn't mind waitin til after dinner. I guess they're plannin some sort of goin away party."

"Yeah," I remembered. "Now that I think about it, the counselor did mention something about it in group. Shows how much I pay attention. Supposed to be a real shindig, she said. Think I'd just as soon get it over with and go home myself."

"Oh, I don't mind," Lilah said, smiling a little. "Been in and outta this place so long now, few more hours ain't gonna kill me."

"Guess not, huh?" I agreed.

"You gonna go down and watch Preacher Man?" she asked, looking at her watch.

"Is it time for that already? Damn," I whispered, remembering his speech at Jessica's graduation. "You know, I saw him speak when I was a little girl. My Uncle Ray's girlfriend's college graduation. They got it on in the lounge?"

"Yeah," she laughed. "Guess Sylvia's supposed to be in there yellin back at him every time he tries to say something."

"Ooh, sounds like a show we can't afford to miss then."

Preacher Man, the Speaker who delivered the address at Jessica's graduation, had called a press conference to announce that after two unsuccessful previous attempts, he would not be seeking the voters' approval in the 1992 presidential election. He was explaining why when we entered the lounge.

"Cause you ain't got a chance in hell!" the phlegm ghost hacked at the television. Lilah and I slipped quietly into the back and stood against the wall. "Three things my daddy told me I'd never have to worry about," Sylvia went on, arm sticking up in the air. "Paying taxes, dying poor, and the chance of a Negro presiding over the government in the glorious free world."

When a reporter asked the Speaker if he was backing out because he realized the American people would never elect a black president, Sylvia hacked again. "Damn right!" she yelled, nearly choking on her own spittle. "What'd I just say?"

"No, no, that's not the reason at all," Preacher Man answered. "On the contrary, I believe the people of this country are more ready than ever to put a person of color at the head of state. For the world is fast approaching a new era. An era that transcends the boundaries of nations as well as nationalities. An era in which the people of *all* races, of *all* genders, of *all* spiritual beliefs and practices will hold their heads high in solidarity because the age of hate will finally have been defeated by the age of awakening. And the American people understand the necessity of installing a leader who will keep hope alive while this new era is materializing, maturing. I have simply come to realize that during the embarkation my leadership is still needed in the arena of spiritual guidance."

"Ha!" the phlegm ghost barked again, still holding her cigarette in the air. The striations in the shoulder muscle of Sylvia's extended arm bulged and twitched as she coughed, causing Lilah to lean over and whisper that in just the three months Sylvia had been here, the muscle had grown three times its natural size. The running joke on the ward was that in the rare moments Sylvia was able to let the arm rest at her side, the muscle feigned such a glaring deformity, one of the ward's new young doctors thought she suffered an advanced case of elephantiasis.

As we giggled to ourselves in the back row, the last of the cleaning crew wheeled their carts past the door of the lounge. Between Sylvia's hacking and the nauseating smell of ammonia that permeated the ward, it became increasingly difficult to concentrate on the Speaker's message. My thoughts instead turned to Agnes, wondering if the patients in lockdown had access to television.

"Seems like I heard that someplace before," Bobby sneered from the doorway. He was leaning against the doorjamb with his coat hung over his shoulder. His fedora was tipped down over his eyebrows and his hands were stuffed in the bottoms of his pockets. "Ol Preacher Man don't never give up, do he?"

"How long have you been standing there?" I asked, crossing Lilah's field of vision to greet him.

"Long enough to know dung seepin from the heifer's ass when I smell it."

"An hour, huh?" I mocked, glancing up at the clock.

"What can I say, lil sis?" he said, shrugging his shoulders. "Things come up. Your big brother's a busy soldier." We moved into the hall, where we could speak more freely. "So, how they been treatin you up in here?" he asked, eyes searching for the bandage.

"Oh, you know," I said, folding my arms across my chest so he could see it easily, "treatin me. Or trying to, at least. Speaking of smellin dung," I joked, "I see you're still partial to that Armani mixture."

He cocked his head back and howled an exaggerated laugh. "Now see how you are, girl?" he said, still laughing. "It's called hygiene. A brothah's got to smell sweet for the sistahs. It bother you?"

"No, not really," I answered. And it didn't; it was just nice to have something light to focus on for a minute, to laugh about with my brother again. Even forced, it had been a long time. "It's kind of a nice change, actually," I added, smiling. "Compared to this place."

"Yeah, well," my brother Bobby said, "that ain't hard to come by."

"No, guess not, is it?" Standing there laughing with him, I almost forgot about that huge fundamental wall of difference we'd erected between us. It seemed like it should be so easy to let all the pain wash away and just be family again. But experience had long ago taught me that moments like these are fleeting, that the erosion of mortar along with the knocking down of walls often takes years, and it began to feel a bit awkward, standing there feeling so comfortable. "So, where's my surprise?" I asked, changing the subject.

"What surprise, girl?" he teased.

"The one that was so important, you had to pull me out of group to tell me about it ahead of time."

"Got ya thinkin about it, huh?" he laughed.

I laughed with him. "Hard not to," I said, "with the big fanfare and all."

"I left it back in your room, girl. Go on and check it out. I'll be along in a minute... to see how you like it."

When I pushed open the door to my room, Onya was sitting on my bed like an oversized, impossible to wrap, Christmas present. And though Bobby had emphasized the word surprise, for some reason when I saw her sitting there, I wasn't.

She was draped in a fake fur coat and wool scarf. Her eyes stared down at her feet, her heels clicking together above the floor. Her hair had just been pressed and the crisp fried ends crept cautiously from beneath the scarf to curl around her ears. A plastic jug of water with orange rinds in it teetered on the mattress next to her.

I didn't know whether to grin or be mad. Grin because it must have been ten years since I'd last seen her. Mad because of all people, Bobby should have known this was the last place either of us would have chosen for the reunion. And it occurred to me that the three hours that passed before his arrival in all likelihood were spent trying to convince Onya she was strong enough to visit here.

I propped open the door to let some air in, then picked up a plastic visitor's chair and moved it closer to the bed. "Still trying to quench that thirst?" I asked, straddling the seat.

"Hi, Po," she whispered, looking down at the floor. "How've you been?"

"Better, at times. Guess Bobby told you about Dad?"

She took a sip from the jug and nodded. "I came for the funeral," she said.

"Yeah, thought maybe you might."

"Are you going?" She was still looking at the floor.

"Don't know, yet," I shrugged. "Haven't made up my mind."

Keeping her head down, she glanced at the bandage from the corner of her eye. "Does it hurt much?"

"Sometimes," I answered, watching her. "Mostly at night, when I'm sleeping. But I guess that's to be expected, since I don't take the medicine they give me. Never know what all might be in it."

She nodded her head, as if in agreement, then took another sip from the jug.

The last time I saw Onya, everything I valued and thought worth keeping was stuffed in the bottom of a duffel bag hanging from my shoulder. It was the year after Uncle Ray kidnapped Lisa Marie and shot himself. Two men in white jackets had just carted Onya away on a stretcher, toward the flashing red lights of a waiting ambulance. Her arms were restrained at her sides and she was heavily sedated. I was sixteen.

Things moved pretty fast in the wake of Truly's accident. The specialist called in by the hospital announced that the paralysis to the driver's wife was, indeed, permanent. And just months after my parents returned home from sitting by Uncle Ray's side at the hospital, we were hit with the lawsuit. No one was exempt. Even Truly and his family were named. And to make matters worse, in the process of having everything we ever owned taken from us or attached to liens, in addition to the deception involving Jessica, it turned out that my father had been keeping other secrets.

When the driver's accountants came to examine the store's balance sheet, they discovered that sometime before the celebration in which my mother had broken the record for turning out batches of potato salad, my father had been doing some cooking of his own. He had gambled away the store's profits and doctored the books to keep my mother from finding out.

The whispers about town grew so loud and plentiful, it took only twenty-four hours for the news of our decline to reach the ears of my sister all the way out in Columbus.

"It's simple," my mother responded, when Onya phoned to verify. The money was gone. That ship MacArthur had such a good time jawing her about? Well, it decided to lift anchor and return from whence it came. The spring semester had already been paid for, but come fall, Onya would have to choose: she could drop out of school and go to work, or apply for financial aid. If she could come up with a better way, more power to her, but that smooth free ride to which she had become accustomed was no longer free, and chances were, it would no longer be smooth. To be honest, said my mother, how Onya planned to finish college was the least of her worries right now. And as far as she was concerned, it was the least of Onya's as well. In the months prior to the accident, even as we celebrated the winning of the store, my father had fallen behind on the mortgage payments to the house. It was only a matter of time before the bank foreclosed on the loan. We had to move, she told my sister, and Onya was needed at home to help us pack.

In the middle of labeling boxes, Onya announced she was going for a walk. She needed some air, she told us, the dust from the boxes was making her nauseous. So after stopping in the kitchen to fill up her water jug, she started a long journey. A journey that would lead her to the cheers and cries of a varsity afternoon basketball game, the psych ward of a hospital, San Diego, and Cleveland before it would reach its end.

From the moment she entered the gym, witnesses recounted later, Onya was antsy. She never sat down, they said. And as the first half of the game drew to a close, she began to draw attention to herself by pacing despondently back and forth along the edge of the baseline. At one point, the players became so distracted by the woman under the basket swinging a jug of water back and forth like it was a pendulum, their shots trajected straight through the air into the frenzied arms of the crowd instead of bouncing off the rim or swishing through the net like they were supposed to. Twice, the referee had to interrupt the game to ask Onya to please sit down.

She never did, it was remembered. She moved out of the way alright, back to the corner, where—hidden by the bleachers—she was less of a distraction, but she never did sit down. And the students and parents sitting in the seats above her fidgeted and grew nervous watching her pace.

When the final seconds of the half ticked off the clock (to the relief of the students and parents in the bleachers), Onya at last stopped pacing and ran out of the gym. Had it not been for a last second strategic time-out called by the visiting team's head coach which delayed the final buzzer, the usually boisterous and raucous crowd might never have heard the crash of the glass. But the time-out was called, and when Onya put her fist through the window lining the school's hallway, the gym was silent. The sound of breaking glass resonated so loudly throughout the gymnasium, it caused some in the crowd to believe a garbage truck full of empty beer bottles had dumped its entire load smack in the middle of the hallway.

"What the hell was that!?" a man's voice yelled, as the mass of spectators ran into the hall.

What they saw confused them. The young woman who only minutes before was pacing despondently along the baseline swinging a jug of full of water now stood perfectly still, blood dripping from a glass-imbedded right arm hanging limply at her side, weeping in front of the broken pane of glass. The jug of water sat on the floor just left of her feet.

Though few recognized her when she was pacing as the captain of the award-winning cheerleading squad that rooted its team to the state championship three years before, as soon as the shock wore off, the voices started to buzz.

"Oh, my God! Isn't that...?"

"Hey, that's Onya Childs."

"Frank, isn't that... that Childs girl?"

And while they stood there mesmerized, dismayed, and whispering, without warning Onya raised her left fist in the air and put it through the glass just as she had done with her right. The women in the crowd gasped and screamed, burying their heads in the chests closest to them, while the men to whom the chests belonged hid their terror by shaking their heads in disbelief.

At last, after turning around to face them, Onya collapsed to the floor. Slow and methodical, arms still limp at her sides, she started to hum a discordant tune, rocking back and forth as she hummed. There were no tears, witnesses said. Just the eerie and discordant humming.

When we got the call, the Salvation Army had just finished hauling away the last of the boxes and furniture that hadn't been tagged for auction. My mother was standing in the center of the empty living room, staring through the curtainless window, drinking a glass of wine, the half-empty bottle cradled tightly in her arm. I stood in the foyer watching her, wondering how long I could stand the numbness before disappearing into my room to cut it out.

Onya had already been sedated by the time my mother and I arrived, and the sheriffs were busy dispersing the crowd. As we watched the ambulance back slowly out of the driveway, I fixated on the fact that Onya had forgotten to mark her boxes.

"She never told us which ones she wanted keep," I said to my mother as we ran to the car to follow the ambulance. "Which of the boxes did she want us keep?"

We followed the ambulance to the emergency room, where an exhausted nurse told us to have a seat and wait. But the room was overflowing with all types of infirmity: from those who were seriously ill to those who were new to the business of child-rearing and had rushed their infants to the doctor because of sudden inexplicable coughing fits. All the chairs were taken so we found an empty space along one of the walls, and leaned against it.

A young brown-skinned boy bearing shackles on his ankles stood a few feet away. He was surrounded by four stern policemen who seemed not to notice the man dressed in army fatigues yelling obscenities at one of the nurses. She had misplaced his admittance form, and though she apologized profusely, it would be another hour before he could see a doctor.

"Bullshit!" he yelled at her. He'd already waited for two motherfucking hours and he'd be damned if he'd wait one more just because she couldn't find some stupid piece of paper.

"Mrs. Childs?" another nurse called.

"I'm Mrs. Childs," my mother answered.

"Come this way, please." We followed the nurse down the hall to a side room where a doctor was waiting for us. Onya was going to be just fine, he said. That was the good news. The bad news was that when he told her we were in the waiting room, Onya refused to see us.

"What do you mean, refused?" my mother cried out, indignant. "I'm her mother!"

Be that as it may, the doctor answered, Onya was over eighteen, an adult licensed to make her own decisions. As her physician, whatever those decisions were, he was bound by oath to honor them. No visitors, she told him. Especially family. Give it some time, he advised my mother. They were going to keep her under observation for a few days, maybe by then she would come around.

But she never did. And the image of her, eyes vacant and arms strapped to a stretcher would be the one I held onto until I pushed open the door to my own hospital room to find her sitting on my bed like an oversized Christmas present, staring at a pair of clicking feet.

Every other year or so, the obligatory card at holiday time told Grandma Margret that she was alive and working. Reception jobs mostly, this town or that. But since there was never a return address and each corresponding postmark was from a different city in the tri-state area, we were never able to determine if she was well nor able to inform her that, a little over a year after Onya refused to see her, my mother had died of an illness three different doctors had failed to identify.

The clock on the wall ticked off seconds that felt like hours. We sat and stared at each other in silence like two girlhood friends seeing each other for the first time after one of our fathers had moved us away to the promise of work in the city. We searched the quiet for something meaningful to say.

"So how you two gettin on in here?" Bobby interrupted, rapping on the door.

Onya looked up from her feet to acknowledge him.

"Now is this some kinda reunion? Or is this some kind of *reunion?*" Bobby asked, grinning. He hung up his coat on the hook behind the door, then sat on the bed next to Onya.

"Oh, yeah, Bobby," I sighed, staring at the fake fur sleeves that covered Onya's arms. "Some kinda reunion."

"When's the last time the three of us were sittin up in the same room?" he asked, shaking his head and laughing at the marvel of it. "Must be what, ten, twelve years now?"

"Can't remember, actually," I said, giving the obligatory response. Curious about the depth of Onya's wounds, I searched my pocket for my cigarettes.

"Devil's still got you on that crutch, I see," Bobby noted with derision as he watched me stick a cigarette in my mouth.

"Yeah, well," I said, pausing to light it, "we all got our crutches, Bobby. Some got Allah; some got water; guess mine's cigarettes."

Onya took another sip of water.

"And some got knives," Bobby snapped back, wounded. "Yep," he said to Onya, changing his tone and patting her leg as he looked at her. "Musta been at least ten years. How long you think it's been, Onya?"

Onya shrugged her shoulders, then glanced around the room as if she were seeing it for the first time.

Bobby's forehead wrinkled as he watched her. "No matter," he said, shaking his head. "Important thing is that we all here now. You talk this girl into it yet, Onya?"

She shook her head no.

"I've decided not to go," I announced, blowing a single smoke ring through the air. I watched the ring float up toward the ceiling, then looked at Bobby and waited for his response.

"What!?" he answered. It wasn't the decision he expected.

"I said, I'm not going," I repeated, still watching him. His eyes rolled back in their sockets as he cocked his head to the side in one deliberate quick motion. He bit down on his bottom lip and inhaled long deep breaths through his nostrils in an effort to remain calm.

Onya reached for her jug of water.

"Alright, lil sis," he said, exhaling through his nose, then breathing in again. "I let you play out your little game, cause I figured after a few days' rest you'd come to your senses. But we talkin bout your father here, Po. You owe it to him to pay your respects."

"Gregory Taylor Childs stopped being my father long before his heart stopped beating, Bobby. You wanna pay some respect," I said, locking onto his eyes to let him know I was serious, "that's your business. I'm not going."

"Them some harsh words, lil sis, for the man who brought you into this world. Ey," he added, clearing his throat nervously, "I'll be the first to admit Pops wasn't no saint; Allah knows, ain't one of us that is. But what'd the man ever do to you that was so bad?"

"First off," I answered, getting up to flick my ash in the styrofoam cup next to the bed, "the person who carried me into this world wasn't no man, and maybe if the woman who did was still in it, she could answer that question for you."

"Oh, I see," he said, beginning to understand. "You still holdin onto that."

I grabbed the styrofoam cup off the nightstand and returned to my plastic chair. "Aren't you?" I asked, catching Onya's eyes as I brushed passed her. They were scared and longed to be someplace else, to be any place, as long as it wasn't here.

"No, no, lil sis," Bobby answered. He got up to walk over to the window. "I let that go a long time ago," he said, staring through the bars. "Had to. See, Allah made me realize cradlin it to my bosom like some raggedy ol teddy bear wasn't gonna do nothin for me or her. And it ain't gonna do nothin for you either," he added. His back was to me. He was still staring out the window. And he spoke soft and low, as though he were trying to convince himself of what he was saying rather than me. "Gots to throw that bear out, Po," he finished, turning back around and smiling. "Throw it right on out."

"Yeah, well, you can do what you want with yours," I responded, returning the grin. "But if I choose to pluck out its eyes and chew off its ears rather than throw mine away, it'd still be my bear."

"And Allah's, lil sis," he said starting to pace the room. The smile disappeared. "And Allah's," he said again. "Who demands that we give all our possessions over to Him and tells us to honor our father." He was sermonizing now. "Your father, Po," he spun around to face me, "deserves a proper burial, overseen by the mournful eyes of his loving children. You owe him."

"Yeah?" I continued to bait him. I couldn't help it. "And what about my mother? What do I owe her? You and Onya wanna do right by your God and go, go. I'm staying home."

"Home, huh?" he laughed manaically. He was beginning to lose control. "That what you call this place? White man's got you deeper in his grasp than I thought, girl. Look around you."

Onya started crying.

"You too, Onya," he shouted, lunging and grabbing her by the back of the neck like you'd pick up a kitten. "Look at this place!" he demanded, pointing her head at various objects around the room. "I know you recognize it. Whitewashed walls, whitewashed halls. Ain't this the devil's house?"

"Let her go, Bobby," I said, watching the gag-and-barf chick push her portable I.V. up to the door and glance through the square glass window.

"There go an example of his work right now," Bobby screamed, pointing at the gag-and-barf chick with one hand while holding onto Onya with the other. "People walkin around talkin to themselves, fraid of their shadows, hackin up blood. Everybody runnin around this place is bein injected with the white man's poison."

Onya didn't make a sound. In fact, she had gone limp and in Bobby's large hands resembled a life-sized rag doll.

I put my cigarette out and stood up. "Let her go, Bobby," I ordered again.

He looked at me and smiled maliciously, then shoved Onya's face deep into the bed sheets. "Remember that smell now, Onya? Go on now," he said, still looking at me. "Breathe real deep. Ain't this his stench? All bathed and dressed in disinfectant, tryin to hide that sinister odor."

"Let her go, Bobby!" I screamed, "or I'll get security!"

Black eyeliner poured down Onya's cheeks as she started to cough.

"So you gonna turn on me now, is that it?" Bobby asked, still pressing Onya's face into the disinfected sheets. "Gonna choose the white man over your own flesh and blood?"

"Let her go," I yelled for the last time.

"Everything alright in here?" It was the floor nurse. She stepped into the room, flanked by two orderlies, one black, one white. None of us spoke. "Mr. Childs?"

Still there was silence. Bobby just stood there, holding Onya's neck and smiling. The whiteness of his teeth flaunting his contempt for the nurse's uniform and her matching white skin.

"We heard yelling," the nurse continued. Her voice was uneasy. "We thought there might be a problem."

"Is there, Mr. Childs?" the black orderly asked.

"The name is Muhammad," Bobby said, finally. "Minister Robert Muhammad. Ain't no problem," he added, releasing Onya's neck before straightening his suit and tie. "Me and my sister were just leaving."

As Bobby grabbed his coat and started for the door, Onya found a tissue in her purse and started to wipe her eyes.

"Let you in on a little secret, Po," he said, stopping in front of the nurse and the orderlies. "No matter where it is, your dingy apartment, your little girlfriend's, or this place, everywhere you lay your head gonna be the house of the devil till you give it up to Allah. You gonna learn, lil sis," he said, looking into the eyes of the black orderly. "Gonna learn quick. Ain't no love in the world like the love of your family. Pay your respects, Po. Pay your respects. All praise be to Allah!" he shouted, then cocked his head back and strutted through the door.

Face streaked with makeup, Onya retrieved her water jug, then followed behind him.

"Bye, Po," she whispered, when she reached the door.

"Onya?" I called to her.

Her feet stopped abruptly as though they ran smack into an invisible barrier but her head remained bowed and her eyes refused to look at me.

"It was good to see you," I said, wanting to say more.

"You too," she mumbled quickly, then vanished down the hall behind Bobby.

Bobby
1983

Bobby was the one who found her answering phones and scheduling appointments in the Fairborn Family Dental Clinic. It was the last decree of his induction into the Ministers of Allah. "You must seek out those persons in your past," the senior minister informed him, "to whom you've done grievous wrongs or with whom you've conspired to carry out the biddings of the white-faced demon."

The Ministers considered Onya one of the former. And though Bobby disagreed with their assertion that the harsh words he'd once leveled at her—accusing Onya of wanting to be white—constituted wrongdoing, with a slightly exaggerated air of humility, he yielded to their wisdom and set out to track her down.

The task of finding her, however, would not be easy. Perhaps, Bobby thought, the Ministers already knew this and sent him on his quest not with the belief that he would succeed, but as a test of his faith and endurance. For Bobby had briefed them on the letters with varying postmarks, hedging that if Onya didn't want to be found, chances were she wouldn't be.

But the Ministers dismissed it, calling Bobby's logic nonsense. No one can hide from the all-seeing eyes of Allah, they scolded, even if their souls are entrenched in the bowels of the devil himself. Bobby, they said, was the prime example of His unparalleled power. Look how lost he had been, when the great hand of Allah reached into the pit to rescue him from the white man's fire of drugs and illness. If Bobby could be found, so could Onya. "Go with faith, Brother Robert," they told him. "Let the clean conscience of Allah be your guide."

He began his search in the summer of 1983. A summer whose coming was celebrated and praised after an unusually harsh winter, two-and-half years after my mother's death. On a well-traveled road that lifted him above the dank grime of the city into the sanitized woods of Tudors and Colonials nestled between the birch trees in the hills that lined the river.

After the Tudors, the well-traveled road carried him back down to the valley, across the river and into the trash country. Country whose landscape, for as far as his eyes could see, was covered with trash. Empty and broken beer bottles along with crumpled-up candy wrappers, potato chip bags, and abandoned bicycles adorned the shoulders of the road, stretching back far into the thickets of the woods. But the most striking sight of all was the row of Pampers trees. Trees whose trunks contorted and stooped from the stench of dirty diapers hanging from their limbs. Stench that was so bad, Bobby had to roll up the windows to keep from vomiting as he drove through the stifling August heat in a car without air-conditioning.

He was on his way to Berea, the town whose name graced the postmark on the last card Grandma Margret received from Onya. The one in which she'd told her not to worry because she'd finally found decent work filing rejected applications in the admissions office of the College.

Though Bobby had scoured the one page note with sponge-like intensity before he left trying to find the smallest clue to her whereabouts, he needn't have. For with the sole exception of the type of work found, all of Onya's letters were identical: no return address, no phone number, and not a single mention of the name of a friend through which she could be reached in case of emergency.

Dear Grandma (they all read),

I sincerely hope this letter finds you healthy, well, and still at the same address...

Once again, I've found myself out of work for several months. And though, for some time now, my finances have teetered on the precarious, this new job seems promising.

I don't believe I'm up to any sort of reunion just yet. I only wish to let you know that I'm okay. Please inform the rest of the family.

Will write again soon,

Onya.

Berea surprised him. When at last the well-traveled road rose up out of the forest of Pampers trees, at once he found the town gentle, beautiful and white. And though her whiteness splayed on a bed of rolling hills at the foot of the Appalachians was to be expected, the gentleness in her beauty was not. It beckoned, caressed his cheek as he entered. Her people smiled at him as he drove down her coiffed and decorated streets. The drivers motioned him ahead when he stopped at unmarked intersections. And her passersby flagged him down, offering unsolicited directions when they sensed that he was lost. The whiteness of Berea opened her arms to Bobby. And it was precisely that flagrant showing of hospitality that made him uneasy.

"Take care, Brother Robert," the Ministers had warned. "You will enter many foreign worlds, the likes of which you have never seen. The devil will attempt to use this knowledge to improve his credibility. He will tempt you with a kindness bred purely from guilt, then seduce you with the lecherous and often irresistible charms of his women. Resist, Brother Robert. Do not be fooled. The devil's good deeds are but mere illusions to distract us from the purpose at hand."

Except for a few early and eager arriving freshmen, when Bobby pulled into the college parking lot, the campus was deserted. He felt inside his suit jacket pocket to make sure he'd remembered the photo.

Back in '79, when he left our parents' house for good, it was the only reminder of Onya he'd wanted. He had pocketed a prized possession from each of us. An autographed copy of *I Know Why The Caged Bird Sings* from me. The gold-plated locket with the broken clasp from my mother's jewelry tray. When opened, it revealed the only photograph in existence of the grandmother we never knew. The others had either been consumed in the fire that took her life, or misplaced and forgotten in the apartment my parents rented before moving into their dream house. From my father, Bobby stole the first vibraphone my father had purchased with his own money, the one he played when he sat in with Miles. When my father was clearing his things out of the closet, it was the revelation of the vibraphone's absence that led us to discover the other items missing.

He wondered what Onya looked like now. The photo was almost seven years old, taken on the night of her senior prom. He never really thought it favored her. Neither did Onya. Perhaps that's why she liked it so. Of all the pictures my mother strategically placed around the house: the one at age seven with the lopsided ponytails; age twelve, when she made alternate for Drill Team; the eight-by-ten glossy at fourteen when she had that embarrassing acne problem; even over all the Kodak moments in her cheerleading uniform in which she was captured by professionals in the midst of various splits and turns and flips, the only photo Onya liked was the Polaroid my father snapped of her on prom night. It made her look like a lady, she said. A princess adorned in opera-length gloves and a white chiffon gown, lifted right from the pages of a fairy tale. She didn't exactly look happy, Bobby noted as he fingered the photograph's edges. She didn't look sad either. But it was the only time any of us could remember, since the onset of that insatiable thirst for water, that her face wasn't fixed in a desiccated expression. Perhaps that's why Bobby liked it, too. The absence of the expression afforded him the luxury of remembering while not remembering.

After one of the eager freshmen pointed him toward the Administration building, Bobby entered the first office from which he heard voices: life, in an otherwise forsaken and (even in summer) drafty building that repeated his footsteps as he walked down its hall. White, he thought as he stepped into the room. Even the building was white.

He stood in front of the desk for nearly five minutes before a shrunken and hunchbacked elderly woman scurried around the partition to notice he was there.

"Help you with something?" she asked, peering over a pair of wire-rimmed glasses. Suspiciously, she took in the creases of Bobby's suit. "I can save you some trouble," she added, before he could respond. "If you've come in here selling something, there's no one here to buy it. Nobody but me, anyway. And my mother taught me a long time ago never to keep any change on my person." Her dark blue eyes narrowed as she spoke. Her lips seemed permanently pursed, as though she'd spent the last forty years of her life sucking nicotine from the filter of a cigarette.

Now this was the white Bobby remembered. And the comfort brought on by its familiarity gave his shoulders cause to relax a little. For contrary to the Ministers' warning, he had met this woman before. Even though they had both been a little younger then, a little softer around the edges, he had no trouble identifying her. At that first meeting, when he was young and naive, she intimidated him. Made him believe he was unworthy to meet her in that naked place hidden behind the eyes. But now that each had watched the other grow old and wary from a safe and tolerable distance, he'd come to recognize her for what she was: yet another of the devil's concubines. And he would handle her the way he handled all the others: with a white-toothed grin and a pair of steadfast eyes, blazing bright with the glory of Allah.

"Well, I thank you for that bit of insight, ma'am," he said, smiling, reaching in his pocket for Onya's picture. "I truly do. But I'm afraid it won't be necessary. You see, I ain't sellin anything. I'm lookin for a woman. I think she might work here, or used to anyway."

She seemed confused by his smile.

"My sister, actually," Bobby continued as he handed her the Polaroid. "Here, I have a picture. Her name is Onya, Onya Childs."

Again she peered over the rims of her glasses at the old, worn-out photograph. "Oh, she's pretty," she exclaimed. "But she's never worked in this office. This is Records. Are you sure she said she was working in Records?" Her arms overflowed with important-looking documents stuffed in manila folders.

"Well, no, actually," Bobby answered, remembering the letter. "I believe it was Admissions. Said she was filing rejected applications in the Admissions office."

"Well, like I said," the woman responded, pausing to wrestle with one of the folders that had slipped from her grasp, "this is Records. The Admissions office is down the hall. But nobody'll be there for another week or so."

"Look, ma'am," Bobby started. He was growing impatient. "I drove a long way, from across the river. I don't have a week or so."

"Well, Mr... What did you say your name was again?"

"I didn't," Bobby answered. "But my sister's name is Onya, Onya Childs."

"Well, Mr. Childs..."

"Muhammad," he corrected.

"Excuse me?"

"My name's Muhammad. My sister's name is Childs."

"Well, as I was about to say, Mr... Muhammad, is it?"

Bobby nodded.

Losing patience herself, the woman shifted the weight of the folders, and dropped them on the desk in front of her. "I guess you're clean outta luck," she said, dusting off the front of her dress with her hands. "But if it's any consolation to you, even if you were to come down next week, it wouldn't do you any good."

"No? Why's that?" Bobby asked, frustrated, but still smiling.

"The age of computers, Mr. Muhammad," the old woman answered as she moved around to the other side of the desk and sat down in a wooden chair. "Everyone knows admissions information is kept on computers these days." One by one she started opening and leafing through the manila folders. "And any jobs doing filing and such are reserved for the work-study kids who come down from the mountains." She stopped going through the folders and looked up at him. "Your sister wasn't a work-study student, was she?"

"No," Bobby answered, smile starting to fade. "She wasn't a work-study student. Look," he said, all but giving up, "maybe I'll go on and come back next week. Thanks for your help, ma'am." He turned to leave.

"Well, you can do that if you like," she yelled after him.

Bobby stopped in the doorway and turned around.

"But, like I said," she went on, "they won't be able to help you in the Admissions office either." She removed her glasses to clean the lenses with a used tissue, then put them back on and peered over the rims to meet his eyes. "I know you folks think you have to figure things out for yourselves these days. But believe me when I tell you, Mr. Muhammad, come back next week and you'll have wasted two trips instead of one."

"Listen," Bobby tried, extending the photograph one last time. "Why don't you have another look at that picture? It was taken a long time ago; maybe she looks a little different now, older."

"I don't have to," she said, shaking her head as she cut him off. She got up from her chair and walked back around to the front of the desk. "No way in the world I'd forget a pretty face like that, with such an unusual name to match. All grown up, or not."

"Well, thanks again," Bobby said snidely, as he put the Polaroid back in his pocket.

"Mr. Muhammad," she called as he turned to leave for the second time.

This time Bobby stopped, but he did not turn around.

"We've got a nice little town here," she offered, giving him some advice. "Full of good Christian people. And the best food kitchen you've ever seen, south of the Ohio. You should walk around a bit. Stretch your legs and have some lunch before you drive all the way back to...Where'd you say you were from again?"

"Across the river," answered Bobby, his back still to her.

"That's right," she remembered. "You know one of my grandson's moved up across the river. I've never been too fond of city life myself," she went on, as though she were reminiscing with an old friend. "But he seems to enjoy it. Oh, well, sorry we couldn't be of more help to you. If you do decide to try out our kitchen, though, I hear the hotel has a very good lunch menu today."

"Thanks," Bobby muttered as he stepped into the hall. "I might just do that."

When he returned to the Ministers, frustrated and empty-handed, he said the whole quest was nothin but a game, a wild goose chase.

The Ministers weren't surprised. "Your search has just begun, Brother Robert. She'll turn up. But not before you believe in your heart that Allah will provide."

In the months that followed, Bobby's search took him through one cornfield town after another, where Onya had boasted such jobs as check-out girl in a grocery store, substitute teacher for the county school district, and radio dispatcher for a local cab company. Each time he came back empty-handed, no closer to the truth of Onya's whereabouts than when he first started.

"You do not believe, Brother Robert," the Ministers warned, when they sensed he was about to give up. "Allah will not reveal the truth to you until He is satisfied that you truly believe."

Bobby decided to give it one last try when he got a tip that Onya had been spotted in Cleveland. On a visit to the city, one of the Ministers' cousins claimed Onya was the woman who had signed her up for welfare. Surely, the city of Cleveland kept records of employment. Even if she were no longer working there, they would at least have an address to which they had forwarded her final paycheck.

In the beginning, Cleveland seemed promising; the cousin's story checked out. And for the first time in nearly six months, someone actually knew who Onya was. Of course she remembered her, the plump round woman behind the counter told him.

"She was that quiet pretty young thing, kept to herself all the time. Only worked here bout a month, as I remember. Never seemed to eat mucha nothin, either," she added, eyes widening as she talked. "Just drank a whole lotta water. Didn't even take no lunch break. I tried to get her to come over to my place and sit down to a real supper with me and my husband, cause you know, our folks, we gotta stick together best we can. And since the kids done got all grown and started families of their own, woulda been nice to have some young energy givin life to the place for a change. But you know," the woman frowned, "she just flat out refused. Kept to herself and just flat out refused. Punched in early; punched out early, drinkin glass after glass of water all day long. Brought it in her own jug, too," she added, smacking her teeth. "Like the water we drank wasn't good enough or somethin.

"Now, let's see," she said finally, typing Onya's name into the computer. "You know, I'm really not s'posed to do this, but you know, our folks, we gotta stick together best we can." Her whole body giggled as she laughed. "O-n-y-a. C-h-i-l-d-s," she read as she typed. "Says here she never gave no address, just a post office box and a phone number. I can give you that if you like. She's not in any trouble, is she?" she asked, overly curious. "You know, I just hate the way our young people get into trouble these days. No? Oh. Well, I sure do hope you find her. Sure was a pretty young thing. You know, if you was gonna be in town awhile," she pried, body giggling again, "I'd invite you to come have supper with me and my husband. You married?" Her eyebrows climbed all the way to her hairline in anticipation, then lowered with suspicion when Bobby said no. "Now how does a handsome young man like you get away with not being married? Bet you could use a good home-cooked meal right about now, couldn't ya? Alright," she said, body still giggling. "Maybe next time. You take care now."

He took the information he received from the welfare office and looked immediately for a pay phone. Just as he had expected, the number had long been disconnected. And when he returned to the Ministers to deliver his findings, they were also just as he had expected.

"Believe, Brother Robert!" they told him. "Believe."

He was about to give up the whole show, induction to the Ministers and all, when something happened that no one could have predicted, except for maybe Allah Himself.

Six months after Bobby began his search, the younger brother of one of the Ministers had been arrested for trespassing. He was being held without bail in the Fairborn jail, denied access to counsel. The Ministers organized a protest. Followers drove from all over the county to come to the young brother's aid.

"Charge him or let him go!" they chanted. "Charge him or let my brother go!"

It was smack in the middle of their chanting that the thing nobody could have predicted put an end to the entire demonstration. Without warning, the senior minister who was sermonizing up on the podium clutched the side of his face and collapsed to his knees. The crowd let out a giant gasp as he rolled around in agony behind the podium.

The whole thing played like an old black and white reel of silent news footage in which the heralded religious leader gets gunned down in the middle of his sermon. An eerie quiet hovers briefly over the crowd before all chaos breaks loose and the bodyguards brandish their guns running this way and that, trying to figure out who the shooter was.

Only this time, there was no shooter. And when the crowd finally managed to get a hold of itself, the commotion at last dying down to a whisper, it turned out that the senior minister had been brought to his knees not by gunfire, but by the onset of an excruciating toothache that required emergency surgery.

The rally was disbanded immediately. After the upheaval surrounding the senior minister's fall from the podium, the organizers believed re-establishing order would be next to impossible. And though a handful of locals elected to stay behind and risk arrest (slinging racial epithets in the direction of the police station), the majority of the crowd piled into their cars to parade behind the sleek black limousines of the Ministers.

Honking their horns as they went, the impromptu caravan resembled a cross between a funeral procession and a stock car race. The four stretch limousines peeled around the corner onto Main Street, with the cars of the protest crowd hot on their heels. Onlookers stopped their shopping and lined up along the sidewalk to watch. Diners, thinking it might be the President, interrupted their meals to wave as the Ministers' cavalcade screeched to a halt in front of the Fairborn Family Dental Clinic.

The advance men filed in first with Bobby leading the way, lining up one after the other along each of the lobby's walls. The bodyguards marched in next, six of them in drill team formation down the middle of the empty lobby, pairing off in twos to make way for their ailing leader. He was led in by the minister he had chosen to succeed him, dragging his feet and holding an ice pack to his jaw, wearing the pained expression of someone who had just been punched in the face. The protest crowd gathered outside the door.

"We need some help out here!" the Chosen One yelled to the back of the clinic. "Hey! Is anybody back there? I said, we need some help out here!"

The dentist, followed by two nurses in fashionable white caps, burst through the door that led to the back of the clinic.

"What's going on out here?" he asked, turning his gaze from side to side as he happened upon the twenty black men in tailored black suits that had taken over his lobby. Beads of sweat studded the bald spot on top of his head.

"The Senior Minister's got a terrible toothache," the Chosen One informed him. "He's in need of immediate attention." The rest of the Ministers remained alert in ready formation: balls of their feet spread twelve inches apart, hands clasped at the smalls of their backs, eyes resting stoically on those of the dentist.

The nurses traded nervous glances between the Ministers, the dentist, then back and forth at each other.

The dentist seemed at a loss for what to do. Everyone stood facing each other as though they were at the crossroads of a tremendous impasse. With the taunts and cries of the protest crowd ebbing and flowing on the other side of the entrance doors, an uninformed passerby might have thought the unfortunate brother whose sudden incarceration instigated this chain of events was being held without bail in the back room of the dental clinic. Only now, instead of yelling "Charge him or let him go," the protest crowd screamed, "Treat him! Treat him! Treat my brother now!"

But just as things threatened to get out of hand, just as the dentist stammered something about the Senior Minister having to fill out a number of forms before being treated while the veins were popping out of the Chosen One's neck as he reiterated the need for swift and timely treatment, just as the hands of the lesser ministers fell from their clasps to form clenched fists at their sides and one of the nurses ran behind the reception window to dial 911, just as the chants of the protest crowd turned into inaudible roars, Onya stepped through the double glass doors with a half-eaten bologna sandwich lodged in her mouth. Before anyone—the dentist, the Chosen One, or even the nurses—could release a sigh of relief worthy of the one face who might diffuse the situation, Bobby broke the stoic ranks of his comrades and dropped to his knees.

Believe, Brother Robert, he heard the Ministers say as he kissed the ground in front of her. *Believe.* Raising his arms high in the air, he yelled, "All praise be to the mighty Allah!" Then, forgetting perhaps (for the briefest of moments) his subordinate position and the reason they were all gathered there in the first place, he jumped to his feet and ran straight for her. "Girl!" he cried. "Where the hell you been? Do you know how much gas I wasted, drivin all over the damn nation, tryin to find you?"

All eyes were on them. Onya didn't answer, just stared straight ahead like a mouse after the trap has sprung: eyes fixed in no particular direction, mouth primed to bite down on the cheese. Purse hung over her shoulder, potato chips to go with the sandwich in one hand, half-empty water jug in the other, she just stood there staring, with Bobby staring back at her, until the Chosen One, the dentist, the nurses, the protest crowd and the rest of the Ministers—losing all hope of mediation—returned again to the argument whose outcome would determine when, if at all, the ailing senior minister would receive treatment.

Completely unaware of the commotion surrounding them, Onya and Bobby stood silent, staring deep into each other's eyes, acknowledging, perhaps for the very first time, that the curse eating away at the other's soul bore a striking resemblance to the one corroding his or her own.

Resurrections
1982

While Onya had been reinventing herself across the country, Bobby had pretty near killed himself, two times. The first time, piece by piece. The second, vein by vein. Yet he qualified for resurrection, twice. Maybe it had something to do with the fact that each of Bobby's revivals involved a different deity. According to my mother and Grandma Margret, it was Jesus who saved him the first time. According to Bobby, Allah the second.

The first time, Hmm Hmm and Try Try were no longer with us. Sometime after Bobby had scooped Debbie's uneaten grits back into the pot kept warm for second helpings, their presence simply disappeared, vanished. My parents stopped setting places for them at the table. And Bobby no longer talked to them. In fact, except for Christmas morning, when he knocked on my door and told me to look in his eyes, he no longer spoke to anyone. Just shuffled around the house in his slippers, yellow eyes glowing, followed by the aura of one who senses he's about to die.

"You think he killed them, too?" I had asked Onya.

It was Christmas Eve, 1977. We were rolling butter balls in the kitchen (although Onya was eating more than she was rolling). My parents were in their bedroom wrapping presents. And Bobby was sleeping.

Just after Thanksgiving, the illness took a dramatic turn for the worse and kept him completely bedridden. To ease his discomfort, my father moved the television into his room, and my mother put a bed pan next to his nightstand. Onya and I took turns serving his meals on t.v. trays and, after doing so, had to wash our hands with a special soap the doctor prescribed to keep from catching his germs.

"Of course he did," Onya answered, sipping a tall glass of water through a straw. "I'm just sorry he didn't do it sooner. It's about time we returned to some normalcy around here."

"How do you think he did it?" I asked, using a spoon to scoop some batter from the bowl, then rolling it between my palms into a ball.

"How do I know?" she snapped, plopping a butter ball in her mouth. "And why should I care? But since you asked," she added with her mouth full, "he probably strangled em, like he did Debbie."

"What makes you think he strangled Debbie?" I asked, carefully placing my newly rolled ball onto the cookie sheet.

"Oh, come on, Po. You saw his hands that day. The way the veins popped out as his fingers wrapped around that plate. The only reason it didn't break was because he was so weak from the hepatitis. If those weren't the hands of somebody trying to strangle someone, I don't know what is."

"You think he buried them?" I asked, scooping up some more batter and repeating the process.

"Oh, yeah, right," she shrieked. "In separate graves even. And the minister blessed their souls before they went to heaven."

"He buried Debbie," I said, putting another ball on the cookie sheet. And I truly believed that he did.

"No, he didn't," Onya laughed hysterically. The sugar was starting to get to her. "He just rinsed her down the drain." She shoved another raw ball into her mouth, then washed it down with water. "Po!" she yelled after swallowing. "We're talking about imaginary people here! They never existed."

"To Bobby they did," I defended.

"Yeah, well, a whole lot of things that aren't real exist in Bobby's mind," Onya joked. "His brain's so ravaged with illness, he oughtta start digging a grave for himself."

"You think he's going to die?" I asked, eating one of the raw balls myself.

"Of course he is," she answered, pausing to take a deep breath and press on her stomach. "Doctor said there's nothing left to do but wait," she continued, still holding her stomach. "I just wish he'd go ahead and get it over with."

"You don't mean that," I said, getting up to put the cookie sheet in the oven.

"Oh, yes, I do," she insisted through clinched teeth. Her stomach was killing her. She was doubled over in pain, but she kept going. "And I'll tell you what else I mean," she said. "I can't wait till this year's over, so I can go to college and get away from this place. Here," she gagged as she slid the bowl of batter across the table, "get this away from me, I think I'm going to be sick," then ran off to the bathroom.

Even accompanied by water, that last butter ball proved one too many; Onya's stomach rejected it. She barely reached the door to the bathroom before puking all over the floor. My mother had to interrupt her present wrapping to clean it up and put Onya to bed. All told, she threw up eight times during the night. And though by the third time they were mostly dry heaves, her body was so dehydrated and exhausted by daybreak, she was forced to spend all of Christmas day lying in bed, eating stale saltine crackers, and drinking flat soda.

At about five o'clock in the morning, while Onya was making her final trip to the bathroom, Bobby knocked quietly on the door and entered our room.

"Look at my eyes," he said, flipping on the light.

"What?" I answered groggily.

We could hear Onya heaving in the background. My mother was in the bathroom with her.

"My eyes!" he said, excited. "Look at my eyes!"

I sat up and rubbed the sleep from mine as he plopped down on the bed to show me.

"What?" I said, peering into his eyes. "I don't see anything."

"Do they look white to you?" he asked. He sounded alarmed.

I looked again, but I still didn't know what he was talking about. "What do you mean, white?" I asked.

"The whites!" he said, frustrated, tilting his head back so I could see better. "Do they look white or yellow?"

For the third time in five minutes, while Onya was throwing up her guts in the bathroom, I looked into Bobby's eyes. At last I saw what he wanted me to see. "White," I said, finally understanding. His excitement was catching. "They look white!" I said again.

"That's what I thought," he said, as we jumped up and down on the bed to celebrate. "But I had to make sure I wasn't seein things." It had been a long time since I'd seen Bobby so happy, expending so much energy without getting tired.

"Mama!" we yelled at the same time, leaping off the bed and running into the hall to find her. "Mama, come here, quick!"

We'd only made it two feet down the hall when my mother scurried out of the bathroom to intercept us. "Are you trying to wake your father?" she scolded, ushering us back into the room. "Keep your voices down!" she whispered sternly. Onya was still in the bathroom, heaving. "Now what is it?" she demanded, still whispering. "I have to get back to Onya."

"Bobby's eyes are white," I whispered, but she didn't believe me.

"Po," she doubted, "it is too early in the morning to be playing games."

"I'm not," I responded, raising my voice in protest. "His eyes are white." I pointed at Bobby's eyes. "Look!"

"Shsh!" my mother ordered as she closed our bedroom door. She took Bobby by the arm and pulled him under the light so she could see. "Oh, my Jesus," she whispered, struggling to restrain her emotion. She looked Bobby in the eye. "How do you feel, sweetie?"

"Hungry," Bobby answered.

"Don't move!" she ordered, then ran down the hall to wake my father. "Gregory!" she screamed as she ran. "Gregory, baby, wake up! Bobby's eyes are white and he's hungry!"

Within seconds, we heard my parents' feet pounding the rug as they ran down the hall toward our bedroom. "Praise Jesus!" my mother kept yelling as they hurried closer. "Praise God Almighty!"

It was a miracle. Not the modern-day kind, when the Lord always manages to provide after you've exhausted all your resources trying to make one dollar look like two. But a true miracle of old. It ranked right up there with Moses parting the sea, and Paul going blind. Jesus had reached into the grave and given Bobby his life back. And He'd shown His appreciation for flare and style by resurrecting him on His own birthday.

Onya was all but forgotten. She was still in the bathroom heaving when my parents threw on their coats to rush Bobby to the emergency room. Guess it wasn't really a miracle until the Lord's work was verified by medical science.

"What about Onya?" I asked as they pushed Bobby out the door.

"Shit!" my mother screamed, stopping to think for minute. "Call your grandmother," she said at last. "Tell her what happened and that we need her to come look after Onya till we get back. Tell her we'll phone!" she yelled over her shoulder as she ran down the sidewalk.

When she called from the hospital, Grandma Margret, Uncle Ray, Jessica, and Lisa Marie were all at the house. The miracle had been confirmed. As suddenly as it had risen, Bobby's white cell count had returned to normal, and the doctors were unable to detect a single trace of hepatitis left in his body. To be on the safe side, they said, we should continue washing our hands with the special soap he prescribed, and the dishes Bobby used while he was contagious should be thrown out immediately. Bobby, they cautioned, needed to ease into recovery slowly. No strenuous activities. And for the next couple of weeks at least, he should remain in bed and be monitored closely. Then, once his strength started to come around, he could take an occasional supervised walk. Of course, if the jaundice returned or if his appetite decreased again, we should bring him back for further testing. But for the meantime, they were giving Bobby a clean bill of health.

My grandmother and Uncle Ray were standing in the front door before my parents pulled into the driveway. Jessica was taking care of Onya, who had finally stopped heaving. And I was watching over Lisa Marie, who was sleeping on the sofa. They had barely made it in the door, when Grandma Margret threw her arms around Bobby and started offering prayers of thanks.

"Oh my sweet Jesus!" she wailed, squeezing him tighter. "Thank you, thank you Jesus! For seein fit to save this precious, precious lamb."

Bobby's nose was squished against her breasts as she cried; he seemed to be having trouble breathing.

"Give the boy some room, Mama!" Uncle Ray yelled, laughing. "Unless you fixin to make the Lord's work in vain."

"Oh my goodness," she cried, laughing along with the rest of us. She backed away as tears of joy streamed down her cheeks. "I got so carried away I almost... Oh, Lord! Did I hurt ya, baby?"

Bobby shook his head no.

"Did ya see that, Lillian?" she cried again. "Po thing. Lord barely breathed the life back into him, and here I come, tryin to take it back away."

"It's alright, Margret," my mother soothed as she rubbed the back of Bobby's head. "Nothing can ruin this day. Bobby's going to be just fine. Aren't ya, sweetie?"

Bobby didn't answer. Just stared at Lisa Marie still sleeping, as though he wished he could trade places with her. When everyone settled down, my father offered a round of celebratory eggnog.

"Put a little pinch in mine," Uncle Ray whispered so that Grandma Margret wouldn't hear.

My mother excused herself to check on Onya, then went into the kitchen to fix Bobby a bowl of Campbell's tomato soup and dry toast. It was the first full meal he'd eaten in nearly a month. And as he swallowed the last bite of bread, we all clapped and congratulated him. After Uncle Ray slapped him on the shoulder and said "Welcome back, son," my mother suggested we celebrate the day in our bedroom, so that Onya wouldn't feel left out.

As we ripped open the presents my parents had spent all night wrapping, my grandmother started to sing *We've Come This Far by Faith*. My mother took it up immediately.

We've come this far-ar-ar by faith
leaning on the Lor-ord.
And we are trusting (trusting in His holy word)
because He's never (He's never fai-ai-ailed us yet).

And oh, ohhhhh, oh, ohhhhh, oh
can't turn arou-ou-ound.
We've come this far-ar-ar by fai-aith.

But even after they completed two verses and a chorus, no one else elected
to join in. Onya, Bobby, and I continued to demolish the wrapping on our
presents. Onya received make-up, clothes, and a new water bottle that came
with its own straw. Bobby was given puzzles and games that he could play
while lying in bed. And I got a pair of ice skates along with hardback
editions of some of my favorite books. While Uncle Ray showed Lisa Marie
how to pull the string that would make her doll talk, my father and Jessica
watched on, avoiding each other's eyes and sipping their eggnog.

It was the last Christmas we would celebrate with so much zeal. For
even though—separately—my mother and Grandma Margret would offer
more prayers in the following years than they had prior to the resurrection,
combined, Jesus would only cure one of Bobby's illnesses. The other one,
the big one that afflicted us all, the one that drained Bobby's blood as he
hacked off piece after piece of his soul, was of a different variety. Imbedded
in its make-up was the ability to mutate. And halting it, required a plan of
attack the Lord was too busy to formulate.

The second resurrection happened in 1982. On the night of Uncle
Ray's last suicide attempt, when he tried to swallow a garden hose filled
with carbon monoxide, Bobby left Grandma Margret's house for good.
While his uncle was fighting for his life behind a curtain in the hospital
emergency room, Bobby went down into the basement, found himself a
new box and moved into an enclave of elms, nestled among the chipmunks
in the heart of the city park.

Every once in a while during the summer, Grandma Margret would
receive a call from one of the Bid Whist girls, saying she had spotted him
begging for change on Race Street when she was coming out of Newberry's.
Or had seen him dozing on the sidewalk, under that broken street lamp
over on Plum, while she was waiting for the bus.

"I was so tired and it was so hot," she remembered. "If I hadn'ta had all
them packages and I thought I could get back up, I'da laid right down on

that concrete and gone to sleep with him."

But on toward October, when the leaves started to turn and the air was finally breathable, the calls stopped coming. Either he was dead, Grandma Margret concluded (which would explain why nobody had seen him), or the sightings had become so commonplace, folks no longer considered them news.

The former was only half true. Nobody had seen him, but he wasn't dead. At least no more dead than the rest of us. For in the final days of 1982, while the city holiday crew decked the streets with bells and folly and Grandma Margret's Bid Whist girls pulled the mothballs from their furs, Bobby was being resurrected for the second time in five years. Only this time, the miracle had nothing to do with the flare and style of our blessed Messiah. It was the result of hard work and menial diligence. And, according to Bobby, all praise belonged to the Ministers of Allah.

Under pressure from the local business association, to ensure that this season's tourists enjoyed a pearly white Christmas, the mayor created a temporary task force whose sole purpose was to remove the indigent from public view. Bobby's box in the park was considered unsightly. And as the harshness of the weather took hold, he was forced to spend his days in hiding, his nights looking for shelter and searching alley dumpsters for food, all while trying desperately to persuade one dealer or another to extend him some credit.

As Bobby tells it, on the morning of one of the year's coldest Tuesdays, he was passed out in an alley under a stack of old newspapers when the brother minister assigned to take out the garbage opened the alley door of the building nearest him

"Wake up, my brother," the minister whispered, after disposing of the trash. Methodically, he started clearing away the newspapers. Bobby shivered from the sudden burst of cold.

"Time to wake up, my brother," the minister said again as he removed the last newspaper from Bobby's body. "The dawn has arrived in which you will seek your place among that which is new. For the truth that you've been seeking in all the wrong places is about to be shed upon you." The minister kneeled down beside him. "What's your name?" he asked Bobby.

"What?" Bobby answered, shielding his eyes from the daylight.

"Your name," the minister repeated, smiling and extending his hand. "No need to hide from the sun, my brother. For the sun is a gift, courtesy of the generosity of the mighty Allah, whose light overfloweth with truth and love."

"Am I dead?" Bobby asked as the minister pulled him to his feet. "Some kind of dream?"

"No dream, my brother," the minister grunted, slinging Bobby's arm around his shoulder. "By the grace of the Lord of the dawn," he said before he helped Bobby inside, "your slumber has come to an end. Now what is your name, my brother?"

Though still a bit confused, he finally answered, "Bobby."

"Pleasure to meet ya, Brother Bobby," the minister said, relieved. "My name is Troy. Minister Troy Muhammed." Minister Troy laughed. "For a minute there," he said, "I thought I was going to have to tell my brethren you didn't have no name."

After leading Bobby inside, Minister Troy showed him to the shower, gave him a clean change of clothes, then fed him a home-cooked meal of broiled fish, steamed spinach, and twice-cooked bread baked from scratch in the Ministers' own kitchen by sister Yolanda X Moore, who stood off to the side waiting to serve on Troy's order.

"Slow down, my brother," Troy cautioned as Bobby tried to inhale his plate. "Give your digestive system time to do its job."

Bobby just looked at him.

"You see, Brother Robert," Troy preached. "It is food that keeps us here." Bobby was about to receive a lesson, the first of many that Troy would teach him. "Is it okay if I call you Robert?" Troy asked.

Bobby swallowed and nodded his head.

"Good," Troy said. "For Bobby is akin to Boy. And both represent a ploy by the demon to take away your dignity. Now, as I was saying, Brother Robert, it is essential that we partake of the food which gives and maintains life. But that same food can also destroy life, Brother Robert. So we must choose wisely that which we would put into our stomachs, and ingest it slowly.

"You will find no swine here," Troy expounded, opening and closing the kitchen cupboards so Bobby could see that he spoke the truth. "No nuts, no white flour, starches, no sweets—although on occasion, we do allow Sister Moore here to bake us some bean pies with only the finest brown sugar. For all of these foods destroy us," he lectured. "And the white devil knows this. That is why he stocks the aisles of our supermarkets with the poisonous foods I've just mentioned. Oh yes, poison," Troy said, nodding his head. "You will soon learn, Brother Robert, that the devil has at his disposal an arsenal of poisons. Not just that which you have been shooting into your veins."

When he was finished eating, Troy introduced Bobby to the rest of the ministers as his new project.

"Allah delivered him to me while I was taking out the garbage," Troy said, smiling.

"The garbage?" the senior minister echoed.

"The garbage," answered Troy.

"Does this mean, Brother Troy," the senior minister queried. "That you have come to understand the purpose inherent in removing deadly bacteria from the house of the Lord?"

"I believe I have, Senior Minister," Troy responded, humbly. "By the grace of the wondrous Allah, I believe I have."

"Well, Brother Troy," the senior minister ended, smiling, "may the wonders of Allah never cease to amaze."

For the next three months, Brother Troy never left Bobby's side. He held his arms while he suffered through withdrawal. Stood beside him through endless hours of street ministry. Sat next to him during the senior minister's sermons. Educated him on the necessity of eating only one meal per day. And when he felt Bobby was ready, at night when they were alone in their room, he instructed him on the verses of the Holy Qur'an into the wee hours of morning.

"Repeat after me," Brother Troy commanded. They were standing in the center of the room facing each other. "Say: I seek refuge in the Lord of the dawn."

"I seek refuge in the Lord of the dawn," Bobby echoed.

"From the evil of that which he, Yakub, has created."

"From the evil of that which he, Yakub, has created."

"And from the evil of intense darkness when it comes."

"And from the evil of intense darkness when it comes."

"And from the evil of the envier when he envies."

"And from the evil of the envier when he envies."

That last verse sent Bobby's body into convulsions. Violently, he fell to his knees, thanking Allah, as he began to cry.

Brother Troy wrapped his arms around him and pulled him to his chest. Held him for some time. "It would appear you are ready, my brother," Troy said at last. "To go forth on the path of righteousness that Allah has set before you."

The Ministers had succeeded where Jesus had failed. Not only had they given Bobby the strength and the courage to kick his habit, but more importantly, they taught him how to respect himself. How to hold his head high and walk down the street with dignity. Although we may have had our doubts as to the veracity of his saviors, the next time we laid eyes on him, there was no denying it; we were smiling on the face of a truly saved man.

Lilah's Big Day
1991

Mary didn't look well. She showed up a full hour before she was supposed to, juggling in her arms a carton each of Marlboro Lights and Camel Filters.

"I hope these are okay," she mumbled as we walked into the visitors' lounge. Forcing a smile, she dumped the cartons on the table, then dropped herself heavily into one of the chairs. "I couldn't remember the brand," she confessed, avoiding my eyes.

She had on the same clothes she was wearing during the last visit: a faded gray sweatshirt with paint stains on the sleeves that had belonged to her father, and an old pair of convent blue sweatpants that sagged in the bottom. Her hair was oily and hung lifeless in front of her face, which was drained and pale. Her eyelids were propped at half-mast, robed in the puffiness of a night spent crying instead of sleeping.

"I guess with everything that's gone on," she added, pushing her hair back behind her ears, "it's my memory for detail that isn't working so well now. Maybe it's your turn to use the cane on me." This time she looked at me and let out an awkward laugh. "It was so strange, baby," she went on, looking away agian when I didn't respond. "When I got up to the register, all I could do was stare. Just stand there and stare at all those cartons of cigarettes, with the woman behind the counter all but growling at me to make up my mind, thinking, God, I can't even remember which kind she smokes. And then I thought, Wow, did I ever? Know what brand you smoke, I mean." Her shoulders started to shake and her voice began to quiver as the floor nurse came into the lounge to remind us about the party. There were no tears, just the shaking, as though her body hadn't had time to replenish the ones from the night before.

"Funny, isn't it?" she started up again, as we watched the floor nurse return to the cafeteria. "How you can close your eyes at night and open them every morning to the same face for two years, have every pore etched in your memory. Then, when it all ends, you haven't the slightest idea what brand of cigarettes she smoked."

"It's fine," I said flatly, watching Sylvia float awkwardly past the glass door. "They all pretty much lead to the same place."

The ward was a continuous buzz of preparation. The nurses were running around, barking commands at the orderlies who were hanging balloons and streamers from the ceiling. And the patients were chatting it up more than usual as they put the finishing touches on their handmade presents. Lilah's big moment had finally arrived and the ward was throwing her a party.

Everyone was invited. All the patients (except, of course, the ones in lockdown), the doctors, staff, relatives, friends, and anyone else who just happened to be visiting or whose duties brought them to Ward 6 to drop off a file. They wanted to do it right this time, Cheryl explained in group. The last two times, after she'd signed her name at the bottom of the release form, the head nurse simply patted Lilah on the back and wished her good luck. And like Lazarus and Christ before her, each time, on the third day, Lilah had returned—disheartened and terrified of the world beyond. But this time everyone involved figured a big send-off would give Lilah the ingredient of confidence intrinsic to success.

They planned an event meant to rival the Big Bang itself, certainly bigger than anything the ward had ever seen. Perhaps, the doctors conspired, the idea would light a fire under the butts of some of the other patients to get well themselves. The ones they had never really deemed sick in the first place, or as Agnes might put it, the ones in whom they had lost interest or no longer found anything groundbreaking to write about in the pages of their medical journals; patients whose insurance coverage was about to run out and whose beds needed to be emptied for the truly afflicted with the means to pay for treatment.

After exhausting the subject of cigarettes and feeling too much like strangers to begin so soon on another topic, Mary and I made our way to the cafeteria to help prepare for Lilah's day. Once again, Lilah's husband had been summoned to the 'funny' ward at City General. And once again, his two girls sat obediently beside him, crimped and bowed in their Sunday best, waiting for their mother to come out.

Red, yellow, and pink balloons with the words Good Luck stenciled across their faces danced excitedly on the ends of elastic strings tacked to the cafeteria's ceiling. Rainbow-colored streamers crisscrossed the room. And three orange birthday candles sat proudly atop the three-layer cake the kitchen staff baked special for the occasion: two small ones—representing each time Lilah embarked on this journey before—on either side of a larger defiant one (in the shape of the number three), signifying that on this occasion, the outcome was going to be different.

For their part, the patients constructed handcrafted presents, consisting of rudimentary baskets hastily thrown together in weaving class and dark abstract paintings whose haunting images had been summoned during mandatory art therapy sessions. The gag-and-barf chick gave Lilah a photograph of a smiling round woman that nobody recognized. And someone named Anonymous put together a notebook, three-hole punched and bound with yarn, that had a different dried flower pasted on each page. The inscription read: To remind you that beauty still exists.

Aside from the small table on which the cake sat, the table with the presents was the only other piece of furniture in the room. Cheryl wanted people to dance, she said. And to ensure that end, the entire staff had pitched in and sprung for a band. A local jazz ensemble, to pay homage, they all agreed, to Lilah's complex and dissident heritage. The only thing missing from the elaborate celebration was its guest of honor.

Only minutes before Mary arrived juggling two kinds of cigarettes,

Lilah had gone to her room to pack and, in her words, slip into attire befitting the occasion. For, like Cheryl and the nurses, she too wanted to do this right. But the nurses were starting to get nervous. A full hour had passed since Lilah first closed the metal door to her room, and the nurses had been so busy barking out commands and making preparations, they had forgotten to send someone to check on her. An orderly was dispatched immediately. Remembering the last time Lilah barricaded herself behind a door with no lock, the whispers started to hum.

"You think it's happening again?" one of the patients asked.

"Wouldn't that be just like her," a floor nurse tsked.

"And after we went to all this trouble," another one added soberly.

Cheryl cautioned, "Now let's not jump to any conclusions." While the orderlies and the kitchen staff produced dollars from their pockets and started making wagers, the doctors discussed what an embarrassment this would be to the ward.

"I was against it from the beginning," one of the older ones reprimanded. "A party! We all knew her history; it never should have been authorized."

The jazz ensemble was fidgeting; unlike the rest of us, they were in the dark concerning the contents in Lilah's file. Their fingers were starting to catch cramps from waiting so long to play. Sylvia increased the decibel level of her hacking and—perhaps sensing the air of impending doom—stepped up the frequency of her trips up and down the hall.

At last the orderly returned without Lilah. The whispers hushed abruptly. Cheryl shot him a worried look. Except for the resonance of Sylvia's hacking, the ward was eerily quiet. Lilah's husband sat expressionless as the orderly cleared his throat to deliver the news.

"Everything's fine," he said, shrugging his shoulders. The ward exhaled a collective sigh. "Girlfriend's just havin a little trouble with her make-up. Get this," he laughed. "She says it's been a while."

"Strike up the band!" the desk nurse yelled, laughing nervously alongside him. "I thought this was supposed to be a party!"

The face of Lilah's husband broke into a wide-toothed grin, as orderlies and doctors took turns slapping him on the back to congratulate him.

Delightedly, the jazz ensemble launched into Herbie's *Cantaloupe Island*, and patients and nurses alike started to dance.

I could hear my father's voice as they eased into the groove. *He's no Herbie*, it said in that short staccato tone, *I suppose he's studied, alright, but his soul's not in it.*

Eddie, the ward's forty-year-old stutterer, grabbed Mary's hand and tried to ask her to dance. She looked at me, confused.

"He wants to dance," I said, bopping my head up and down to the music.

She withdrew her hand and silently mouthed the words, "No, thank you," into his face.

"He's not deaf, Mary," I said, rolling my eyes. "He stutters."

"No, thank you!" she repeated again, this time loud and slow. "I don't wish to dance."

"Oh, go on," I nudged. "It's not like he's asking you to have his baby or anything. It's just a dance, Mary. And even if he was," I added coldly, "what do you have to fear? If he starts to go a little nuts, security's only a scream away."

A terrified look washed over her face. "That's not funny, Po," she snapped, disgusted.

"Go on and dance with him then," I challenged, letting the music seep into my soul. "Trust me, if you refuse, you'll never get rid of him. Here," I said, extending my hand and giving her no alternative, "I'll hold onto your purse."

It took a little more prodding, but reluctantly, Mary finally agreed. And when Eddie put her arm through his, she actually smiled as he escorted her onto the dance floor.

At first they moved awkwardly. Mary stood in one place bouncing up and down to the backbeat while Eddie wiggled his knees hesitantly and stumbled over both their feet. But after a chorus or two, their bodies seemed to relax and they agreed on a rhythm. We all watched, amazed, as they began to spin and twirl like an amateur version of Astaire and Rogers. Every now and then Eddie's hand would slip down to cop a feel on Mary's sagging ass, but each time, Mary would swat the roving hand away before it reached its destination. The ritual enchanted him. And when Mary mouthed over the music that she'd had enough, and turned on her heels to leave as the ensemble segued into *Sookie Sookie*, Eddie ran around in front of her and mimed for her to stay.

He was harmless, really, Eddie was. His mouth just had trouble forming the words that appeared in his head, so his body had to do his talking for him. The doctors still hadn't figured out the cause. A battery of tests eliminated any physical reason. And all they could get from Eddie's parents was that it started sometime when Eddie was a little boy. Agnes claimed it was because Eddie's father had sexually abused him, and as a result, Eddie's brain went into severe shock, taking away the words he would use to tell someone.

About three years ago, it was rumored a hot-shot young resident got the bright idea to give Eddie a pen and pad of paper. Told him to write down whatever words came into his head. It was a brilliant idea, the chief of staff told him. The only problem was the thing preventing Eddie's mouth from forming the words that appeared in his head also affected his motor ability. Every time he would put pen to paper, his hand would get stuck on the first letter. And at the end of each session, the hot-shot young resident would leave the room dejected, carrying a single sheet of notebook paper, filled from top to bottom with row upon row of capital A's, E's, and sometimes Y's, no closer to the cause of Eddie's stuttering problem than when they first started.

The guitar cat's no Wes, my father's voice continued, as I watched Mary and Eddie dance. *And that horn player. Naw. Naw. He's tryin too hard, too hard to sound like Miles.* Miles was God, as far as my father was concerned. And anyone who tried to sound like him, mimic his style, didn't know the first thing about jazz. "Even if," he would say, "he spends his life married to the needle. Even if. He wouldn't be able to dream of going where Miles has gone. Wouldn't even be able to sit down in the same house."

When I was younger, I believed my father welcomed the numbness brought on by the curse. That while the rest of us were doing whatever we could to feel something, anything, he was trying hard not to. That the reason he turned his back on Uncle Ray, the night he shat all over himself in our bathroom, was because he was angry. Angry at his brother for bringing back the feeling. Now I wondered if I was wrong. If numbness, rather than feeling, was the natural reaction to the horrible things witnessed. If, like Miles, when he turned his back on everyone and sat down at the piano, calling up the ghosts of Billie, Bessie, and Bird, he was playing the feeling back in, instead of playing it away.

Maybe that's why he believed Miles was God. Because Miles succeeded where my father and Uncle Ray failed. In my father's eyes, Miles had beaten the curse. Every time he blew that horn, the holes and track marks lining his hands and feet gave testimony to it. Perhaps, like my father, Uncle Ray believed in Miles too and shot junk into his veins, hoping to find the music inside himself.

All these years, I believed my father had given in and I resented him for it. Blamed him for letting the curse take his soul. For leaving my mother behind to fight it on her own. But now, as he spoke to me, I realized that, like the rest of us, he'd been fighting all along.

Mary's chance to slip away from Eddie came when the ensemble's drummer halted abruptly during a rendition of *Alfie's Song* to break into a drum roll. Lilah was making her entrance. Everyone stopped dancing and turned their attention toward the cafeteria's entryway.

If she truly did have trouble applying her make-up, no one would have known. Truth be told, the confident, striking black woman wrapped head to foot in gold kinte cloth gliding effortlessly across the cafeteria's thresh old gave off the impression she'd never had trouble with anything. Not coping with a hostile world, not balancing the gourd of a shoulder-breaking legacy, and certainly not a task as simple as putting on an even foundation and a line of lipstick.

Lilah's husband was speechless. Mesmerized, he sat unmoving in his chair, with his two girls crimped and bowed beside him, as though he were living anew all the reasons he'd asked this woman to share his life.

As Lilah approached, the drum roll stopped. Her husband rose to his feet, his hand motioning for the two girls to stay behind. Slowly, he inched toward her. The ward held its breath. The only sound that could be heard was Sylvia's hacking.

The hacking seemed to be getting louder, closer, and a phlegm-filled dying cough echoed every step Lilah and her husband took. Step. Cough. Step. Cough, until the dying cough entered the cafeteria and caught up with them, mirrored them step for step, like a graveyard satire of an old Amos and Andy skit in which a translucent Sylvia, arm sticking straight up in the air, sneaks up behind Lilah, planning to take her by surprise. Only the incessant hacking announced the phlegm ghost's presence before the desired moment, foiling the plan.

Everyone except Lilah was in shock, as though the hose of a giant vacuum cleaner had sucked all the color from our faces. The doctors in their bleached white coats, mouths gaping open, practically falling to the ground; the nurses in their pinched-at-the-waist knee-high dresses and half-moon caps, frozen in their white stockings of disbelief; while the band members, in their white satin suits and black bowties, clung tight to their instruments and stared, dumbfounded. Not at the spectacle of Sylvia, Lilah and her husband, but at the patients, who were whooping, hollering and jumping up and down, drunk on excitement—more intoxicated than any of them had been since retreating from the wide open spaces locked away outside into the confinement, safety, and sterility of the ward. And then there was Mary, finally free from the roving hand of Eddie, glancing nervously about through the mockery of it all, anxiously searching for the nearest escape.

Lilah's husband stopped first, a terrified and confused expression washing over his face. He'd never met the phlegm ghost before, and his eyes combed Lilah's wantingly, seeking an explanation. But Lilah didn't seem to notice Sylvia was there, closing in swiftly behind her. Or that her husband had stopped and leaned back on his heels. She just kept walking, opening her arms to embrace him, her smile growing wider with each step.

Perhaps she was caught up in the realization that she was finally going home. Or had become so used to Sylvia's hacking, she neglected feel the subtle drops of spittle, spraying the hairs on the back of her neck. Maybe she'd mistaken *wantingly* for *wantonly* and couldn't wait to be alone, within the safety of their bedroom, to feel her husband's full lips on her breast, inhaling his scent as he lowered his weight down upon her. Whatever it was, Lilah moved through the discombobulated scene in the ward's cafeteria as though she hadn't a care. And she probably would have continued that way if Sylvia's heart hadn't exploded when it did, causing Sylvia's body to go off-balance and topple into her. Just kept on gliding without a care into the outstretched arms of her husband, then over to collect her crimped and bowed girls, leading all three out of the haven of the ward's pale green walls into the life of uncertainty awaiting them on the outside.

But Sylvia's heart did stop. And with it erupted Lilah's fantasy of things being different. Of being able to escape unscathed. To walk—for the first time—through those double glass doors on the main floor with her head held high, leading her impressionable little girls not by the hand, but by example. When Sylvia's soul floated up from her time-ravaged body, it took a piece of Lilah with it. Not a big piece, but a necessary piece. Ample enough to remind Lilah that around every vacant corner lurked a corpse that wasn't quite dead. That the fantasy of things being different was just that, a fiction, forever bound to the pages of her mind.

Sylvia hacked up her final cough when Lilah was just inches away from the wanting face of her husband. And, to the horror of the orderlies, whose feet—for the life of them—couldn't move fast enough to intercept, the lifeless corpse crashed into Lilah from behind, sending all three—Sylvia, Lilah, and her husband—spinning out of control into the patients' pile of handmade presents. But as the presents, Lilah, and husband tumbled to the floor, Sylvia kept going. The strangely unbalanced corpse bounced like a pinball from the table that supported the presents, to the outstretched arms of the intercepting orderlies, over to the cake, where it lost all momentum and teetered briefly, before falling—face first—into the top layer of frosting. When the orderlies finally caught up with her, as Lilah and her husband lay stunned on the floor, surrounded by the crushed and broken presents, Sylvia's pale body lay splayed across the now-defiled triumphant pastry.

The silence that accompanies death quieted the room. With the exception of Lilah and her husband crawling around like the blind trying to get their bearings, the rest of the ward stood stock still, motionless, staring transfixed. Not at Lilah and her husband, or even Sylvia for that matter, but at the marvel of the cigarette, still lodged and burning between Sylvia's index and middle fingers.

In time, the room started to breathe, like in the aftermath of a great disaster in which the survivors all stagger around, dazed and stunned, trying to figure out what just happened and how they can piece their lives back together. How they can reach back through the flames without getting burned, to retrieve the seared snapshot of the great-grandmother they never knew. Rescue the handkerchief or the legacy that had been passed down through the ages. Then, when at last the cinders have finally cooled down, they fumble desperately through the wreckage to see if there's anything left to salvage. A shattered piece of china. A fork from the sterling set of silverware that same great-grandmother bequeathed in her will. Anything that might mask the reality of having to start all over. That's how Lilah and her husband moved, once the ward started to breathe again— charred and stunned. Like they were searching the wreckage for a piece of that feeling they shared before Sylvia's heart exploded. A hint, even, of the optimism that had told them it had been okay to hope. To believe, this time, that things could be different.

Sylvia was pronounced dead immediately. And after shooing the patients back to their rooms or into one of the lounges, the staff started in on the clean-up process. The orderlies removed the cigarette butt from Sylvia's fingers, then lifted her corpse onto a gurney and carted it away towards lockdown. The kitchen staff wrapped up the remains of the cake in a tablecloth and carried it back to the kitchen. The jazz ensemble quietly packed up their instruments. And the doctors called an emergency meeting to assess the damage. By the time the elevator doors closed—without fanfare—on the dazed faces of Lilah, her husband and their two girls, the cleaning crew had the place reeking of ammonia again, and Mary and I found ourselves back in the visitors' lounge, sitting across from each other at one of the tables.

"Some party, huh?" I offered, laughing awkwardly and shaking my head. I couldn't think of anything else to say and I was tired of the silence. "You and Eddie were sure cuttin up the rug."

"Po, I can't do this anymore," Mary said, looking me square in the eyes. This time it was my turn to look away. I knew where she was headed and I didn't want to have that conversation just then. Didn't want to admit that the scene that just went down in the cafeteria was indicative of the shambles my life was in.

"Do what?" I asked, eyeing a pair of nurses who were huddled together, whispering, just outside the lounge.

"Visit you in this place," Mary answered, reaching across the table and taking my hand in hers to gain my attention. Still, I refused to look at her.

"Well, you won't have to after tomorrow," I said, pulling my hand away.

"Everyone's insane around here," Mary stated emphatically as she got up to pace around the lounge. "Even the nurses and the doctors," she went on, still pacing. "The scary thing is that every time I come here, it feels a little more familiar. The patients smile and say hi to me like I'm one of them, like I belong. And when it's time for me to leave, I have trouble remembering how to function again in my own life. I swear," she said, stopping to make sure that I was listening, "I'm beginning to think I'm just as crazy as the rest of you."

"Maybe you are, Mary," I broke in, giving her no chance to respond. "Maybe that's the solution. Maybe the whole world should quit their jobs and check into their local psych ward." At the moment, I truly believed it. But Mary wouldn't buy it.

"I'm serious, Po," she said, waving me off with her hand. "The things that go on in this place are unnatural. I don't even know who you are anymore. It's like you're caught up in some kind of nightmare and I'm trapped in there with you. I need to wake up, Po. Why can't we just open our eyes and have everything be like it was before?"

"Before what?" I asked, starting to get angry. "Before my father died? Before my mother died? Your parents? Before my uncle Ray tried to blow his brains out while he held his baby girl in his arms? How far back do you wanna go, Mary?" I started to laugh uncontrollably, as though hysterical laughter was the only way my soul knew to cleanse itself. "Maybe it's all a bad dream," I said, snorting as I laughed. "Maybe Hitler never really slayed the Jews, and genocide and slavery are just figments of our imagination. Maybe we're not even here having this conversation, and there's nothing for us to wake up to."

"God, listen to you!" Mary screamed, shaking me from my hysterical stupor. "I can't even talk to you anymore. Everything always has to be a fucking riddle!" she yelled. A nurse stuck her head in the door to make sure everything was alright. Mary nodded to say all was okay, then sat down in the chair next to me. "I just wanna go back to the way things were before you checked yourself in here," she whispered, taking my hand in hers again. "Is that too much to ask? I want you to tell me stories, Po." Her voice began to rise again. "Tell me a story, baby. Finish the one about your family."

"Mary..." I started, but she cut me off.

"Come on, Po! Finish the story." Now she was the one in a frenzy.

"Mary..."

"Your uncle just blew his brains out, and your family went bankrupt. What happens next?"

"Mary, stop."

"What happened to your mother? And your father?"

"Stop this!" I demanded, grabbing her shoulders and shaking her. "You know what happens! Why are you doing this?"

She just looked at me. Tears welled up in the corners of her eyes.

"Look," I said, still holding her. "Maybe you should go on home."

"I can't," she pleaded. "Not yet. Please, Po," she begged. "Please, finish the story." She was sitting on the edge of the chair, clutching her purse as I held her. Her eyes were watery and wide and took up most of her face. She was grasping for something familiar. Something she knew more intimately than the hospital's pale green walls. Something she could take with her, hold onto to help maintain her balance when she left. A part of me wished I could give it to her, wanted to tell her that we could go back. To believe it myself. But we both knew it wasn't true.

"Mary, I can't," I said. "Don't make me do this." The tears started pouring down her cheeks as she collapsed onto the floor.

"Look at me, Po!" she cried. "I'm begging you. Please!"

Sitting there, watching her sob, I suddenly realized I couldn't feel anything. Without warning, the numbness had completely enveloped me. I must have been distracted by the day's events and let my guard down, because I never even saw it coming. "Get up, Mary!" I ordered, trying to lift her to her feet.

"Please, Po," she whispered as I struggled with her.

"Get up!" I said again. I wanted this to end. I wanted to cut, but I had nothing to cut with. "My mother's dead," I said. "And so is my father. Your parents are dead, too, remember? End of story. Now come on, get up. Before the nurse returns." I tried one last time to get her to her feet, but she was too heavy. So I sat back down and left her there, crying. Collapsed in a pile on the floor and crying.

When she finally stopped, a strange smile came over her face, as though something inside had shifted, resolved itself. Pushing her hair back behind her ears again, she climbed into the chair and searched her purse for a tissue. "Sorry," she said as she dabbed her eyes.

"It's alright," I said, forcing myself to go through the motions. "You okay?" I asked.

"Oh, yeah," she sniffled. "It's just that I haven't had much sleep lately, you know? Guess everything's finally getting to me."

"You sure?"

"Yeah, yeah," she said, brushing it off as though she had just tripped or something. She put the dirty tissue back in her purse, then stood up and straightened out her sweatpants. "But you're right," she added, as I stood to face her. "It's late. I should be going."

We stared at each other awhile in silence, inhaling the fumes from the ammonia.

"Me too," I answered finally. "I want to see if they'll let me say good-bye to Agnes." She nodded her head up and down as I spoke.

"So, is... Bobby picking you up tomorrow?"

"I don't know yet," I heard myself say. "We had an argument when he was here earlier. Never got a chance to ask him."

"Well, if you need a ride..." she said, still nodding her head.

"I know. I'll call." We held hands as we kissed each other's cheek to say good-bye. I felt nothing.

WEDNESDAY

Onya
1984

Onya had been living a lie. Everyday for a full year the clinic's bookkeeper had been issuing Onya's paychecks to someone named Twyla Fairbanks, until Bobby and the Ministers burst into the Fairborn Family Dental Clinic promising the wrath of Allah if their leader didn't receive immediate treatment. Miss Fairbanks was the other self Onya created while she was living in San Diego. The self she longed for during most of her childhood. A normal self whom she could love, who had the same normal adventures of other children. Children whose families lived their days free from legacies and curses.

It was easy, she told Bobby, when he asked how she did it. They were sipping tea in one of the new cafés in the city's 'revitalized' district. Initially, they had planned to meet in the park, where they could be assured of privacy. But the night before they were supposed to meet, a late season storm dropped two feet of snow on the ground and forced them to retreat inside.

After she was released from the hospital, Onya took a bus back to Columbus, cleaned out her dorm room and withdrew from all her classes. Since the semester had just started, and since Onya submitted her withdrawal slip prior to the add/drop deadline, the university gave her a full refund.

She just wanted to disappear, she said. Go away. Forget.

So after changing the university's refund check into travelers' checks, and donating all the books and clothes she couldn't sell to the Salvation Army, she fled as far west as the bus driver would take her. To freedom, she told Bobby. A new life. One in which she could be whomever she wanted to be. In which she could choose the memories that haunted her, the family she came from, and the house she grew up in. A house that wasn't possessed by demons and relatives who told you that everything happening to you—that was ever going to happen to you—would always be tied to some stupid curse. Along with the new life would come a new childhood, filled with games and innocence. Slow country drives on lazy Sundays, picnics in the park on anxious Saturdays, and boyfriends, lots of them, wooed by the depth of her coffee brown eyes, who never once looked over their shoulders to see who might be watching. Not a childhood of grown black men flopping around in excrement like fishes out of water. She wanted a life in which she could blend, she said, just blend deep into the fabric of things, without anybody taking notice.

But San Diego didn't bode well for Onya. Not because she couldn't be who she wanted to be. For ninety dollars and the right smile, she was able to purchase an official state I. D. that to the untrained eye looked just like the real thing. But not long after she arrived, the curse caught up with her. And even in a land where it's said just about anyone can lose themselves if they really try, Onya found it difficult to blend in.

The memories that continued to stalk her, jump out at her when she wasn't looking, were from the life she left behind, not the new one she created. Even as she concocted believable tales about her father the college professor for the ears of carefully selected friends, or not so believable ones about the inheritance she was to receive when he died, past images surrounded her. Whenever she walked down the street, she was joined by visions of Bobby running around in his pajamas. The specter of her father tangled up with Jessica disappeared behind the meat counter as she strolled down the aisle of the supermarket. And the sight of a woman scrambling to gather papers swept up by a gusting wind brought to mind the figure of my mother running through the house, chasing wildly after the smell of violets. So in the end, Onya abandoned San Diego, choosing instead to return to the life that wouldn't let her leave, to see if she could hide within it.

"Twyla Fairbanks?" Bobby questioned, knocking over his tea as he shook with laughter. "Praise be to Allah!" he yelled. "I do believe I've heard it all." He was still laughing when he called for the waiter to bring a towel. "How'd you ever come up with a name like Twyla Fairbanks?" he demanded.

Immediately, Onya was on the defensive. "I don't see what's so funny about it," she snarled, as she ripped open a packet of sugar and dumped it in her tea. "Some very creative people have been named Twyla."

"Like who!?" Bobby asked, incredulous.

"Twyla Tharp, the dancer, for one," Onya retorted.

"But, Onya," Bobby scoffed, raising his eyebrows as he tried to get her to recognize the obvious. "Twyla Fairbanks?"

"What?" she insisted, sipping her tea unamused. "It's a nice name."

"Girl," Bobby grinned, "ain't no way in the world you look like anyone named Twyla Fairbanks. Now how you expect to go unnoticed, usin a name like that?"

"Look, Bobby," Onya reproved, "I didn't agree to meet you just so you could make fun of me. You said you had something to tell me?"

"But, Twyla Fairbanks?" Bobby teased one last time. He just couldn't let it go. Onya pushed back her chair and stood to leave.

"Okay, okay," Bobby jumped up to stop her, as the waiter wiped up the tea. "Sit down, girl. I'll stop, alright?" Onya just stood there.

"I'll stop, I promise." He held out his hand, motioning for Onya to take her seat. "Come on, girl. You didn't come all this way just to turn around and go back now, did ya? Sit on back down here." Slowly, Onya returned her seat.

"First," Bobby said, trying to wipe the grin off his face with a napkin, "I wanna apologize for gettin you fired from your job and all. But seriously, Onya, how was I to know you was usin a phony name?"

"It wasn't just the discovery of my name that lost me my job, Bobby," Onya mumbled dejectedly.

"Alright, alright," Bobby conceded. He didn't want Onya to walk out again. "I'll give you that. Maybe the Ministers did come down a little too hard. Maybe we did go a little overboard in puttin the man in a chokehold," referring to the dentist. "But maybe it was all meant to be, Onya. You ever thinka that? Maybe Allah decided at that very moment it was time to snatch you back from the white man's grasp and bring you home. You know it wasn't just coincidence we ended up in that particular dental office. We was led, girl. You hear me? I'm talkin led."

Bobby went on to say that the reason he called Onya to the coffeehouse was to make amends. That the last time she saw him (and all those times before), he was lost. Messed up on the devil's poison.

"I was sprung, girl," he confessed, sheepishly. "Half the time I didn't even know myself what was comin out of my mouth. But see," he was beginning to preach, "that's just how the white man works. Fills your head with all them negative vibes and self images, then sends you spinnin around all confused, never knowin whether you goin this way or that. But Allah saved me, Onya. Reached out His hand just when I was about to spin off the edge and stilled me. Showed me how to look into my heart and see who I really was."

Onya sat quietly across the table from him, slowly stirring her tea.

"Now I know this all might sound a little crazy," Bobby admitted, smiling and shaking his head. "A little too convenient right about now. I know you skeptical, but it's the truth, Onya."

He misread her silence. What Bobby failed to understand was that during the past four years, Onya had fought long and hard to forget certain occurrences. Events that, when faced openly without the aid of protective barriers, threatened to shatter the fragile nature of her existence. It was a battle that was still raging. And in just a few hours, without meaning to, Bobbie had stripped Onya of her armor.

"May Allah strike me down dead if I'm not a changed man," he continued, unaware of the affect he was having on her. "Look at me, Onya. Look at me!" he implored, spreading his arms wide and tilting his head back as though he were looking up into the heart of heaven. "I'm still sittin here, ain't I?" He paused. "I love you, Onya Childs," Bobby beamed. He leaned into the table to make sure she heard him. "That's what I came here to tell you. I love you, and Allah loves you. Now I don't expect you to believe everything I'm sayin right here in this coffeehouse. That's how the white man operates. I want you come to a meetin, whenever you ready, and feel Allah's love for yourself."

Tears started to roll down Onya's cheeks as she haphazardly swirled her spoon around the teacup.

"That's alright," Bobby went on, oblivious. He was looking at her, though he wasn't seeing her. If he had been, he would've realized that after he reminded her of how messed up he used to be, she hadn't heard a word he'd said. She was too busy feeling the sting of the arrows piercing her armor. "Go ahead and cry," Bobby tried to comfort. "I cried too the first time. Feelin Allah's arms wrapped around you has a way of doin that to you. Now I know it's a lot to take in all of a sudden like this. But I want ya to think about somethin, big sis. Allah wants you back in His house, where you belong. He's not gonna force ya. Might squeeze you a little bit to let you know that it's time. But, ultimately, He wants you to turn to Him on your own. So what you think?"

Onya didn't answer, just kept crying and swishing her spoon around her tea.

"You know, Dad's been around." He tried a different tact. "To the meetins, I mean. Hasn't answered the call yet, but it's only a matter of time. He misses you, ya know. I showed him your letters."

Onya started weeping harder; a steady stream of water poured from her chin into her tea. The waiter came over to make sure everything was alright.

"Oh yes," Bobby said, reaching across the table to squeeze Onya's hand. "We just havin a little reunion here; it's kind of emotional."

"What about Mama?" Onya sighed, as the waiter turned to leave.

"That's somethin else I gotta tell ya, Onya," Bobby said, nodding his head up and down as if to say he knew this was coming. He hesitated and took a deep breath. "I was gonna wait awhile before I brought it up, but since you askin..." He stopped, then stared at the veins in Onya's hands. He didn't mean to. His eyes just came to rest on them while he searched his mind for the proper words. They were popped out and spastic as Onya held fast to her tea cup, anticipating what Bobby might say. "Mama..." he started, then stopped again. But there were no correct words, and there was no gentle way to break it. "Well, Onya," he began again, jerking his eyes away from her hands to look at her face. "Mama's dead."

"What?" She was stricken, as he knew she would be.

"Been called home to Allah," he soothed.

"How?" The word caught in her throat and the tears fell even harder.

"Don't nobody really know," he answered, shaking his head. "Doctors never figured it out. Grandma Margret thinks she went looking for Great-grandma Shirley."

Onya wiped her eyes with a crumpled napkin. "When?"

"Bout three years ago. We tried to find ya. Lord knows we tried. Even put ads in the newspaper... Guess Allah didn't think it was time."

"I want to see the grave," she whispered. A brief silence fell over the table before Bobby realized she was serious and tried to talk her out of it.

No need to rush things, he said. It was freezing outside. The path to the tombstone would be so deep in snow by now, they'd never be able to find it. Better to wait till spring, he argued. Let the emotion of the last few weeks die down a little. Besides, now that they had found each other, there'd be plenty of time. They could go as soon as the snow melted. But standing around lost, knee-deep in the middle of a bunch of snow-capped tomb-stones, wasn't about to do either of them a bit of good. And it would probably make them sick.

"I want to see it," she quietly demanded.

"Onya..."

"I want to see it, Bobby. If you don't want to take me," she finished, blowing her nose, "then tell me where it is, and I'll take myself."

"I knew I shoulda never agreed," Bobby told me later. "But when the women in this family put they mind to somethin, it's like turnin water to wine tryin to change it."

I imagine the two of them driving to the cemetery in silence. Onya's shoulders offer the occasional splutter or shiver, while Bobby curses him-self and shakes his head, thinking he should've known better. During the drive the snow starts falling harder, becoming so thick in spots that Bobby has to pull off the road and wait for it to thin out. It's dark by the time they reach the turn-off. And when they finally pull up to the gate, Bobby puts the car in park and leaves the engine running. He hesitates to get out.

"Show me," Onya demands, stepping out of the car.

"Onya, look at this place," Bobby yells through the open door. "Ain't nobody been here in days. Let's come back tomorrow when it's daylight. Maybe the sun'll come out and melt some of this snow away by then."

"I said, show me," she yells back, remaining outside.

Reluctantly, Bobby turns off the motor and steps out into the cold. Onya closes the door and follows behind. "I think it's this way," he says, after passing through the gate.

The air smells like the comfort of a wood-burning stove. As they plod through patch after patch of undisturbed snow, their boots sound like twigs crackling over the fire, while their breath creates little clouds of fog in front of their faces every time they exhale. Finally, deep in the heart of the cemetery, Bobby turns off the main path—as I have done many times before and since—and cuts across three rows of concrete slabs, caked with snow.

Onya gets caught up in a snowdrift and falls behind. After crossing the second row of headstones, Bobby stops to wait for her. "You alright?" he asks, when she reaches him.

"Yeah," she answers, out of breath. "Let's go."

"You sure? You need a rest?"

"I'm sure," she insists. "Let's go."

At the third row, Bobby turns left, walks four paces, then stops in front of an empty space.

"Why are we stopping again?" Onya asks, beginning to get annoyed.

"This is it," Bobby tells her, squatting down to clear away the snow. "Didn't have no money to pay for a raised headstone," he says, breathing heavy as he clears. "Barely had enough for the little flat piece, buried under all this snow. But Grandma Margret refused to see Mama remembered as one of the unnamed, so she scraped together the little she had and borrowed what she didn't. One of these days," he adds with conviction, "I'ma get her a proper one." Hands cupped like a bowl, he scoops away layer after layer until they can see the beginning of the letters. "Hey, Mama," he says when he's finished. He steps back to let Onya see. "There, you seen it. Now can we get outta here and back into someplace warm?"

But Onya ignores him. Just stares at the letters that spell my mother's name, then, cautiously, sits down in the snow and lays her hand on the grave, as though she expects to feel my mother's presence. Immediately, the cold wet snow saturates her pants. "I'm sorry, Mama," she whispers. "I couldn't... I didn't... I'm sorry."

Hesitantly, Bobby puts his hand on Onya's shoulder to comfort her. Offers soft words about how my mother is better off with Allah now. But Onya doesn't hear them. Just sits there, inhaling the smell of a wood-burning stove, letting the cold turn the snow in her pants to ice, whispering, "I'm sorry," over and over. By the time Bobby persuades her to make the trek back through the cemetery into the warmth and safety of the car, though her body will take a few days to catch up, Onya's mind has already returned to Cleveland. The fight to forget the events of the past is over. And both Onya and Twyla have lost.

Of all the towns in which she tried to hide, Cleveland was the only place Onya felt safe enough to use her real name. She didn't know why that was, she explained to Bobby, it just was. Perhaps it was because my mother and Aunt Florida had both grown up there, and even as she was trying to forget them, the ancestors protected her. Or maybe it had something to do with the fact that Cleveland was so troubled with curses of other kinds, the one troubling Onya had to take a number and wait in line. Whatever the reason, the decision was made, and Bobby could say nothing to unmake it.

She was not running, she told him, when he implied as much on the way to train station. On the contrary, she had finally stopped. To prove it, she told him she would call with her new address and phone number as soon as she was settled. She needed to lay the past to rest, she added. Cleveland was as good a place as any to lay it.

She'd been there seven years when Bobby called to tell her about my father. The longest she'd lived anywhere since going off to school. The thirst was still there, and there were still those times—when she was waiting at

the bus stop on her way home or sitting alone in a crowded movie the-
ater—that she broke down and cried for no apparent reason. But, all in all,
Cleveland agreed with Onya. After getting rehired at the welfare office, her
superiors were so impressed by her performance, they promoted her to
assistant supervisor. And though it had taken a full seven years get there, she
no longer flinched when she was asked her name.

Violets
1980

My parents waited at the hospital for three days before the doctors decided it was okay to move Uncle Ray from Intensive Care. For a man who only 72 hours before blew a hole the size of a dime through the side of his head, his vital signs looked excellent. They had repaired all the tissue damage, and the latest CAT scan revealed no sign of remaining bullet fragments. Of course, the recovery period would be considerable, but given time, his functions should all return to normal.

Bobby was already gone when my parents got home. And not until my father discovered that Bobby had stolen his prized vibraphone did either of them show any concern. As soon as they walked through the door, my mother told Onya to pack her things; she was taking her back to school. My father headed straight for the telephone, then got back in the car and drove to Mercy General to check on Truly.

In the following months, my parents hardly spoke at all. Except for polite and cordial discussions of the lawsuit in the presence of their attorney, the few words that passed between them were rare and ugly. "Don't you think you've had enough of that?" my father would chide, whenever he caught my mother with a bottle. "Funny," my mother would snap back as they passed each other in the hall, "the drinking habits of Jessica never concerned you all that much." Finally, to avoid any confrontation with her, my father took to staying away from the house as long and as late as possible.

We never saw Jessica after that. As soon as she found out Uncle Ray was going to be okay, she and Lisa Marie moved to Connecticut to live with Jessica's parents. The rumor mill had it that my father had taken up with another white woman, a transfer student at the College, who was ignorant of his history.

"Well, Mama," my mother whispered, when she heard. "Guess you were right. No matter how light my children turned out, it would never be light enough for Mr. Gregory Childs. Too many demons, Mama. Guess the man just had one too many demons."

One night, after staying away for a week, my father returned to pack his bag. My mother was collapsed on the floor in a corner of the living room, surrounded by a pile of dirty clothes, quietly weeping. One hour later, he left without ever speaking to her, carrying a single suitcase.

Once it became clear that we would lose everything, my father and his new girlfriend decided to leave the state. He came to see us one last time before he left. It was dark out, and we were in the middle of the season's worst snowstorm. My mother was sitting on the sofa, with a bottle, smoking a cigarette.

"If there's anything left, it's yours," he told her in that voice that soothed even as it pierced. "Not that I expect you to believe this, but I never meant to hurt you, Lil."

"What about Ray?" she answered coldly, watching the snow fall through the window. "Or the children? Did you mean to hurt them?"

My father didn't answer. Instead, he took me aside and told me that even though he was going away, he would always be there for me. Whenever I needed him. "I'll always be your father, Po," he said, as he walked out the door. "Always."

When she heard the door slam, my mother—dressed only in her nightgown—put down the bottle, jumped to her feet and ran into the snow behind him.

"Goddamn it, Gregory!" she yelled as she ran. "I'm not going to let you do this! I'm not gonna let you do this!"

"Lil," my father said as she jumped on his back. "Lil, baby. It's the only way."

When they tumbled into the snow, I ran outside after them, shoeless. The severity of the cold burned my feet. My father's new girlfriend sat in the car, looking on, horrified.

"What about the kids?" my mother screamed. "How can you do this to them? How can you do this to me, you bastard?"

At one point, my father managed to get up, then lost his footing and fell back down. Both of them lay flat on their backs. On impulse, I lay down beside them and started making snow angels.

Thinking about it now, we must have looked quite a spectacle. And except for the fact that neither my mother nor I had any shoes on, if it had been daylight, someone driving by might have thought he was witnessing the nostalgic wonderland scene of a loving family at play in the snow.

Finally, my father made it firmly to his feet. And after throwing my mother off his back, he got into the car and drove away. Ten years would pass before I saw him again.

When the car was out of sight, my mother and I carried each other back in the house and huddled without speaking under blankets on the sofa. And after recovering from the colds we each got from running around in the snow with no clothes on, my mother's affinity for the bottle graduated to prescription pills. Librium at first, just to help her relax a little, she told the doctor. Then onto Valium when the Librium wasn't enough.

The snowstorm never let up. The following morning, the school board gave us a two-week vacation from school. Because my mother spent most of that time sleeping, sitting on the sofa, or staring out the window, Grandma Margret made daily trips from the city to bring us food.

She couldn't continue to do this, she told my mother one afternoon. Exasperated, she stormed over to the sofa, snatched my mother up by her nightgown and started shaking her.

"This is not gonna happen!" Grandma Margret yelled. "You hear me!? You have a child to take of, and another one in the street you need to find and bring back home. Where would our people be if every time we were wronged we just gave up hope? If every time we were disappointed, we gave up on livin? Where would you be now, if your mother's mother—bless her heart—had just given up when her eldest child died in that fire? If you ain't gonna do it for these children," she said, "then do it for the woman who set aside her grief so you could have a chance in life. My hands are too fulla worry for my own kids, child. Ain't no more room to be holdin up three more."

"Onya's grown," my mother slurred under her breath.

"Who's talkin bout Onya? I'm talkin bout you, child. Cause right now you ain't actin no more grown than that youngest of yours."

I'm still not sure which of my grandmother's words made it inside that day. But something she said caused my mother to break.

"Oh, God, Margret," she sobbed as she threw her arms around my grandmother's neck. "It hurts so much. It just hurts so much."

"I know, I know," murmured my grandmother, patting her back as she held her. "But you gonna be alright. Gonna be alright. Little worse for the wear, maybe, but what don't kill ya can only make ya stronger. And you can start makin that so by gettin up off that sofa and puttin some clothes on. And after you done with that, you can put some of this soup I brought over in a bowl and serve your child some supper."

It was Grandma Margret who talked my mother into moving. Even if they let us keep the house, she said, we needed to put it up for sale and get on out. Let the memories go on and have it.

She wouldn't stand for any arguing. We were to begin immediately. Pack up the house and move on into her place. Then, when my mother found work, we could find a place of our own. But just when things seemed to be turning around, just months after my mother emptied the last of her pill bottles into the toilet, Onya refused to see her, and the illness three different doctors failed to identify sprouted the roots that would take hold and suck up her life.

She was tested for every disease the doctors could think of but each time the results came back negative. Although she said she was eating more than she ate during her three pregnancies combined, she was steadily losing weight. On his final visit, the third doctor said he could find nothing wrong. It was as though my mother's body had decided to stop working. By the time it was all over, my grandmother would claim she died of a broken spirit.

It all started when Onya refused to see her. Before my sister decided to leave pieces of her flesh in the window of the high school's hallway, my mother couldn't get out of the house fast enough even though the bank had generously offered to let us stay until it secured a buyer. She wanted to get a head start on the memories, she said. Wanted to be settled someplace new before they realized she was gone and came chasing after her. But before we could get on our way, Onya refused, and when we returned from the hospital to finish packing, the urgency to leave had dissipated.

Every time I would pack up and seal a box, my mother would peel off the tape and sort through it again. Every time I would throw some useless, seen-its-better-days item into the trash, she'd look up and holler, "Don't throw that away just yet," or "Let me look at that a minute," and "Here, set it over there; I haven't made up my mind about that yet."

"You trying to leave this place?" I'd finally asked, frustrated. "Or have you decided to take the bank up on its offer?"

But she'd never give an answer. Just open up the box, pull out some keepsake she'd forgotten about and reminisce. "Oh, remember this?" she would say. "Mama gave this to me when I had my first caller," or "Lord, I haven't worn this thing since you were a little girl. Probably can't even get into it now," and "My, my, my! Will you look at this picture? I don't believe I've seen Mavis since... Lord, child, I can't remember when. Wonder what ol Mavis is doin these days?"

Pretty soon she stopped having anything to do with boxes altogether. Just sat on the sofa in her nightgown, fingering the faded auction tag tacked to the sofa's arm, staring through the window. "Sure is cold out today," she'd say. Every once in a while she'd take a sip from her wine glass and comment about the temperature. "Does it feel hot in here to you this morning?"

"No, Mama, it doesn't."

After a while, looked like the only way we'd ever leave that place was if the new owners themselves put us out on the curb with the discarded furniture. Items the lien holders hadn't been able to sell and had thrown in with the house. Old furniture—like the sofa—for which it was determined there could be no future use. And in the fifteen months it took the bank to secure a buyer and close escrow, other than a second trip to the hospital to find out that my sister had been released and gone on her way, my mother left the house on only two occasions: once because Uncle Ray's fascination with a branch on the oak tree towering above our front yard demanded that she do so; and once to be transported by silent ambulance to the mortuary, to prepare for her own funeral.

That second hospital trip to find Onya occurred just a few days after the first one, somewhere between the time Mama started reopening boxes and fingering auction tags. She decided to make it an event, and before we left the house, she unpacked her favorite Sunday dress (a silky black little number, with white violets stamped all over it), then threw on her best hat and overcoat along with a pair of black leather gloves. "Want Onya to see she's got something to come home to," she said.

But when we got to the hospital, Onya was already gone. "I'm sorry, Mrs. Childs," the doctor informed us in the lobby. "Once we removed the glass fragments and bandaged her arms, your daughter insisted she was fine. We tried to call you, but your phone seems to have been disconnected."

"But where?" she asked, glancing around the lobby. "Where did she go? And why wouldn't she come to her mother at a time like this?"

"Can't answer that, ma'am," the doctor said. "Other than the emphatic refusal to see you, we never got much out of her. I can tell you one thing, though. Your daughter may be physically fine, Mrs. Childs, but emotionally, she's a very depressed and troubled young woman."

"Aren't we all?" asked my mother.

"Mrs. Childs?" he responded, confused.

"Depressed," she said matter-of-factly. "Isn't everybody a little depressed and troubled?"

"Uh, no, ma'am," the doctor answered, looking questioningly at my mother. "No, I don't believe we are, at least not to the extent your daughter seems to be."

"No?" my mother replied. "Well, I never would've figured. Can I see where she was?"

"Ma'am?"

"Her room," she specified. "Can you show me where it was?" She left the lobby and walked down the corridor, peering through the little glass windows of random rooms as she went.

"I really don't see what good that would do, Mrs. Childs," the doctor said, chasing after her. "Besides, I can't," he explained when he finally caught up. "It's already been disinfected, and it needs to remain that way for the next patient. Hospital policy."

Back then, like the doctor, I couldn't understand for the life of me why my mother wanted to see the room. All hospital rooms looked the same to me. You'd think, after spending so much time in one or another with Uncle Ray, my mother would've committed their contents to memory. But looking back on it now, I guess she was hoping to find the answer to the question she asked the doctor. Some remnant or feeling Onya may have left behind that the clean-up crew had missed which could tell her the why of things. Like Onya, needing to lay her hand on my mother's grave. Like Bobby searching for meaning in needles and Allah. My father looking in the keys of the piano. And me, thinking the answer was in knives and razor blades and carving up my skin.

"Go home, Mrs. Childs," the doctor finally told her as he put his body between my mother and the rest of the corridor. "Your daughter's probably sitting on the doorstep, waiting for you as we speak."

But she wasn't, and my mother never saw her nor mentioned her again. If she was thinking about Onya at all, she never let on. And if anyone even thought of bringing up the subject of that second trip to the hospital, she shushed us before we got started. So no one talked about it—the trip or Onya. At least not in the presence of my mother. Not me, not my grandmother, not Uncle Ray. Bobby was busy living off in the street somewhere, too strung-out to notice. And even though inside we thought about her almost every moment of the day, outside we moved through our lives as though Onya never existed, my mother steadily losing weight as we went.

The trip to the hospital happened in February. Spring passed, summer followed, and red and yellow leaves covered most of the ground before my mother left the house again. It was night time. A boy claiming to be a friend of Bobby's was ringing the doorbell. Other than the worn-out sofa, boxes half-full of books and clothes, a couple of mattresses on the floor, some wine and two or three dishes in the cupboard, the house was empty. The stereo was gone. So was the piano.

When the bell rang, my mother was sitting in her usual position on the sofa, staring out the window. I was reading one of the books that had been stuffed in the bottom of my duffel bag. The boy had come to tell us that Bobby was over in Xenia, living in a cardboard box down on Main Street. But when we opened the door, instead of telling us the story of Bobby and his box, he blurted out something about a large black man fiddling around with a bedsheet and a butter knife, trying to hang himself from the giant oak tree towering above our front yard.

If my mother hadn't been losing so much weight and the apparitions of Bobby, Onya, and my father hadn't been screaming their presence in the empty rooms, the scene might have been almost comical. Uncle Ray had chosen the lowest of the branches on the giant oak. It hung just five feet above the leaf-strewn ground. Given Uncle Ray's six-foot-five-inch stature, the impossibility of the act was apparent to everyone but Uncle Ray.

He was standing flat-footed on a pile of tawny leaves, slip-knotting the bedsheet—first around the branch, then around his neck. But when he lifted his feet into the air, very few seconds passed before he was standing firmly again on the pile of leaves. Three times, while we were standing there, cursing as he went, he undid the knot around his neck, shortened the sheet, retied it, then stood back down on the leaves. And if my mother hadn't called out to him when she did, he probably would have never known we were there.

"Ray?" she called, leaning all of her weight on me to keep her balance.

"Oh, hey, Lil," he answered, in that gravelly voice. "What you doin out here this time a-night?"

"Honey," she said, tired and already winded. "I believe the question is what are you doing?"

"Oh," Uncle Ray answered, knotting, untying, then reknotting the sheet.

"I'm just out here tryin to figure out how I can shorten this sheet."

"I see," my mother said, looking up at me for help. I shrugged my shoulders. "Listen," she told him, "I got a bottle of Chardonnay chilling in the refrigerator. I'da opened it a long time ago, but my hands don't seem to work so well anymore. Why don't you come open it for me? Maybe together we can figure out the best way for you to shorten your sheet."

"Ya know, I am a little thirsty," he said as he wrestled with the sheet.

"Bet you are," my mother answered, fighting back a smile. "Shortening sheets can be mighty exhausting business. Come to think of it," she said, yawning. "I'm pretty tired myself. Been unable to catch my breath all day long. Tell you what, I'm gonna go back inside and sit on the sofa. Why don't you come on in with me, quench that thirst and rest your head awhile?"

"Ya know, Lil," Uncle Ray said, feet standing back on the leaves for the fourth time. "I might just take you up on that. Gimme a minute though, I'ma try to do this one more time."

"Alright, baby," she said, tapping my arm to lead her back inside. "Take your time. I'm gonna go back inside now. You come on whenever you're ready."

We never did find out what the butter knife was for. But fifteen minutes later, when Uncle Ray burst through the front door, cursing that damn, not worth the price his mama paid for it, no good sheet, he still had it in his hand. And it stayed there, too, clutched in the palm of his large and powerful, handsome black hands, even as he and my mother opened, then finished an entire bottle of wine. Finally, after promising she wouldn't let it out of her sight, my mother talked him into turning the knife loose and leaving it on the table, then convinced him to lie down on one of the mattresses and rest his eyes. When he woke in the morning, Grandma Margret was there to take him home.

The last time my mother left the house, Onya had long since stepped off a Greyhound into the promise of San Diego, and Bobby had been home one month. A few weeks after Uncle Ray tried to hang himself, my grandmother paid the boy claiming to be Bobby's friend ten dollars to show us where Bobby's box was.

The box was really a three-sided shelter, made of three or four boxes taped hastily together—long enough to lie down in if he bent his knees, and tall enough to sit up in if he hunched his back. It smelled like a combination of sweat, feces, and stale beer. A pile of soiled clothes was pushed in the corner on one end, and a waterlogged plastic bag, full of empty pop cans, hung from a rusted nail shoved through the side of the other. During the day (when he was home), the open side of the box faced the street. So he could see what was going on in the world, he said. At night, or when he was out, the box was turned toward the brick wall of the abandoned building it leaned against. He was skinnier than I'd ever seen him, and he greeted us with the sort of crooked-toothed grin reserved for an old forgotten friend.

"Hey, Grandma, Po," he sang, when we walked up. "Y'all doin some shoppin round here?" His eyes were nearly closed, and the little you could see of the whites was glazed and bloodshot. The butt of a cigarette, with an ash the length of a full one, dangled from his fingers.

Grandma Margret started crying as soon as she saw him.

"Mama's sick," I said, staring at the box.

But before he could answer, Grandma Margret started tearing apart the shelter, screaming things like "Uh-uh! You cain't do this to me, Lord. You just cain't."

"Hey! Grandma!" Bobby slurred, ducking a flying piece of cardboard that just missed his head. "What you doin!?"

Grandma Margret didn't answer. She just kept tearing at the boxes, yelling, "No! No! No!"

Bobby made a move to try and stop her, but he lost his balance before reaching the box and fell, hitting his head on the sidewalk. Grandma Margret didn't even notice he'd fallen until she'd finished ripping the shelter to shreds and thrown the last of the soiled clothes into the middle of the street.

"Now look what you done gone and did," he yelled, holding his head as he got up. "Where I'm s'posed to sleep tonight?"

When we picked him up and put him in the car, he was still yelling.

"Nobody asked y'all to come out here," he screamed from the backseat.

"Didn't nobody ask y'all for nothin. You can't just walk up and tear apart a man's home like that. Who you think you is anyhow?"

"I'll tell you who I is," my grandmother yelled back, tears pouring down her face as she drove. "I'm the one who diapered you when your parents had to work to earn the money to feed you. Who cleaned you up when you messed in your pants. Held you in my arms when you was too sick to hold yourself. I'm the one who loved you more than I loved myself, beggin the Lord to take me instead when we thought we was gonna lose ya. And I'll tell you another thing, you ain't no man. Not yet, leastwise. You a lost and confused little boy, and if you keep runnin off at the mouth the way you are, when we get home, I got a good mind to get my switch."

Bobby stayed quiet until we pulled into the driveway and started dragging him to the house.

"You gonna have to tie me down to keep me here," he yelled, when we got to the door. "And even if you do, you know I'ma figure out a way to get free."

But my grandmother refused to argue. She just locked his one arm in hers, while I held the other, reached into her pocketbook and pulled out her house keys. When she opened the door, the house greeted us with the sweet smell of stewed potatoes, chipped beef and the musty odor of over-cooked greens. Without speaking, we dragged Bobby down the hall to my mother's room.

She was lying on the mattress, half-awake, in a nightgown that no longer fit. A bottle of wine sat on the floor next to her, to ease the pain.

Bobby just stood there, hands in his pockets, staring.

"Bobby," my mother said, groggily. "That you?"

"Yes, Mama."

"Praise, Jesus," she whispered. "He finally brought you back to me?" She sat up on her elbows to get a better look at him. "Lord, child, you skinnier than I am. You been eatin?"

"Yes, Mama," he said, looking down at his feet.

"Now you know it's not right to lie to your mother," she scolded from her deathbed. "When's the last time you ate something?"

"Couple a days ago." Even that was a lie, but my mother let it go.

Guess she figured there was too little time left to spend it arguing with her only son.

"That's what I thought," she said, smiling triumphant. "Lucky for you, your grandmother made a delicious pot roast. Ate so much I had to come and lay down a spell. Margret, fix this boy a plate. I'd do it myself, but I'm just so tired."

"That's alright, Mama," Bobby said, looking at her for the first time. "I, uh... I ain't hungry."

"Nonsense," she argued, waving a limp hand at him. "Go on and fix him that plate, Margret. And you, Bobby," she ordered, pointing an even limper finger. "Come on over here and let me look at ya." She felt his arms as he sat down. "Just like I thought," she said. "Skin and bones. Now tell your ol mother about how the world's been treating you."

After telling my mother lies about his well-being, Bobby found his way into the kitchen, nibbled on some of the pot roast Grandma put in front of him, then said he needed to lie down. I moved the other mattress into his old room. In the week that followed, we would have to tie him down. Not so much to prevent him from leaving, but to keep his hands from tearing at the veins crawling violently beneath his skin.

One day, Grandma Margret walked through the door, dragging another mattress behind her, saying she was moving in. Just temporarily, she told my mother. Long enough to help us pack. "Spend all my time down here, anyhow. Don't make no sense to keep wastin all that gas, drivin back and forth."

The real reason was twofold: the first, to make sure Bobby didn't kill himself during withdrawal; the second (and perhaps the more urgent), she knew my mother was barely hanging on. We all sensed the time was near, and Grandma Margret wanted to make sure she was present when it arrived.

She left Uncle Ray to fend for himself. The demons that were haunting him had gone into hiding, and for the time being, at least, he was doing much better. Only a few days after the incident with the bedsheet, he woke up and put on a suit. Then told my grandmother he was going to see a man about a job.

"Oh, it's no bother," Grandma Margret assured my mother. "Fact is, it's kinda selfish, really. Big ol house a mine has been so empty lately, what with Ray workin and all. Guess I'm just anxious to get y'all packed and moved into it. Maybe the kids'll breathe some life back into it."

As much as we could, we tried to keep Bobby's withdrawal a secret from my mother. But we were quickly running out of answers to her questions, concerning his whereabouts and the death cries calling to her from the other end of the hall.

"You know young boys," my grandmother said one evening, when she brought my mother her supper. "Always got somethin goin on."

"Still seems he could find time to make a trip down the hall to say 'hey' to his mama."

"Give him time, Lil," Grandma Margret asssured. "He'll come around."

"But is he eating enough, Margret?" my mother asked, as Grandma Margret turned to leave. "He's so skinny, you know. I worry about his eating."

"Now, child," my grandmother said from the doorway, "you know as long as I'm in this house ain't a soul gonna go hungry."

But Bobby wasn't eating. Not yet, anyway. He was too busy throwing up his insides, trying to get rid of the poison.

"Help me, Po," he whispered one day, when it was my turn to watch him. I was sitting on the floor, with my back against the wall opposite his mattress, thumbing through a copy of Baldwin's *Another Country*.

"Help me, Po," he pleaded again from his soiled mattress, louder this time. I didn't answer. Just sat on the floor, back against the wall, and watched as he struggled to loosen the rope that bound his wrists.

"Goddamn it!" he yelled as he writhed. "If you cared anything about me, you'd fuckin help me!" Still, I just sat there, watching, wondering what he would have me do. Untie him? Go into the street and find him some smack? Kill him? Get out my knives and cut him, like I'd been cutting up myself? If that was it, I'd have to tell him that it hadn't been working so well for me. That since my mother started losing weight, even before (when Uncle Ray stole his baby girl and put a bullet through his own head), the numbness had stepped up the frequency of its visits. Took to coming earlier and staying later, until, like Grandma, it just moved on in. That even though it was May, it was a good thing it was still cold out. Because by now, I had so many scars on my legs and arms, I was embarrassed to wear shorts or sleeveless shirts. If that was it, I'd have to tell him that I could try, but like me, it probably wouldn't do him any good. So I went back to the pages of *Another Country* and let him scream. Writhe and scream, cause there was nothing else to do.

The morning he finally came out of it, he woke from his first fitless sleep in over a week to the overwhelming smell of violets. It was Grandma Margret's doing. Thinking it might help my mother, she bought three fresh bunches from the nursery and placed some in every room of the house. I was reading *Tar Baby* when Bobby propped himself up to look at the vase full of violets sitting on the windowsill. Before either of us could say anything, my grandmother appeared in the doorway, holding a tray with a bowl of chicken broth on it.

"Thought you might be hungry," she said, setting the tray on the floor in front of him.

Bobby took the soup without answering.

"You know I can leave here whenever I get ready," he said, when my grandmother went back to the kitchen. He blew on the soup before tasting it.

"I know," I answered, turning back to *Tar Baby*.

"Yeah, well, just so you do," he slurped loudly.

"You ever read that book?" I looked up and asked.

"What book?" He answered without looking at me.

"The one you stole from me. *I Know Why The Caged Bird Sings*."

"Nope," he said, concentrating on his soup. "Sold it for two dollars. Sold the locket, too," he announced as chicken broth dribbled onto the tray from the corner of his mouth. "Kept the picture, though."

"Yeah, I know," I said. "We found it when we washed your clothes."

"Y'all undressed me!?" he yelled, incensed.

"Grandma did," I shrugged. I smiled as his face crinkled up at the thought of Grandma Margret seeing his emaciated body.

"I swear," he said, disgusted. "A man can't get no privacy around here."

"What'd you do with the vibraphone?" I asked, still smiling.

"Shit, that ol thing," he laughed. "Gave it away to the first fool that asked. He know it was me?"

"Yeah."

He laughed again. "Was he mad?"

"What do you think?" This time we both laughed.

"Good." Bobby slurped the last of his soup. "So where's he at, any-how?"

"Gone," I shrugged.

"Figures. With Jessica?"

"Nope. Someone else."

He squinted at me to make sure I wasn't putting one over on him. "What about Onya?" he asked.

"Same."

"Can't Die Man?" he said, referring to Uncle Ray.

"Still trying to die." We both laughed again.

"He ain't succeeded, yet?" he asked.

"Nope."

"Damn!" He shook his head in disbelief. "Mama's bout to go, though, huh?"

"Looks that way," I said, nodding my head.

"You don't seem too upset." He acted surprised.

"Nothing to get upset about," I explained. "Lost her life a long time ago. Dying's just what comes after."

He thought for a minute, then rubbed the back of his head. "Well, I might have to get on up outta here fore it does," he confided.

"You and everybody else," I said, turning back to my book.

"What, you think I'm just runnin away?"

"We all are," I said without looking up.

"Then why you still here?" he asked.

"Oh, I'm gone," I said quietly. "Just chose a different path, that's all."

"Uh-huh. You be runnin to them knives." When I looked up he was smiling, like he was holding something sinister just above my head. I just stared at him.

"Yeah, I know," he said, still smiling. "May look all fucked up in the head, but I know what's goin on. That's why you be wearin all them clothes. Hot as a motherfucker up in this house, and you got on all them clothes, tryin to cover up them scars. What they call it? Self-mutilation? Yeah, I'm hip. Seen a lot a kids in the street into that shit."

"Better than sticking needles in my veins." Now it was my turn to smile.

"Oh yeah? Do it work?" he asked, feeling a little too smug.

"What do you mean?" I asked, even though I knew what he was getting at. I just wanted to hear him say it. No one in the family had ever mentioned it out loud. I always knew we all suffered from it, but suddenly, the knowledge wasn't enough. I needed to hear someone speak it, to give a name to the unseen enemy I'd spent my whole life fighting. "Does what work?" I prompted.

"Do it get rid of the numbness, girl?" He mouthed the words slowly, as if he'd read my mind. "You know what I mean."

I was stunned. I knew exactly what he was going to say, and it still caught me off guard. *The numbness.* Out loud, it sounded so airy, so light, so... phony. Yet there it was, night and day, as real as I was, wreaking havoc in our lives.

"Most of the time," I lied. "Yours?"

"Oh, yeah!" Bobby said, letting his head fall back on his neck like he was wishing he was high. "When I'm high, girl, I don't just feel—I feel good. Oughta try it sometime," he taunted.

"That's alright," I said, wondering if he was telling the truth.

"Suit yourself," he shrugged. "But if you ever change your mind..." He stopped in mid-sentence. Grandma Margret had come back in to take his tray.

"Feelin any better, now that you got somethin besides poison in your body?" she asked.

"Yes, Grandma," Bobby answered dutifully.

"Strong enough to get cleaned up and make a trip down the hall to see your mother? She's been askin for ya."

"Guess so," he said, realizing he didn't have much choice.

"Good," she said as she picked up his tray. "I'll run you a bath and bring your clothes."

The violets had backfired. While Bobby's body was busy trying to rid itself of the poison, my mother's body stopped accepting food and no longer opened its eyes. "Don't like the looks of things anymore," she told my grandmother. "Smells are so much sweeter. Don't you agree?"

She mistook the vases of violets for the spirit of my great-grandmother, come to take her home. We toyed with the idea of getting rid of the them, but my grandmother concluded it might do more harm than good. If we were to take them away now, she said, my mother might think Great-grandma Shirley had gone without her and die right there on the spot to keep from being left behind. So we left the vases where they were and tried instead to convince her that the scent she was dozing off and waking up to was not from Great-grandma Shirley but from the fresh-cut violets Grandma Margret bought at the nursery.

She refused to believe us. And three days after the third doctor told us he could find nothing wrong, my mother stopped talking, while she was awake anyway. And the few words she muttered during sleep were reserved for Great-grandma Shirley.

"Whenever you ready, Mama," she'd mumble. "Just waitin on you."

After awhile, we thought maybe Great-grandma Shirley really was there, and that, somehow, the smell of the natural violets was masking the fragrance of the supernatural ones. But then Grandma Margret decided if Great-grandma Shirley's spirit really was in the house, we'd know it. There'd be other signs, she said. A sudden coldness, or the knocking over of things. No, my mother was just suffering from the usual delirium. We'd better get ready, she added. The Reaper was on his way.

When he finally got there, my mother looked more asleep than dead. She was lying on her back in the middle of the mattress. Her eyes were closed, and she had a slight smile on her face as though she were teasing us, playing Dead Man's Bluff, like she used to do when we were little. Any moment now, I expected her to jump up, tickle my ribcage and yell, "Got ya!" but she never did. She just lay there, steadily smiling. And when the coroner arrived hours later to pronounce the time of death, not only was the smile still there, but it had grown wider, like she'd been saying, "Got ya" all along.

Home
1991

Policy. That's what the desk nurse answered when I asked if I could say good-bye to Agnes. Allowing a patient who had been placed in lockdown to be exposed to outside influences prior to completion of the disciplinary period established was against hospital policy. What about food? I wondered. Was the food that was cooked, then carted in from the kitchen, considered an outside influence? Did Agnes have to wait the established seventy-two hours before she could eat again?

"You're welcome to come back and visit tomorrow or the next day," the nurse said, smiling as she flipped through a patient's file on the desk, "if it's still that important to you." She added smugly, "But Agnes won't lose any sleep over it, if that's what you're worried about." The smile disappeared. Vanished. As if a midget Lilliputian controlling things inside her head flipped off the smile switch. "If you come tomorrow," she offered, coldly, "it's unlikely she'll remember your name."

"Well, can I leave a letter for her at the desk at least?" I asked, frustrated even though I had anticipated her response.

"Of course you can, Miss Childs," she said, closing the patient's folder and looking up at me. The smile had returned. "All letters and care-packages addressed to patients in lockdown are kept in a box with their name on it until privileges have been restored."

"Yeah, but will you make sure she gets it?" I asked, annoyed.

"Miss Childs," she said evenly, in a voice that sounded rehearsed. "It is in our best interest to see that patients receive all mail addressed to them. Unless, of course, the doctors deem it harmful or detrimental to their well-being and healing process. It gives them something to look forward to, something to strive for, reminds them of their ultimate goal to become healthy active members of society again. Now," she said, glancing up at the clock, "is there anything else I can do for you this morning?"

"Yeah," I answered, still frustrated. "I need a plastic bag to put my things in."

"Now that I can do," she replied, turning around and rummaging through one of the cabinets behind the desk. "What time is your brother coming to pick you up?" She produced a plastic bag from the drawer and handed it to me triumphantly.

"Ten-thirty," I answered, taking the bag.

"Oh, my!" she gasped. "That's only half an hour away. Doesn't leave us much time, does it? I'd better get your paperwork in order."

While the desk nurse completed my paperwork, I took the plastic bag back to my room to pack and wait for Bobby. There wasn't much to do. Just gather up the clothes I was wearing when I checked in, and the few things that Mary brought. When I finished, I sat down at the plastic table in the corner and tried to think of something meaningful to write to Agnes.

Back at the desk I had wanted to tell her all kinds of things. That I was glad I had met her. That her laugh infected me, constantly ran through my head and made things bearable. That aside from those railroad tracks creeping up her arms, she too was the most normal-looking person I'd seen in this place. But now, sitting at this plastic table, staring around this barren room encased in vomit green walls, none of those things seemed important anymore.

It just didn't make sense to tell her that I wished we had met under different circumstances. That during all I had experienced here, I wondered how it would look through her eyes. Then I remembered the name tag on the desk nurse's uniform. Judy Barns, RN. The desk nurse had a name. All of the nurses had names, as did Lilah, Sylvia, Eddie, Mary, Jessica, Uncle Ray, Lisa Marie, my mother and father: Lillian Louise and Gregory Taylor Childs. Bobby, Onya, Sumner, MacArthur, Truly, Aunt Florida, Grandma Margret and Great-grandma Shirley. We all had names, given to us or chosen, behind which lay stories of survival.

As I was sitting there, I felt someone's eyes on me. When I turned around to see who it was, the gag-and-barf chick was standing in the doorway.

"No, wait," I called to her, as she turned to leave. "It's alright. I mean, you don't have to go, unless you want to."

"I heard you were leaving today," she mumbled, staring down at her feet.

"Sure am. Just waiting on my brother. He's late. You know, family, always on their time." I motioned for her to come in. Pushing her portable I.V. ahead of her, she shuffled to the middle of the room and stood behind it, still staring at her feet.

"Wanna sit down?" I pointed, offering the other chair. She shook her head no. I stood up and fished in my pants pocket for cigarettes.

"Smoke?" I asked, extending the crumpled pack. Again, she shook her head no. "Mind if I do?"

"No," she answered, refusing to look up. I pulled a cigarette from the pack and stuck it in my mouth, then sat back down in the plastic chair.

"What's your name?" I asked, lighting my smoke.

"Sarah," she said to her feet.

"Mine's Po."

"I know," she said quietly, glancing up momentarily. "Not too many people come and go around here without the rest of us knowing who they are."

"How long have you been here?" I asked, realizing Sarah and I had never had an actual conversation. Everything I knew about her, I'd learned from Agnes.

"One month, three days, two hours. Not that I'm counting." She laughed awkwardly. "I used to be in this other hospital over on North Side."

"North Side? That where you live?"

"Yeah."

"Private hospital?" She nodded her head. "How'd you end up in here?" I asked, wondering how anyone with money or health insurance could wind up in City General.

"My parents found out about the experimental treatment program here," she said, eyeing her I.V., "and volunteered me for it."

Bobby rapped on the door and asked, "You about ready?"

"Oh, hey, Bobby." I greeted. I'm not sure why, but I was happy to see him. I guess I was just ready to get out of there, anxious to go home. "Sarah," I said as I stubbed my cigarette in the styrofoam cup, "this is my brother, Bobby."

Sarah waved weakly in his direction, and started pushing her I.V. toward the door. Bobby grimaced at the I.V. and nodded back. "I was just leaving," Sarah said.

"Hey, Sarah," I called after her, as I tied up my plastic bag. "We can keep talking if you want. Bobby can wait a few minutes. Can't you, Bobby?"

"Yeah, but make it quick, Po," Bobby said, rolling his eyes and holding up his watch. "I got things to do."

"That's okay," Sarah answered as she pushed her I.V. past him. "I just wanted to say good-bye." Bobby stepped aside to let her pass.

"Take care of yourself, Sarah," I said, feeling like I should say more. "You know, I do get over to North Side once in a while," I fumbled for the right words. "Maybe we'll see each other again."

"Yeah, maybe," she said. Her mouth smirked with doubt. "Long as it's not in here."

"Ain't that the truth," Bobby muttered as she disappeared.

"Don't start, Bobby," I chided.

"What?" he squealed. "Sanest thing I ever heard anybody say in this place."

"Look, I just don't want to get into it right now, okay?"

"Oh, that's right," he said, stepping further into the room. "I forgot. I'm just the driver, the getaway car. I ain't s'posed to say nothin, right? But you got all kinda time to talk to crazy people don't make no sense. What about your family, Po?" he asked stretching his arms wide. "Ain't you got no time for family?"

"I said, I don't want to get into it now, Bobby." I was tired of arguing. With Bobby, with everybody. Seemed like that's all I'd done since I got here. I just wanted to write my note to Agnes and go home. "How come you're always judging people?" I threw my jacket and bag full of clothes on the bed. "I thought Allah loved everybody."

"Everybody but the devil, Po," Bobby smiled. "Everybody but the devil. Thought you didn't wanna get into it now."

"I don't."

"Then let's get on up outta here."

"You're the one who was late," I snapped. "I've got one more thing to do, then we can go." I tore the flap from the extra carton of Marlboro Lights Mary had bought, then sat back down at the table. On the back of the flap, I wrote:

Agnes:
The gag-and-barf chick has a name. It's Sarah. Remember it and keep telling everybody yours. Along with the story that goes behind it. Carve it into your chest and flash it to someone every chance you get.

"Can we go now?" Bobby asked impatiently as I hid the torn flap at the bottom of the carton, beneath the unopened packs of cigarettes.

"Yeah, but we have to stop at the desk on the way out."

"Thought I told you to take care of the paperwork before I got here," he scolded, heading for the door.

"I did, I just have to sign the forms and drop this off." I pointed to the Marlboro carton, then grabbed my bag and jacket off the bed, taking one final look around the room before I left. As we started down the hall, a small commotion was brewing in the lobby.

"Praise Allah," Bobby said, throwing back his head, agitated. "What now?"

A handful of patients and nurses were huddled together in front of the desk, whispering back and forth. Bobby and I pushed our way to the front to see what was going on.

Two orderlies were pushing Lilah out of the elevator in a wheelchair. Her eyes were half-closed and her body slumped over to the side as though she'd been drugged. Her husband followed behind.

"Lilah?" I said, walking toward her, as the orderlies stopped to sign her in.

She lifted up her head and smiled. Not a big smile, the kind that's flashed when two friends who haven't seen each other meet unexpectedly on the street, but a small vaguely familiar grin. The kind that says 'Hey! I know you. Can't recall the where from just yet, but gimme time, I will.'

"Lilah, it's Po," I said before the orderlies pushed me aside.

"Fine, thank you," she answered to the question I didn't ask. "Still kickin. Not too high these days, but kickin just the same. You know, my grandmama used to say that?" She looked at me and laughed. Then winked, as though she were trying to tell me something.

"All set, Miss Childs?" the desk nurse interrupted.

"What?" I said, twirling around to face her.

"Are you ready to go home?" she asked. The smile was wide.

"Uh... yeah, in a minute." But when I turned back around, Lilah was gone.

"I just need you to sign your name by that big red X on the bottom there," the nurse said, sliding my release form across the desk.

I watched her as I signed. Although a wide smile was plastered across the width of her face, her eyes were numb. Like before, the smile, wide as it was, felt rehearsed, practiced. As though mastering it had been a prerequisite to working on the ward. But the numbness behind the eyes was real. Even the most gifted actor would have trouble faking that. I recognized it. The numbness acquired from years of watching one tormented soul after another fall to pieces right in front of you. And the creation of its protective covering was essential to keeping her own soul intact. But where the nurse's eyes were clear and bright white with pupils so small they could have been nonexistent, the whites in my eyes were hidden by a thick milky yellow film, with pupils so deep and black, anyone who looked into them was struck with the sudden and anxious feeling that they were falling, drifting weightless through a spiraling bottomless hole, devoid of all emotion.

"And your brother here," the nurse nodded in Bobby's direction, "will he be driving you home?"

"What?" I asked, somewhat distant. I was still trying to figure out what Lilah was trying to tell me.

"Your brother, will he be driving you home?" she repeated.

"Yes," I answered. I felt myself drifting further away.

"Policy says we have to ask," she said to Bobby as she looked over the form. "Well, everything seems to be in order."

"I wanted to leave these cigarettes for Agnes." I said, passing the carton across the desk. "I won't be needing them."

"Cigarettes!" she exclaimed, beaming with a practiced joy. "What a thoughtful gift. I'm sure it'll be the first thing Agnes asks for when she returns from lockdown. Cigarettes are like money around here," she commented to Bobby. "Hard to come by unless family or friends bring them in from outside." Bobby nodded his head politely in acknowledgment. "Okay, Po," she said, handing over my copy of the release forms. "I guess that's it. And on behalf of the staff, I want to wish you the best of luck."

"Thanks." I ignored her extended hand. "Let's get out of here," I muttered to Bobby while starting for the elevator, as the desk nurse tsked loudly.

"Right behind ya, lil sis," Bobby answered, following closely. "Most sensible thing you said all week."

He popped in the cassette tape as soon as we got in the car. A live recording of the senior minister's most recent sermon. Except for the sermon and the echo of amens from the congregation, the first half of the drive to my apartment was silent. The last few days had taken their toll. My body was exhausted and my eyes still needed time to adjust to natural light, so I fastened my seatbelt and closed them, letting my head fall back on the headrest.

"The life of a true soldier," the minister boomed through the speakers, "a committed soldier, is tiresome."

"Yes, Brother Minister," echoed the congregation.

"He can never relax. He must always be on the lookout for the devil's mischief. For the white-faced demon will stop at nothing to seduce our brothers and sisters away from the fold."

"Yes, Brother Minister."

"He will disguise himself as your friend."

"Go on, Brother Minister."

"And he will pretend to understand your pain. Be warned, brothers and sisters, for the devil is disguised in all walks of life. From the reverend in the pew, to the bum on the street. And though they may not realize it..."

"Tell it, Brother Minister."

"Though they may not realize it, each one carries in his heart a fatal disease. The number of souls we've already lost is staggering. Simply staggering. We got brothers sleeping in doorways, injecting the white man's poison into their veins. Sisters standing on the corner selling the wares of Allah's temple for money. We got our menfolk bedding down with each other, and our women doing the same."

"Who? Where?" a voice in the congregation shouted.

"Our young people are out there killing and swallowing each other whole, like frogs do flies. And I'm here to tell ya, brothers. Yes, Allah has called me as the humble messenger, brothers and sisters. The majority of our people are horribly afflicted with the disease of the white man. It is a killing ground out there, brothers and sisters. It is a killing ground. And, yet and still, the mighty Allah provides."

"Yes, Brother Minister."

"And, still...," his voice quieted. "The mighty. Allah. Provides. All praise be to the mighty Allah."

"Praise be to Allah," the congregation shouted.

"So we cannot rest, brothers," he went on. "And sisters. Must not rest. Until we have recovered and cured all those afflicted. Until we have won. Won—I say—our beloved sovereignty."

"Amen, Senior Minister," Bobby whispered as the congregation erupted in applause. I felt the car slow down and veer to the left. I opened my eyes and stared out the window as we crept past dilapidated houses. We were nearing my apartment.

Sovereignty. I wondered what the word meant to Bobby. Freedom? Or power? Supreme power over those afflicted like me. The playing of the tape was staged, a prop meant for my benefit alone. Bobby had heard the sermon before. Many times, I was sure.

"You hearin this?" He reached over and turned down the volume.

"Can I help it?" I answered, still staring at the slow-moving houses.

"But are you listenin?" Bobby asked again, looking right at me.

I sighed emphatically. "I'm listening, Bobby. Wanna keep your eyes on the road?"

"I'm cool," he said, smiling. He glanced at the road, then turned back to me. "Allah's got it all under control. You know you can count yourself among those lost souls the senior minister's talkin about," he continued, returning his eyes to the road.

"That why you agreed to pick me up?" I asked, laughing at his transparency. "Hoping that I would sit here and listen to your minister's words, then fall to my knees and praise Allah for helping me to finally understand what's been wrong for all these years?"

"Sounds a little melodramatic," he answered, laughing with me. "But somethin like that."

"That what happened to you? Someone take you aside and play you a tape that finally shed some light on the nature of your illness?"

"Exactly," he said, tapping his fist on the steering wheel. "And the fact that Allah saved me means that He can definitely save you." We pulled to a stop in front of my building. A homeless man was sleeping on the sidewalk.

"As I recall, Bobby," I said, unfastening my seatbelt, "it was Grandma Margret who pulled you out of that box, not Allah."

"But Allah cured the numbness, girl," he said, shifting the car into park and turning to face me. "Allah resurrected me. Stopped the curse dead in its tracks, then helped me to recognize it for what it really is."

"And what is that, Bobby?" I asked, looking him in the eye. Suddenly, I was interested.

"Ain't no curse, girl, I can tell you that much," he assured. "Curses are cast by superior beings, and Allah's the only superior being I know. Naw, girl, white man brought this on. Got inside our heads and made us believe wasn't nothin we could do to stop it."

"And you think there is?" My hand rested on the doorhandle.

"I know there is," he said with conviction. "I'm livin proof, girl. I'm alive, Po. More alive than I been all my life. I notice things now. Birds chirpin up on top of telephone poles. Flowers, bucking the weight of the concrete, sproutin buds through the cracks in spite of it."

"Well, Bobby," I said, hand still on the door, "after the past few days, I'm inclined to agree with you, at least on some points."

"Yeah?" he laughed. "Which ones?"

"That we can stop this train. White man may have put us on it, but we're the ones who stayed on board. And we're the ones who can step off, any time we please. But I don't go in for all that stuff about needing help from some superior being."

"Allah help you, Po," he said, shaking his head as he turned off the ignition. "Allah help ya. But that's alright, I ain't worried. I know it ain't you talkin."

"No, who is it then?"

"White man. White man and his illness. But Allah bout to cure that."

"Whatever, Bobby," I mumbled, exasperated, opening the door.

"What, you don't think you sick?"

"No, Bobby, I don't. No sicker than you and the rest of the world."

"This comin from a girl who just got released from a mental hospital."

"I checked myself out," I corrected, looking at him. "Just like I checked myself in. Of my own free will, so I could rest and figure things out. You should try it some time."

"Ha! That'll be the day. That what that bandage is all about?" He nodded his head at my arm. "Figurin things out?"

"Maybe."

"And you don't call that sick?"

"No."

"Ha!" he yelled, banging the steering wheel. "I do."

"Yeah, well, if turning my mind and everything I own over to some little man claiming to be selling the will of God means being well, then sick I'd rather be."

"Listen to you, girl. Devil's got you talkin all kindsa crazy mess."

"Seems to me it's your thoughts and actions that are still being dictated by somebody. Addiction is addiction, Bobby. Curse, Allah, or junk, you still got something controlling your mind."

He licked his lips and thought a minute. "Cept that now I ain't doin no harm to myself," he said quietly. "And now I can feel. Can you say the same thing, Po?"

"Look, Bobby," I said, avoiding the question as I placed one foot on the curb. "Through all your shit: Hmm Hmm, Debbie, and Try Try; the illness; the drug addiction; the Ministers; I let you be you. And nobody, not Mama, not Grandma Margret, not Onya, not even your father ever questioned or stopped loving you during any of it."

"I love you, Po!" Bobby said, placing his hand on my leg to keep me from leaving. "Why you think I'm tryin so hard to save you?"

I sat there a long time before answering. One foot in the car, one foot out. My head hurt and I was tired. Tired of arguing with Bobby, tired of explaining to Mary, tired of fighting with myself. Bobby made it all sound so easy. If ever there was a time I could've let someone else have it. Just given up, that was it. Remove the armor and let someone else fight the battle. But I couldn't. Deep down inside, I knew I couldn't.

"Then let me be, Bobby," I said, finally. "If you love me, let me be who I am. Let me make my own decisions and suffer the consequences. Even if it means I end up on a path different from yours. If there's any saving to be done, I gotta do it myself."

"Can't do that, Po," he answered warmly, raising his eyebrows. "Can't do that. Allah won't let me."

"Alright, Bobby." I stepped out of the car. "Thanks for the ride. I'll see you later."

"Tomorrow, right? At the funeral?"

"Yeah, right, Bobby," I sighed, slamming the door closed. He started the engine and pulled away from the curb, shaking his head as he roared off down the street.

I stood in front of my building and stared before going in. It had only been three and a half days, but the ivy crawling up the crumbling brick facade seemed to have climbed higher. When I opened the door to my apartment, everything was just as I had left it. My books were still on the floor. The sheets and the patch of rug next to the bed were still bloody (although the blood was dry now and no longer red). The phone remained teetering on the desk, the receiver dangling from its cord above the floor. The only thing that was different was the snapshot of my Aunt Florida. When Mary and I left for the hospital, it was lying face-down in the center of the mantle. Now it had moved to the edge nearest the door and was no longer lying, but standing up, tar black eyes and the burning cigar pointing toward the door as though she'd been expecting me. Even in death, as she had done in life, Aunt Florida kept watch over the members of the family she thought needed the most looking after.

It was Aunt Florida who kept Grandma Janie from falling apart when her husband left her. Then, when she died in that fire, it was Aunt Florida who consoled Great-grandma Shirley and helped her to raise my mother. And it was Aunt Florida who notified my parents when Great-grandma Shirley passed, then flew down from Cleveland to help my father take care of my mother and Onya. She spent that whole year with us, my father told us. Didn't even think of leaving, he said, until the day my mother woke up claiming the house was filled with violets.

I tried to leave the photo behind. When I first took the apartment, I tried to forget about it. But every time I turned around, it always found its way back into my duffel bag.

The summer after my mother died, Grandma Margret took Bobby and me back to the city to live with her and Uncle Ray. Then, when fall came, we both enrolled in school. Grandma Margret seemed pleased even though Bobby only went to class when he felt like it which wasn't too often. And though he was two years older than me, because of all the time he missed when he was living in Xenia, we were both in the same grade— juniors. I hadn't cut myself in months. And I spent my afternoons working shifts at the Big Boy across the street from school. Uncle Ray was steadily gaining power over his demons. He'd held onto the job he got through the school district as a substitute teacher for nearly an entire year.

He lucked out. One of the teachers he once subbed for at the high school suffered an irreparable stroke; they called on Uncle Ray to take his place. He would still be a substitute, they told him. His tendency toward suicide prevented them from hiring him full-time. He would prepare lessons, facilitate class discussions, and grade papers just like the regular teachers. But even though his students would come to adore him, he could be fired at any moment without provocation, and he would never be eligible for benefits.

It was almost the first anniversary of my mother's death when things started to fall apart. Grandma Margret made us all get dressed up and drive to the cemetery to pray and lay flowers on my mother's grave. It was still a few weeks before the actual date, but Grandma Margret wanted to go early—so we could beat the Memorial Day rush.

Except for my grandmother, none of us really wanted to go. Bobby said he didn't see what good dropping a bunch of flowers on a slab of concrete was going to do anybody. Uncle Ray complained that he had too many piles of exams to grade to be wasting an entire day standing over a grave. And I just didn't want to reduce my mother's life or death to a box of flesh and bones decomposing under a tombstone. But Grandma Margret insisted, and three weeks before the official date of her death, the four of us stood over my mother's grave with our eyes closed, each in our own way wondering what we were doing there.

Other than a flat tire on the way which delayed us considerably because we didn't have a spare, the trip to the cemetery was uneventful. Grandma Margret praised God for giving us beautiful weather, and just as she had hoped (except for a groundskeeper picking up trash and mowing the grass), we were the only ones there. After laying the flowers on the grave, Grandma Margret had us hold hands while she thanked Jesus for letting us keep my mother in our lives as long as He had and asked Him—in addition to watching over her soul in heaven—to please continue taking care of the rest of us, including the troubled souls of my father and Onya, wherever they may be. When she was finished, Bobby put a cigarette in his mouth and told us he'd meet us at the car. Grandma Margret pursed her lips as he walked away, then told the Lord to especially look after that one. Uncle Ray told my mother he missed her and that the world just wasn't the same without her. I just stood there, playing with my fingers and watching the groundskeeper, waiting for my grandmother to say it was time to leave.

Maybe it was the flat tire and the fact that my grandmother had to shell out forty dollars to have it repaired, or perhaps it was because the Lord's beautiful day had been replaced by dark clouds and showers during the ride home. Whatever it was, when we got back to Grandma Margret's, everyone seemed on edge. Grandma Margret snapped at Uncle Ray because he ran over part of the curb when he pulled into the driveway.

"We just paid to have it fixed," she yelled. "Think you could make it last awhile before we have to do it again?"

Bobby glared at anyone and everyone who even looked like they might try to say something to him. Uncle Ray cursed his maker three times when he fumbled with the key, trying to fit it in the lock. And I had a sudden uncontrollable urge to cut something.

In the following weeks, it was hard to tell who would crack first. Bobby started spending every other night away from home, pushing the hands on the clock so far into the evening on the day of his return, eventually, he graced us with his presence only one or two days a week. Grandma Margret—who could whip up a mouth-watering meal with her eyes closed—started burning up dinner with such regularity, one week we ate Kentucky Fried Chicken seven days in a row. Uncle Ray flat out ignored the piles of exams on his desk. Instead, he paced around the house with a bottle in his hand—ruing the day "that white bitch" who took his child had ever been born. As for me, I measured the sharpness of every knife in the house with renewed intensity. And we all displayed extreme levels of paranoia, watching each other like hawks to make sure whoever leapt first didn't try to take the other ones with him.

As it turned out, it was Uncle Ray. And I was the one who found him. It was six-thirty in the morning, three days before the anniversary of my mother's death. I had just left for school and was on my way to the bus stop when I noticed Grandma Margret's car parked on the street in front of the house. The motor was on but nobody was in it. A strange object was stuck under the back fender. As I got closer I saw that it was the end of a garden hose, protruding out of the exhaust pipe. And after following its trail around the car through a crack in the driver's side window, I discovered the unconscious body of my uncle Ray, curled up in the back seat like a sleeping baby. The other end of the hose was shoved deep inside his mouth.

He'd been there all night, since sometime after my grandmother and I had gone to bed; the car was almost out of gas. Grandma Margret was just about to go upstairs to wake him for breakfast when I told her. Once again, the doctors at the hospital scratched their heads at the impossibility of it. Uncle Ray, they said, had enough carbon monoxide in his system to kill an elephant. And once again, he'd survived with no apparent brain damage.

He was released three days later with a doctor's clearance to return work. But when he showed up at the school, doctor's note and graded exams in hand, the principal informed him that he no longer had a job. The school board considered Uncle Ray a liability, he said; and they had already hired a sub to replace the sub.

One year later, after graduating from high school, I enrolled in the summer session at City College and moved into my own apartment.

"I'll be alright," I told my grandmother. "Besides, you got your hands full with Uncle Ray. Last thing you need is to be taking care of me, too. It's not like I'm leaving the country. If anything happens, if you need anything, I'll be just up the road."

I guess like Onya, I thought a change of surroundings would make the numbness go away. If I could just leave that other world behind—the one that had spirits telling my mother to lay down and die, and self-imposed curses which forced a grown man to shove a garden hose down his throat— if only I could distance myself, maybe it would forget all about me. If only... As with Onya, this wouldn't prove so easy. Like Agnes once said, "If ifs and buts were candy and nuts, we'd all have a wonderful Christmas."

Aside from my duffel bag, my grandmother's bureau and an old photograph of my mother were all I wanted to take with me, but Aunt Florida insisted on coming along. When I asked Grandma Margret if she was the one who kept putting the picture back in my duffel bag, she said she didn't know what I was talking about. Finally I just gave in, figuring if Aunt Florida was that bound and determined to watch over me, I'd better let her.

I collapsed on the blood-stained sheets and looked up at her, waiting for the tar black eyes to speak.

So what you gonna do now? they asked, staring at me.

"I was waiting for you to say something."

Course I am. Everyone else done had they say. So, what you gonna do? Just gonna lay there, like you laid up in that hospital?

"You got something better in mind?"

No, guess not. Not if you don't.

"What's that supposed to mean?"

Nothin. I done lived my life. You don't wanna live yours, that's your business.

"Oh, so now I'm not living?"

Not if you call cuttin your skin all up and layin up in bed feelin sorry for yourself—cause it's all not what you expected—livin.

"You think I'm giving up."

Givin in is more accurate.

"Givin in to what?" I asked.

The curse, that's what. I thought I taught you better than that.

"There is no curse," I said, folding my arms behind my head.

Ain't no curse? What was all that stuff bout Uncle George then? You think I was makin it up?

I thought about it. "No. I just think you were trying to scare us."

Scare you into what?

"Acting right."

Oh, is that all it was?

"Look, if our family was cursed," I said defensively, "we put it on ourselves." I was trying to convince myself of that fact more than Aunt Florida.

On ourselves, huh? she asked, incredulous. *So let me get this right. You sayin that Uncle George and his kinfolk kidnapped themselves from Africa, shackled themselves in chains, sold themselves into bondage, then passed the legacy on down to us?*

"No."

Sounds like what you sayin to me.

"That's not what I mean. I'm just saying that we have a choice."

A choice in what?

"A choice in how we decide to deal with it."

Like choosin to carve up your skin?

"No, like not letting it take hold in the first place."

And what if it already has?

"Then we need to realize that we're the ones letting it live. It needs us to believe in it to keep on breathing."

You mean like taking a stand?

"Exactly."

Well, took you a little while to get here. But looks like I taught you right after all.

"What?" The black eyes stared at me.

Uncle George made his choice, baby, just like the rest of us. Just like your mama did, just like your father and his brother did. Don't mean you got to make the same one. You'll be strippin our lives of meaning if you do.

"But why does it have to fall on me? Let Bobby or Onya make the stand. I'm tired."

Bobby's already started, much as you don't agree with how he's goin about it. But he can't do it by himself. And what you got to be so tired about?

"Didn't you ever get tired?"

Sure, I did. But it didn't stop me from doin what I had to do. And I was old. You ain't but twenty-seven, you ain't lived long enough to be tired.

"That's just it. You and Mama fought your whole lives, and in the end, what'd it get you? Nothing."

That the name you callin yourself these days, nothin? Ain't you heard a word I said? You the one we was fightin for. All three of ya. You, Onya, and Bobby.

"Yeah, and look at us now. You sorry?"

Lord, no, child! How many times you been left for dead a block away from your home? How many times you had an empty beer bottle broken upside your head, cause you loved somebody you weren't s'posed to? You got your own apartment. You got a degree. Shoot, I woulda licked somebody's boots if I coulda gone to high school, let alone college.

"Yeah, but it still doesn't seem like all that much has changed."

Hasn't. But you can't wipe away four hundred years in a hundred. Give up now, it'll never be clean.

"But look at us. Me, Bobby, Onya. We don't even know each other.

How are we supposed to make a stand against something so big, when we're so disconnected?"

You connected. Fact that you all here makes you so. And as far as knowin each other goes, patterns torn from the same fabric, no matter how different, can't help but know each other. Once you remember that, fightin to sew it back together comes real easy.

My whole body suddenly felt heavy, and I was having trouble paying attention. I crawled under the bloody sheets and closed my eyes.

That's alright, baby, I heard Aunt Florida say, as I drifted off. *We done said all we need to. You go on and rest up. Tomorrow's a busy day. And you got a whole lotta cleaning to do before it's through.*

THURSDAY

Funerals
1991

The rain started sometime in the middle of the night while I was sleeping, sometime between Aunt Florida's words trailing off and the sound of bottles breaking as they crashed into the bed of the recycling truck parked outside my window. I dreamt I was falling with the bottles, twisting and twirling through the air, breasts flapping against my chest as the rain cleansed the soot from my pores. For some reason, I was fighting it—I didn't want to be cleansed; I wanted to stay dirty. Wanted the clouds to be old and experienced and sadistic. To curl the spittle on the backs of their tongues and spray it all over me. I wanted to be shit upon like the heavens shat upon Uncle Ray, because it was easier that way. Easier to ignore the conviction behind Aunt Florida's words and continue on down the old dirt road, echoing the cries of those who'd been victimized. The paved roads of the future were slick with promise, offering an ease of maneuverability that couldn't yet be trusted.

I woke to the aches of one who'd slept too long. Not crooked or crimped or for too many hours on one side, just too long. I was still in my clothes. The last thing I remembered was Aunt Florida saying something about cleaning.

The bloodstained sheets were shoved in the corner at the foot of my bed. I half-expected to look up and see Aunt Florida rolling her eyes at me, fixing her mouth in that familiar setting of disapproval. The way my mother used to look at Bobby before anybody knew he was sick, when she would burst into his room and throw open the curtains to let some light in. I could still hear the derision in her voice. "Planning to sleep your whole life away?" she'd bark at him. "Sun's burning hotter than it has all year, and you got yourself shut up in the dark like you were living in a tomb." But the sun wasn't burning, and Aunt Florida remained silent. Her picture was sitting just as it was when I got home—perched on the mantle and staring at the door as though she were expecting someone.

Mary's leather jacket hung on the doorknob. An odor of dried blood and stale sweat permeated the room. My clothes smelled like institutional ammonia. As the rain eased into a steady 4/4 beat against the window, I pulled the sheets off the bed and tossed them into the trash. Next, I opened the window and hung up the phone. Put the books back on the shelf and washed the blood off the knife before placing it back in the bureau. Other than the stain on the rug which would have to wait for a day or two at least, the scalpel was the only reminder.

I lifted it from the nightstand and held it up to the light the way Mary had done. The sparkle was gone, but the memory wasn't. The memory was still as fresh as the wound, causing me to wince with pain every time I moved my arm, or glanced at the phone. I decided to cut off the bandage. The doctor said three weeks, two at least, but I couldn't wait. I wanted to see the damage.

I expected to find a long gaping hole. To be able to peer in and see clear through to the marrow. As it was, the scar was barely visible. And except for the glaring contrast of black stitching against a tiny patch of new white skin, a stranger who knew nothing of the events leading up to it would be hard pressed to notice it was there.

I sat back down on the bed to study my arm. The scalpel wounds had already begun to heal. Three thin lines with scabs on them were all that remained, like the scratches one receives from a testy cat or an overly playful dog. All that fuss, all that business, all that worrying, and aside from the pain and memory, three thin lines and a patch of black thread were the only evidence it happened at all.

The powerful hospital stench from my clothes started to make me nauseous. I opened the window as wide as it would go but my breath grew moody, coming in short, fitful spasms. Suddenly the room started to spin. And everything in it, with the exception of me and the telephone, started shrinking. Like some almighty governing board unanimously decided it was time to downsize my apartment into a doll's house, but neglected to tell me or the phone, which was swelling fatter as fast as the rest of room was growing smaller.

'Get out!' I heard a voice yell inside my head. I had to get out before the phone rang again. Before the door became impassable and I was trapped inside with the ringing. I ripped off my clothes and ran to the shrinking bureau, just managing to pull a black slip from the top drawer before it disappeared. After pulling the slip over my head, I threw on Mary's jacket, slipped into my army boots, then ducked my head as I ran panting through the door.

When I was safely outside the building, I fingered the lapels on Mary's jacket, then sat down on the stairs to lace up my boots. I knew things had to end between Mary and me, but I couldn't help feeling a sense of loss, sadness. Not because of the echo of Bobby's words which rippled through my head—*You know, li'l sis,* they scorned, *beddin down with the devil ain't gonna bring you nothin but grief*—but because I realized we never had a chance.

The road wasn't always littered with obstacles. In fact, there were months when it was clear for miles, when you could see forever. And its smooth refuge gave me a comfort and ease of motion I'd never known before. Still, it was the wrong way to go, and we both knew it. Knew that as we were gliding atop its slick surface, our eyes combed the branches of the trees that ran alongside for the cure to a malady that could only be healed from inside. And the more desperate the hunt, the clearer the understanding. As long as we continued to seek the remedy in the arms of another, we would never find it.

"You're wrong, Bobby," I said out loud. "We made this mess. You, me, all of us. The shit in our beds comes from our own assholes. Devil didn't have a thing to do with it."

As soon as I tied the laces on my boots, my feet just started moving. They chose no path. Pointed in no particular direction. All I knew was that I needed to walk. Get my legs moving again. Scratch the backs of my knees as the blood started to circulate. Remember what it was like to feel the rain dribble off my nose and plop into my mouth. To walk, a *quidam* through the world, void of any specific plan or purpose. Just walk. One foot in front of the other, without the obstruction of walls.

Before I knew it I was standing in front of the gate that guarded the cemetery. The same gate where Bobby pleaded with Onya to change her mind and come back some other time. Guess my feet knew where they were headed all along. I unhooked the latch and opened it. As I neared my mother's grave, I saw a row of folding chairs lined up in front. A deep hole, the size of a coffin, had been dug beside her grave. I kneeled down to read her headstone. It had been changed. In place of the dull flat plaque my grandmother had barely been able to afford was a sparkling new three-foot-high rounded slab of concrete. The engraving read: *Mrs. Lillian Louise Childs. 1938-1981. Died before her time. Devoted wife and loving mother of three.* My father's stone was leaning against its backside. Except for the name and the dates, the inscription was the same: *Gregory Taylor Childs. 1935-1991. Died before his time. Devoted husband and loving father of three.*

The last time I saw my father, I had been working at the typehouse for nearly a year. President Bush was addressing the nation on the radio, explaining the details of his plan for a new world order. My eyes were tired. The nighttime proofreader had called in sick, and I had just started the second leg of my double shift, when he and Bobby walked through the door. I was proofing a final set of galleys when I looked up and saw him.

He was smiling. Not the bold toothy grin of someone bubbling over with glee to see me, but the sad and tired smile of a man painfully aware that too much time has passed. I didn't let on, but I was shocked at how much he had aged: gravity had taken hold of his face and form, and rearranged him into a slightly stooped and softer framework. The lines on his handsome face had become deeply etched, and his hair had turned to charcoal.

Bobby, on the other hand, was grinning from ear to ear. "Surprise, surprise," he said as they walked toward my desk. "Your girlfriend told us you was here." He emphasized the "girlfriend."

"Feels like I'm always here these days. Hey, Dad," I said, ignoring Bobby's slur and getting up to greet them.

"You've grown," he answered, shaking his head in disbelief. He hesitated, then gave me a hug. A loose one, the kind one gives in moments of uncertainty. I returned his hug without any warmth, going through the motions.

"I understand it happens sometimes," I answered, leaning back on my desk.

He just stood there, shaking his head and smiling, like he couldn't get over it. "I, uh... I'm sorry about your mother," my father said, finally.

"Yeah, me too." I nodded my head up and down awkwardly. "You just find out?" I asked.

Bobby interrupted before he could answer. "You lookin a little tired, Po," he teased.

"Am tired," I said to Bobby, while looking at my father. "And I still got a pile of work to do before I can go home."

"Well, we won't keep ya, li'l sis," said Bobby, looking somewhat relieved. "Dad just wanted to say hi."

"It was good to see you, Po." My father hesitated like he had something else to say, but thought better of it.

"You too, Dad," I answered quickly, as they turned to leave. "Maybe next time it won't be so long between visits."

"No, sweetheart," my father assured, "it won't be," then disappeared through the door.

I didn't ask where he'd been all this time, how come he never called or wrote. I didn't want to know. All I knew was that he had been back in the city a year, and this was the first time he tried to contact me.

I heard footsteps approaching on the grass. When I looked up to see who it was, the groundskeeper was standing over me. He was dressed in an oversized rain slicker, topped with a wide-brimmed, cellophane-covered hat, and wore the sunken, sorrowful eyes of a man who has accepted the calling of watching over the dead. He looked like he could be my grandfather. At least the way I pictured my grandfather would look, if he had lived to be as old as this man. One of the first questions Grandma Margret said she was going to ask the Lord (when at last she saw Him) was why did all our men folk have to die so young. It wasn't just the men folk, I always wanted to tell her. With the exception of her and Great-grandma Shirley, seemed no one in our family ever made it past the age of sixty.

"I'm sorry, miss," the groundskeeper mumbled. "But this section of the park is closed today. Got a burial s'posed to happen any minute now."

"I know," I answered softly, smiling up at him. "The deceased is my father. I got here early so I could spend a few minutes with my mother," nodding toward the headstone, "before the rest of the procession arrived."

He apologized for the intrusion, then tipped his hat and shook his head at my slip before walking away.

I knew my mother's soul had never spent so much as a day trapped under all that dirt and concrete. But kneeling there, I couldn't help but remember the day we buried her. The only similarity between the two funerals was the rain. There were no chairs lined up for the dearly beloved. And aside from the minister, Grandma Margret, Uncle Ray, Bobby, and I were the only ones who bothered to see my mother off. There was no reception afterwards. No out-of-touch friends who'd read about her passing in the newspaper and came to pay their respects in exchange for a free plate of food. It was a quiet unimpressive day just like any other. And except for the thunderstorm that interrupted the middle of the minister's sermon, along with the drunken old woman nobody knew who passed out and fell into the grave, it probably would have gone unnoticed.

As I reached out to trace the letters that remembered her name, I heard the procession enter the gate. The hearse was first, then the limousine carrying Bobby, Onya, and Grandma Margret. All three were genuinely happy to see me. And after helping Grandma Margret into her chair, I turned to embrace Onya and Bobby.

Bobby bent down and whispered in my ear, "I knew you'd show, li'l sis."

"Yeah, well, I almost didn't," I whispered back, slipping out of his embrace.

"But I knew you would. Why I ordered the extra chair," he said a little too confident. He took a step back and looked at me. "Sure is some dress to be payin your respects to the dead in."

"Yeah, well, like I said, Bobby, I wasn't planning on coming. I see you changed the headstone."

"The day we buried Mama," he said, cheekbones flushing with pride, "I vowed that someday I'd have enough money to give her a proper resting place. Now I do."

"Devoted husband and father?" I taunted.

"Po," Bobby said calmly, "you at the man's funeral. Ain't it about time you gave it a rest?"

"You're right, Bobby," I agreed, feeling rebuked. "Truce?"

"Truce," he replied and gave me another hug.

There had been a slight altercation between my grandmother and the Ministers about what kind of service it should be. Bobby and the Ministers believed that, since he'd been a regular at meetings until the day he died, and since they were the ones footing the bill, my father should be given a Muslim burial. Grandma Margret disagreed. He was born Baptist, she argued. As long as the woman who birthed him still had life left in her, Gregory Taylor Childs was going to die Baptist. Even if it meant she had to bury him herself in a brown paper bag. Grandma Margret won. And when the minister from her own church stood up to usher my father into the boat that would carry him to the afterlife, she sat with her hands folded across her lap, wearing the smug expression of a woman who'd finally managed to have her say.

"Brothers," the minister started, "sisters, family, friends. We are gathered here today to say good-bye to a soldier. An infantry man in God's army. Now I know that many of us believe Gregory Taylor Childs was called home before his time. Though we may not always understand or agree with the timing of our maker, we must always remember that God's way is the right way.

"Like all soldiers in God's army, Gregory Childs had his trials in life.

Once again, our prayers go out to those who've been left to grieve: his loving mother, Margret; his brother, Ray; and his three beautiful children, Onya, Bobby, and Po. With the Lord's blessing, I offer but one word to you now. Assurance. Rest assured that there will come a day when the whole of God's army will be called back home. A day filled with joy and jubilation, when we will look once again upon the faces of those who departed before us. Now please bow your heads with me in prayer as we lay the battered soul of a warrior at the feet of the lamb."

As I closed my eyes, my thoughts roamed to Great-grandma Shirley. To the way she devoted her whole life to carrying on the resistance that had been passed down to her. Resistance in the form of love, self love, empowering love. Not a day went by, my mother used to say, when Great-grandma Shirley wasn't sitting on her stoop, snapping beans, and telling one neighbor or another how beautiful he or she was. Whether it was the widow next door or the drunk down the street, as soon as they stepped up onto that stoop, each was enveloped in love. Pure, all-encompassing love that asked for nothing in return. And no matter what form of brutality they had been exposed to the day before or earlier that morning, wrapped in the blanket of Great-grandma Shirley's love, their burdens just didn't seem all that heavy anymore. "You got to relearn how to love yourselves," Shirley would say. "Cause ain't nobody else gonna do it for ya."

Before things fell apart, my parents tried to teach us certain truths. Truths, they said, that would prepare us for the world: our way would be hard in life; we would always be loathed because of the color of our skin; in order to achieve what we truly desired, we would have to work twice as hard as the next person. But somewhere along the way they let the weight of their own burdens get the better of them and they forgot to pass on my great-grandmother's message of love: until we know the joy that can only come from loving oneself, loving each other would be next to impossible.

One by one, after the minister pronounced "ashes to ashes and dust to dust," the well-wishers began filing through the sympathy line. Just about everyone my father had ever said hi to came to pay their respects. From folks I'd never seen before who said they knew him from way back when, to three ex-girlfriends from before my parents were married who had come hoping to meet the woman who had finally found his heart. It was just a shame, they said, that both had died so young. They all agreed Bobby was the spitting image of my father. MacArthur couldn't get over how much we'd all grown. And Truly strolled through the line, smiling from ear to ear, wielding that cane as though he had been born with it. Sumner, they said, sent his condolences. "Woulda been here to give em to ya himself," MacArthur added, but he was still doing time. One of the Bid Whist girls broke down and started sobbing as soon as she reached my grandmother. And as Grandma Margret put her arms around her, whispering, "There, there now," in her ear, it was difficult to tell who was comforting whom.

The reception was held in the gym of the old Y—now home to the city's new Boys and Girls Club. The free food and drink immediately lifted everybody's spirits. While MacArthur (who was now a recruiter for a different BSA, the Boy Scouts of America) spun yarns about my father's exploits in the Alliance, against the Ministers' wishes somebody hooked up a turntable and put on Miles. And as folks started dancing with the unlimited supply of wine wrenching their hips in previously unheard of directions, it was genuinely agreed that things were proceeding exactly as my father would have had them.

Bobby engaged Truly in a discussion of the Ministers' mission and general philosophy. And Grandma Margret vacillated between crying and laughing at MacArthur's stories. Onya and I stood off by the punchbowl, watching—avoiding any mention of the water jug in her hand or the scars that covered each of our arms.

"So what's next, Onya?" I asked, watching MacArthur contort his body in various directions as he charmed the years off my grandmother. "Back to Cleveland?"

"For awhile, anyway," she said, watching the scene and clutching her jug.

"When do you fly out?"

"Tomorrow morning."

"Quick trip?"

"Yeah, I have to get back to work."

"How long you been up there now? Five, six years?" I asked. MacArthur and my grandmother laughed loudly.

"Seven," Onya said, looking at my sleeve-covered arm from the corner of her eye.

I pretended not to notice. "You like it?"

"I think so," she sighed. "But it's not really a city like that, you know, to like or dislike. It just feels like a good place to be."

"Yeah?"

She took a deep breath and looked at me before she answered. "Yeah. I've got a nice cheap place to live, a job that I can leave at the office when I go home. And I've made some good friends. People like me who just sort of ended up there after trying other things, who needed to stop for a minute in a place that would let them be while they figured things out. Don't plan to spend the rest of my life there. But it's nice, you know, to be around people who don't expect anything."

"Any boyfriends?" I asked, nudging her in the side with my elbow.

"Ha!" She tossed her head back and laughed. "A couple, maybe. I don't know," she said embarrassed. "What about you?"

I smiled. "No, Onya. No boyfriends." Grandma Margret let loose another howl.

"That's not what I... I mean what's next for you? Any big plans?"

"See if I still have a job, for one. Look for one if I don't. I don't know after that. Think things through like you, I guess."

While we were talking, two women who could have passed for mother and daughter entered the gym. The older one stepped just inside the door and waited; the younger started walking toward Onya and me. Her step was heavy, tired, like she had seen easier days. A small child was curled up in her arms. A second one skipped along beside her. And her belly was swollen to twice its natural size with what would soon become the third.

"Hi, Po, Onya," the young woman said, smiling.

Onya and I looked at each other, confused.

"I read about it in the paper," she added, eyeing the woman at the door. "And asked for permission to come."

She stared at us through a pair of sad blue eyes, surrounded by dark brown circles that made her look older than she was. Her face was painted heavily with makeup. I figured her for my age or a few years younger maybe, and searched my mind, trying to place her as a childhood friend.

"I thought maybe I might get to see my father," she said, glancing around the room. Her older child had run off to play with some of the other children. "Is he here?"

"Who's your father?" Onya asked, still looking back and forth between us.

"Ray," she said, softly. "Ray Childs. I'm Lisa Marie, but I go by Lisa now."

She was six years old when Jessica whisked her off to Connecticut to live with her grandparents. It was meant to be a place of refuge. And it was for awhile. Jessica's parents fell all over Jessica like she was expecting, and the Childs family—and anyone who knew them—were nearly two thousand miles away. But three years after the move, the demons and memories caught up with her, and Jessica had a nervous breakdown.

It started with panic attacks, Lisa Marie told us. Small fleeting ones, once or twice a month, usually when she was driving. She'd be stuck behind a slow-moving line of traffic or stopped at an intersection waiting for the light to change, when all of sudden her entire body would be stricken with debilitating fear. The attacks would last only a few seconds, then disappear as sudden as they had come on, like unwanted visitors who had a habit of dropping by unannounced. A slight headache and fatigue were the only reminders of their having come at all.

But like most unwanted callers, as time went on, their visits became more frequent and had to be tolerated longer. And along with the headaches and fatigue, she started having blackouts. On one memorable occasion, she woke up from an attack to a chorus of horns blowing in the middle of an intersection, unable to remember how she got there or where she was going. Finally, after a few more near-misses (one involving a police cruiser en route to a crime), her parents took her to see a doctor.

For awhile, the medicine did the trick; the attacks stopped calling and the headaches and fatigue vanished. But it wasn't long before they started up again and this time they brought visions. Horrifying apparitions of my uncle Ray, coming at her with a knife or threatening her with a gun. He was everywhere, she said. Leaning against a fence post when she picked Lisa Marie up from school. Hiding behind a tree when she was walking alone in the park. At one point, she claimed she saw him breaking into her car as she was coming out of the grocery store. But when she returned to the parking lot with the store's security guard, there was no one there and her car showed no signs of tampering.

Her parents wondered guardedly if it might not be an extreme case of exhaustion; that, quite possibly, with all she'd been through, she might be seeing things. Jessica accused them of saying she was crazy. She was not seeing things! she yelled. That's just what Ray wanted them to believe. Think about it, honey, they pleaded. The decision to come back home was sudden. She'd never really had time to process it, what with having to find a job right away and enrolling Lisa Marie in school. Did she really believe that Ray would come all this way just to follow her around and make her think she was crazy? Jessica would have none of it. They were always taking up for him, she argued. Always taking his side. In the past, whenever she called to tell them that he had hit her or that he had pushed her down the stairs, they always wanted to know what she had done to deserve it. That was just not true, they defended. How come no one else had seen him? Why hadn't he shown up at the house or tried to see his little girl? Because he knew they would be there, Jessica yelled. He wasn't stupid, for Christ's sake.

Eventually, Jessica stopped leaving the house altogether, fearing that if she did, Uncle Ray would hunt her down and kill her. But even locked inside he got to her. He was a shadow on the wall, a branch brushing against the window, a caller breathing into the other end of the phone every time she picked up the receiver. Finally, she believed that somehow Uncle Ray had managed to squeeze his six-foot-five-inch spirit into the nine-year-old body of Lisa Marie. And that, in the end, it wouldn't be Uncle Ray who came for her in the middle of the night; it would be the girl, her own daughter, who would deliver the final blow.

"Get out!" she yelled one day, when Lisa Marie entered her room after school. "I said, get out of here! I know who you are! And you can just get the fuck out!" When Lisa Marie cried, "But Mommy, what did I do?" Jessica grabbed the lamp off the nightstand and threw it at her. "I said, get of here, you bastard! Did you hear me? Get out! Get out! Get out!"

When Lisa Marie ran from the room crying into the comforting arms of her baffled grandparents, Jessica locked the door behind her. And except to take a shower during the day when the house was empty, or to scavenge food in the middle of the night while everyone else was sleeping, she refused to come out. It would be three years before she opened the door for good. The day Lisa Marie decided she'd had enough and ran away from home.

One year after she left, Lisa Marie phoned her grandparents to tell them she was okay. No, she couldn't tell them where she was, she just wanted them to know she was alright. How was her mother? she asked. Jessica was much improved, they told her. Seemed like after Lisa Marie left, her mind just snapped back to normal. And after being granted an uncontested divorce (on account that the court had been unable to locate the husband), she had remarried. He was a real nice fella, they added. One of the local businessmen. Was she sure she couldn't tell them where she was? Well, it was nice to hear from her, anyway. Oh, they had almost forgotten, she was a big sister now. Jessica had just given birth to the cutest little twin boys.

After spending five years hitchhiking from one town to another, Lisa Marie had been back in the city a year. She was a court-appointed ward of Saint Elizabeth's, a home for pregnant teens who'd run into the law and had no place else to go. And though her mother would never know it, Lisa Marie had given birth to two boys of her own. The first at fifteen, the second at seventeen, and at the ripe old age of eighteen, she was pregnant with the third. And somewhere between the reign of each of the boys' fathers (all had vanished upon hearing the news), she had attempted suicide twice and been arrested for prostitution once. Now she was looking for her father—who was no better off than she was—to introduce him to his grandchildren. But she was alright now, she said confidently. She was studying for her GED and she was planning to take computer classes so she could bring the boys up proper.

After explaining that nobody knew the whereabouts of Uncle Ray, Onya suggested it probably wasn't the best time to tell Grandma Margret she was a great-grandmother.

"Bobby either," I agreed, overhearing him debate religion with Truly.

Lisa Marie said she wasn't planning on it. She'd only come hoping to find her father. And now that she knew he wasn't here, she was going back to Saint Elizabeth's.

"How long can you stay there?" I asked, eyeing the woman she'd come in with who was stationed by the door.

"Till the baby's born," Lisa Marie answered.

"Then what will you do?" Onya asked, concerned.

"I don't know," she sighed. "Find an apartment I guess."

"Can you have visitors?"

"Yeah, on the weekends."

"Then I'll see you this weekend," I told her. I wrote down my number and pressed it into her palm, then checked to see if Bobby or Grandma Margret had noticed her presence as I hugged her good-bye. "In case you need anything before I get there," I whispered. "Anything at all."

"That goes for you too, Onya," I said, after Lisa Marie had gone. "Cleveland's only a few hours away, ya know."

"I know," Onya answered, glancing down at her jug. "Might not look like it, but I'm doing okay these days. You just look after yourself and Lisa Marie."

"You sure?"

"Sure, I'm sure. Got a job that I like, I'm using my own name. Hell," she laughed, "I might even go back to school."

"Yeah?" I asked, believing she could do it.

"Been thinking about it. Besides," she said under her breath, "Aunt Florida's been stopping by."

"You too?" I cried. "Damn, she's busy."

"Promise me something, Po," she demanded, looking me in the eye for only the second time all day.

"What's that, Onya?" I asked.

"No more hospitals, okay?"

I paused for a second to look at her. Even with the water jug, she really did seem to be doing okay. I wondered how she did it. "Okay, Onya," I said and hugged her, "no more hospitals."

I walked over to Bobby and Grandma Margret to tell them I was leaving.

"See you at the meetin next week?" Bobby asked smoothly.

"Yeah, sure, Bobby," I answered, winking at him. "Just don't go holding your breath."

"You know I ain't gonna give up on ya, Po."

"Yeah, Bobby, I know." I hugged my grandmother long and tight. It was hard to let go. "Can ya make it home alright?" she whispered. She had tears in her eyes from laughing so hard at MacArthur. "I can have Bobby drive ya, if ya want. Won't be no trouble."

"That's alright, Grandma," I said, thinking of the last time Bobby drove me home. "The walk'll do me good."

"You sure?" she asked. "How bout an umbrella? You got an umbrella? It's awful wet outside."

"I'm fine, Grandma," I said, kissing her on the cheek. "I'll call you tomorrow, okay?" But I wasn't fine. The conversation with Lisa Marie and Onya only made the wind of events swirling about my head swirl harder. And as I left the gym, the urge to cut was strong.

The rain had picked up. When I left my apartment, it was nothing more than a harmless drizzle, glistening on the streets the way morning dew moistens the grass. But now, as I descended the steps of the Boys and Girls Club, it fell violently from an endless sea of deep black clouds. I draped Mary's jacket over my head for cover as sheets of water crashed onto the sidewalk. It was as though the heavens had begun a long overdue cleaning. A cleaning that would continue for twenty-six days without interruption, toppling street lamps, washing away foundations, ruining the interiors of cars. A cleaning that would send entire neighborhoods fleeing from their homes. It had all the makings of the latest horror movie. And its longevity and purpose would tax the minds of all the experts before it was through.

As I trudged though the sheets of water, I wondered about things. Why in all these years had I never once heard from my mother, only from

Aunt Florida? Whether it was a picture falling over or the wind chimes ringing in my window, it was always Aunt Florida letting me know if she was pleased or mad. And why had Lilah winked at me? What was she trying to tell me? "Some things have to remain a mystery till you meet the Lord," Grandma Margret always said. "Folks be wastin their whole life looking for the answer to one little thing, just to go to their grave never knowin what it was."

Mary's jacket was useless. When I finally turned the corner onto my street, I was a walking puddle. Puddles in my socks, puddles in my boots. My slip was so wet it chaffed my skin. And Mary's jacket had soaked up so much water, I was sure it had gained three pounds since I first put it on. As I neared my building, I saw a man slumped against one of the cars parked in front of the stairs. His back was to me and it was dark, so I couldn't make him out very well. As I got closer, I could see that he wore the remnants of a soggy newspaper hat on top of his head. He had no coat, wore no shoes, and his hand was holding the back of his neck as though he'd been injured.

"You alright?" I asked, stopping behind him. There was no answer. "Hey, man, you alright?" Still there was no answer. I moved around in front to see if he was conscious. "Do you need some help? Can I..."

...Call somebody, I was going to ask. But as soon as I got around in front of him, the words got stuck on my tongue. It had changed some since the last time I saw him, but for the first time in nearly seven years, I was looking upon the bruised and pockmarked face of my uncle Ray.

His eyes were rolled back deep in their sockets, and foam dribbled from the corners of his mouth. I had mistaken the purpose of the hand. The one that was holding the back of his neck. He was using it for leverage to keep his head still while the other hand, the important one, steadied the needle as it released a brown stream of liquid into his jugular vein.

He never even knew I was there. I'd called out to him just as he had fixed; he didn't answer because he couldn't. Bobby's words echoed through my head, *Naw, girl. You know he all tore up on that poison.*

The food and wine from the reception rose to the top of my stomach. My feet were frozen; no matter how hard I tried, I couldn't move. So I just stood there, soles of my feet plastered to the sidewalk, watching him.

His hand had slipped off the needle and was having trouble finding it again. The hand kept reaching for it and missing, like a dog's paw bats at a fly, only slower. And each time he missed, his body would sway from side to side, causing the needle to bob up and down. When at last his fingers wrapped around the empty rig, in one long fluid motion, they yanked the needle from his vein and dropped it on the ground. His eyes were now closed, and a warm smile spread across his face.

It was standing there, frozen, watching him (the warm smile growing wider and wider), that I finally understood. All those times, all those attempts at suicide, he hadn't been trying to kill himself at all. It was the curse. Like Uncle George and the rest of us, he was still trying to beat the curse.

"That's not the way, Uncle Ray," I whispered, when my mouth could finally speak the words. "Right now you're just feeding it. Only way to get rid of it is to starve it, stop."

He opened his eyes to look at me, but he had trouble focusing. I knew he couldn't see me.

"Ey, li'l man," he said in that familiar gravelly voice. "Got a cigarette? Oh, scuse me," he slurred, correcting himself, "li'l lady. Got a cigarette for a brother, li'l lady?" The smile grew even wider.

As I searched Mary's jacket for my smokes, I thought about telling him who I was. About making him remember, reach back through the high, crawl if he had to, and call up my image or one of my father, mother, or grandmother. It's me, Uncle Ray, I wanted to shout. It's me, Po. Remember? But as I handed him a cigarette, I realized that wouldn't be fair. To force him to crank up the motor of a memory so badly rusted would only confuse and frustrate him. And the thought of watching him struggle through the process made the wine and food mixture rumbling in my stomach rumble even louder. Instead, as he spent match after match trying to light the cigarette dangling impatiently from his bottom lip, I wrote my name and number on a wet scrap of paper, and stuck it in his pocket. I'm still not sure what I thought it would do. Guess I just hoped that when he came out of it, sometime between this high and the next, he might look at it and remember.

When he finally got the cigarette lit, he tipped what was left of his newspaper hat, said good-bye, then shuffled his way up the street slow and uneasy, like a blind man separated from his cane. I watched him feel his way until he turned the corner, then I ran like lightning up the stairs to my building and into my apartment.

Luckily, when I opened the door to my room, everything had returned to its normal size. After hanging Mary's jacket back on the door, I turned on the stereo and put on Billie, then sat down on the bed to take off my boots. It had been a long day and though I was cold and tired, it felt good to be inside. I could feel Aunt Florida watching me.

"I know," I said, pulling the wet slip over my head. "What I got to be tired about?"

Don't know what you talkin bout, child. Been a busy day. Everybody's tired at the end of a busy day. Hell, I'm tired, too.

"Don't worry bout me," Billie sang. "I'll get along..." The wind chimes clanged in harmony behind her.

I let my head fall back on the pillow and closed my eyes. The images of Uncle Ray and my father were heavy on my mind. Not the recent portrait of my father lying lifeless in a grave or the silent footage of Uncle Ray swatting futilely at a bobbing needle, but the strapping and handsome shadows of the black men of my youth. Muscular silhouettes, whose un-wavering belief in a mythical impotence tried to dampen the pages of their memory. All these years I let the shadows tell my story. The shadow of Uncle George, of my father and Jessica, Bobby's soul, Onya's thirst, my scars. The shadow of my mother searching the crevices of a room that reeked of violets for the shadow of my Great-grandma Shirley. I never understood that the shadows' tales, by nature, were false. Had to be. That the real story, the one worth telling, was buried deep beneath the fabric of suggestion, the interception of light. "You're right, Florida," I mumbled. It was time to let the shadows walk silent and embrace the narrative of the whole. I imag-ined Aunt Florida smiling as Billie's voice drifted over me, "Don't worry bout me... I'll get along... Let's say our little show... is over and so... the story ends... Why not call it a day... the sensible way... and still be friends..."

"Goodnight, Aunt Florida," I muttered before falling asleep.

Goodnight, baby, she answered. *Sleep tight.*

Marci Blackman was born in Yellow Springs, Ohio, and grew up there and in Los Angeles. She co-edited the critically-acclaimed anthology *Beyond Definition: New Writing from Gay and Lesbian San Francisco* (Manic D Press). Her writing appears in *Girlfriend #2* (Cleis Press) and *Fetish* (Four Walls/ Eight Windows). Blackman has performed her work throughout the U.S. at bookstores, nightclubs, and festivals including the Albuquerque Poetry Festival, Seattle's Bumbershoot Festival, New York's Nuyorican Cafe, and the Paradise Lounge in San Francisco. She lives in San Francisco.

Manic D Press Books

The Underground Guide to Los Angeles. *Pleasant Gehman, editor.* $13.95

Flashbacks and Premonitions. *Jon Longhi.* $11.95

The Forgiveness Parade. *Jeffrey McDaniel.* $11.95

The Sofa Surfing Handbook: a guide for modern nomads.
   edited by Juliette Torrez. $11.95

Abolishing Christianity and other short pieces. *Jonathan Swift.* $11.95

Growing Up Free In America. *Bruce Jackson.* $11.95

Devil Babe's Big Book of Fun! *Isabel Samaras.* $11.95

Dances With Sheep. *Keith Knight.* $11.95

Monkey Girl. *Beth Lisick.* $11.95

Bite Hard. *Justin Chin.* $11.95

Next Stop: Troubletown. *Lloyd Dangle.* $10.95

The Hashish Man and other stories. *Lord Dunsany.* $11.95

Forty Ouncer. *Kurt Zapata.* $11.95

The Unsinkable Bambi Lake. *Bambi Lake with Alvin Orloff.* $11.95

Hell Soup: the collected writings of Sparrow 13 LaughingWand. $8.95

Revival: spoken word from Lollapalooza 94. *edited by Juliette Torrez,*
   Liz Belile, Mud Baron & Jennifer Joseph. $12.95

The Ghastly Ones & Other Fiendish Frolics. *Richard Sala.* $9.95

The Underground Guide to San Francisco. *Jennifer Joseph, ed.* $10.95

King of the Roadkills. *Bucky Sinister.* $9.95

Alibi School. *Jeffrey McDaniel.* $8.95

Signs of Life: channel-surfing through '90s culture. *edited by*
   Jennifer Joseph & Lisa Taplin. $12.95

Beyond Definition: new writing from gay & lesbian san francisco.
   edited by Marci Blackman & Trebor Healey. $10.95

Love Like Rage. *Wendy-o Matik* $7.00

The Language of Birds. *Kimi Sugioka* $7.00

The Rise and Fall of Third Leg. *Jon Longhi* $9.95

Specimen Tank. *Buzz Callaway* $10.95

The Verdict Is In. *edited by Kathi Georges & Jennifer Joseph* $9.95

Elegy for the Old Stud. *David West* $7.00

The Back of a Spoon. *Jack Hirschman* $7.00

Mobius Stripper. *Bana Witt* $8.95

Baroque Outhouse/Decapitated Head of a Dog. *Randolph Nae* $7.00

Graveyard Golf and other stories. *Vampyre Mike Kassel* $7.95

Bricks and Anchors. *Jon Longhi* $8.00

The Devil Won't Let Me In. *Alice Olds-Ellingson* $7.95

Greatest Hits. *edited by Jennifer Joseph* $7.00

Lizards Again. *David Jewell* $7.00

The Future Isn't What It Used To Be. *Jennifer Joseph* $7.00

Please add $2.50 to all orders for postage and handling.

Manic D Press
Box 410804
San Francisco CA 94141 USA

info@manicdpress.com   http://www.manicdpress.com

Distributed to the trade

in the US & Canada by
Publishers Group West

in the UK & Europe by
Turnaround Distribution